# A Touch of Mother

## Justice #4

# SUZAN HARDEN

A TOUCH OF MOTHER
(Justice #4)
ISBN-13 - 978-1-938745-70-6
Copyright 2020 by Suzan Harden
All rights reserved

Published by Angry Sheep Publishing
Findlay, Ohio

Cover Design by For the Muse Designs
Interior Design by JW Manus

# PROLOGUE

*So it came to pass that Love could not bear the sadness and pain She had caused Mother and Father in forcing Them to release Death into the World. She searched and searched, but when She found no method, no magic, to alleviate Their misery, She sought Her sister Child.*

*Alas, Child had no advice to give Love. So in Her sorrow, Love withdrew from the World.*

*Without Love, women and men felt no desire, no passion, no fervor to lay together. No more children were born.*

*Child grew desperate for her creations. Under Balance's edict, the human race would be no more if they all died without bearing offspring. So Child traveled far and wide, but She could not find Love anywhere. Child sought out Mother for Her counsel.*

*Mother assured Child She would find Love and bring Her back to the World. Mother journeyed to every corner of Creation before she found Love curled in the darkest recess of the Earth, weeping.*

*"You must come back with Me, My Daughter," Mother murmured as She stroked Love's hair.*

*"But I hurt You and Father," Love cried.*

*"Yes, and You tried to make it right, but there are some things even We cannot repair," Mother said. "But You will hurt Your Sister just as much if You allow Her creation to fade from the World."*

*"They do not need Me to have children." Love continued to sob.*

*"You came into existence because the relationship between Me and Father had to be named," Mother said softly. "Your Sister's existence was the result of*

*Your Name, and the human race's existence is due to You as well. Child patterned them after Us. The desire to have children of their own is necessary. You are necessary."*

*Love saw the wisdom of Mother's words, yet She still had doubts. "What about Conflict?"*

*Mother hugged Love. "He is a part of Us, just as You are. We can channel His power into something productive. Defend life, not attack it. But We need You to help Him find a better way."*

*After much thought, Love nodded and wiped away Her tears before She followed Mother back into the World.*

– The Second Book of Mother, Verses XIV thru XXVI

# Chapter 1

The soft knock on my door couldn't be my head of household and personal assistant Sivan with my second pot of tea. She would have simply barged into my office. The jingle of bells as the door opened immediately set my teeth on edge. I wish I could blame my reaction on my visitor. However, my past wasn't High Sister Dragonfly's fault.

Nor was my present predicament her fault. Dragonfly wasn't sleeping with my lover. The saddest part was I liked and respected Sister Claudia of Love, but I could no longer stand to be around her, which was the reason Dragonfly came to my office in the Temple of Balance for the last few weeks instead of me going to the Temple of Love.

"Good morningtide, High Sister." I set aside the latest dispatches from the Issuran home Temple of Balance in the capital. Whatever else my own Reverend Mother prattled about could wait. "Ready for our next round of examinations?"

High Sister Dragonfly's veil fluttered with her sigh. "I hope you've had your first cup of tea, Chief Justice." Her hands clutching the mound of scrolls and bound parchment were bright orange. Whatever currently bothered her must be worse than the audit of Orrin's Temple of Love.

The poor priestess had inherited a royal mess when her predecessor, my birth mother, had been caught in a number of criminal acts, not the least of which were embezzling from her own order, demon dealing, and high treason.

"I already had an entire pot as a matter of fact, but Sivan should be here any moment with freshly brewed tea." I cleared my desk of research grimoires from Light and Knowledge.

Frankly, I was a little surprised the wardens didn't insist on being in the room with us. But it was a terribly tight space between my desk, my tiny table, and the multiple shelves for Balance's records.

And I didn't have all of them. The majority sat in the storage library adjoining my clerks' office.

"What has happened?" I asked as I dropped the last pile in the corner behind my chair.

Dragonfly flipped back her veil. Her shorn cheeks were as bright orange as her hands.

The silk covered her face as required by all the priestesses of the Temple of Love when in public. Here in my office, neither of us stood on ceremony. The times we had met privately at her office, she would often switch between male and female civilian clothing rather than wear the formal robes of a priestess. I could never decide if she made a more handsome woman or a prettier man, but such was the lot of a *berda* in the service of Love.

Neither of which mattered with the feeling of dread in the pit of my stomach. I feared she would announce Claudia was with child.

Dragonfly shook her head, and the bells lining her robes and threaded through her intricate hairstyle jingled. "You are not going to be pleased with this news, Anthea." She inclined her head toward the open door where my squire Nathan stood, awaiting orders. Beyond in the hallway, Balance Warden Jonata and one of the new Love wardens stood guard, a leftover from the demon attack inside the city of Orrin right before the Spring Rituals. No warden would let their priest or priestess go anywhere unescorted.

It had become damn annoying when I had to attend a privy other than the one in my personal quarters.

"Nathan, would you please tell Sivan my morning visitor has arrived early?"

"Yes, m'lady." He bobbed his head and took off in the direction of the kitchen.

Dragonfly closed the door Nathan had forgotten and dropped heavily into one of the sturdy oak chairs on the other side of my desk while I took my own seat. "Gerd has escaped. The Reverend Mother of Love believes she may be headed south."

"What?" This was worse than Claudia carrying my Luc's child. My right hand automatically reached for my sword, but my scabbard and harness hung from their peg behind me. I forced myself to relax and lowered my hand. "How? What happened?"

"No one seems to be sure on the details, according to my Reverend Mother." Dragonfly handed me the top parchment on her pile before she leaned forward and rested her elbows on the scarred oak of my desk.

I ran my fingers over the parchment. There were none of the raised marks used by my Temple for records. Though I wasn't blind like the rest of my order, even my odd sight couldn't quite discern between the ink and the thin skin. Which meant I couldn't read the demon-blasted original.

I rerolled the message. "May I have Donella make a copy of this?"

"That's the reason I brought it," Dragonfly answered sourly. "I rather suspected you didn't know about Gerd's escape yet."

There had been nothing of that sort in the dispatches from the home Temple of Balance in Standora. Why hadn't an alert gone out from the capital? Such news should have been stamped with the priority symbols. The Temples of Balance should have known before Love. Balance's gaol in Standora was where Gerd had been imprisoned.

Unless the Reverend Mother's pride had gotten in the way. Losing a traitor of this magnitude would have our entire order questioning her competence.

I sucked in a deep breath and released it. "Tell me."

"The warden who delivered her evening meal was found in her cell beneath her blankets. Dead. He wasn't discovered until the next morning."

"What about the second warden? No one opens a cell door without a reinforcement." I couldn't see any warden much less any assigned to Balance breaking protocol, especially not with a treason case of this magnitude.

"They haven't found him."

"Balance help us." I wiped my hands down my face. "This is not good." I pushed to my feet. I needed to move.

My birth mother on the loose meant the Reverend Mother of Balance was right. There was a traitor within her own Temple in the capital. Goddess, no wonder she wanted to keep this quiet. The dread in my stomach shifted to fury at her blasted ego.

"Why does your Reverend Mother believe Gerd is fleeing south?" I asked as I paced in the small confines of my office.

"According to the Reverend Father of Child, Gerd's overriding desire is to kill you and torture me."

I stopped abruptly. My robes swirled around my ankles. "You say that very calmly."

Dragonfly shrugged. "It's not the first time Gerd has threatened me."

Which was true. Even though Dragonfly had been Gerd's second, she had never trusted the *berda* and often threatened her with castration if she didn't obey Gerd's every whim and command.

"If it makes you sleep better, Gerd allegedly hasn't decided exactly what retribution to inflict on High Mother Bianca." Dragonfly chuckled.

I shook my head as I rolled possibilities and probabilities through my mind. I still wasn't sure how involved Orrin's seat of Mother had been in Gerd's illegal activities. There were a lot of rumors, but no actual evidence. Gerd could simply be enraged Bianca failed to convince the other Temple seats regarding the false charges my birth mother had brought against me. However, I sincerely doubted the matter was that straightforward.

"Would any of the other Love priestesses here in Orrin help her?"

Dragonfly cocked her head and simply stared at me.

"That was an idiotic notion." I bowed. "My apologies to your sisters for even allowing the thought to enter my head." Gerd and her renegade allies had done worse things than those mentioned by the Reverend Father of Child in order to keep the city's Love clergy under control. Their Temple had been closed to worshippers for a month as they dealt with the physical and emotional damage. Our evaluation of the financial damage was ongoing despite three months of efforts on mine and Dragonfly's parts.

Dragonfly inclined her head in return, granting me a bit of forgiveness for my blunder.

I resumed pacing and tapped my index finger against my chin. "So, who else in Orrin is mad enough to possibly help her?"

Dragonfly laughed despite herself. "Why do you make light of such serious matters?"

"Would you prefer I soil myself?" I grinned at her. "She should have been executed three months ago for demon dealing alone. In the meantime, we gather proof of Gerd's additional misdeeds in your ledgers, and she still hasn't lost her head."

"My Reverend Mother does want a complete picture." Dragonfly patted the topmost record book. "She's already started financial audits in other Love Temples now that we have an inkling of what to look for."

Sivan chose that moment to burst into my office with tea and cups.

"Find Chief Warden Little Bear for me," I ordered as she set down the tray on my desk.

Sivan frowned at my rudeness.

"Please," I amended. "It's a matter of Temple security."

Alarm filled her expression. "What happened?"

"Our dear Reverend Mother managed to lose the Mad Whore."

# Chapter 2

Of course, Little Bear demanded a group meal at midday with our counterparts from the Temple of Light to discuss the situation regarding Gerd's escape. I thanked Balance our cook Deborah put up with our shenanigans. My predecessor Chief Justice Penelope didn't entertain visitors often, if at all. I wasn't sure if it was due to the senility that gradually destroyed her mind before her death or her generally disagreeable nature from the hints from others besides the Balance staff. However, my Temple had become the meeting place for the clergy, the local nobility, the Guilds, and the citizen officials. Mainly, because I didn't tolerate petty politics.

Not when we'd been dealing with the Assassins Guild, demons, and renegade humans for the last year.

My staff rather enjoyed the reaction of the Light personnel when I announced the news from Love. Our visitors would have been less surprised if I'd tossed a Jing flashbang with a lit fuse in the middle of the dining table.

After the initial shock and disbelief, the three junior clergy and the chief warden of Light surreptitiously peeked at High Brother Luc at the opposite end of the dining table from me. As the seat of Light in Orrin, he had a particular cause to dislike my birth mother. Especially after her renegade allies cut off Luc's left foot and delivered it to me in their attempt to force me to turn over a demon grimoire Gerd had obtained and managed to lose.

I spent a great deal of my nights since midwinter, lying awake in my bed and wondering if I had made the correct decision.

"Why foster her escape?" Luc said.

"What do you mean, sir?" Brother Garbhan said. As the newest priest of Orrin's Temple of Light, he was often reluctant to speak up during our meetings. He must be thoroughly rattled to ask questions aloud.

I leaned my elbows on the polished oak surface of our dining table. "He means why isn't she dead. She lost a demon grimoire the renegades wanted. She exposed the Assassins Guild's alliance with the renegades, and by that, ruined the plot to quietly takeover Orrin as they had Tandor—"

"You're forgetting your own contribution," Justice Elizabeth teased. "You're the one who uncovered Samael DiRoy's conspiracy with the previous duke and duchess of Orrin."

The former chief justice of Tandor had remained in Orrin for her recovery from the year of torture the renegades had inflicted on her. Despite her emotional troubles, I was grateful for her presence. My junior justice Yanaba had been suffering from excessive morning sickness. I wished I could say my gratitude was due to the easing of our workload, but I would be lying to myself.

When Gerd tried to illegally end her pregnancy, she left me blind and unable to bear children. Elizabeth had been granted an exception to the recent change in Temple policy, which allowed, well reluctantly encouraged, the orders of Balance and Light to pursue carnal relations. With the increase of demon activity, we needed as many clergy with our particular talents as we could conceive.

But between my inability to have children and the terrible things the renegades did to Elizabeth, we often retreated to my office and commiserated over a bottle of red wine from the Pana Valley. Even now, Elizabeth sat between me and Sister Shi Hua of Light at the table because she could barely tolerate being in the presence of any priest of Light after what the skinwalkers made High Brother Dav, Luc's counterpart in Tandor, do to her.

I cleared my throat. "I found out totally by accident. We've been lucky—"

"You call losing the city of Tandor lucky?" Luc exclaimed.

"Considering we saved a majority of the civilians in the midst of a demon siege and invasion," I snapped back. "Yes, I do." Regret immediately flooded me. "I apologize for taking my anger out on you." I blew out a deep breath. "All of you. I'm worried. Worried Gerd and her Assassins Guild cronies will attack the people I care about while the renegades carry out some other scheme."

"We've been warned she's on the loose, which is a point in our favor." Little Bear ran his index finger around the rim of his ceramic cup. I didn't need to sniff his cup to know it contained water. He might have a tankard of ale on his day off, but I'd never observed him drink more than a sip or two of wine at a communal meal out of etiquette.

"However, I agree with the high brother." Little Bear's gaze fixed on me. "The Assassins Guild doesn't suffer failure. Especially not failure of Gerd's magnitude. If she didn't commit suicide out of loyalty to them, and they didn't silence her, then they need her for another purpose."

"But what purpose?" Yanaba asked to my right. She reached unerringly for the pitcher of milk in front of her despite being unable to see it and poured some into her bowl of oat porridge. Deborah made sure to serve my junior justice something that would agree with her delicate stomach.

Shi Hua sighed. "We could speculate on that subject until the stars fall from the sky. We won't know until the knives are at our throats." As if to emphasize her point, she jabbed her table knife into the slice of roasted duck on her plate and sawed furiously even the bird was far more tender than the dried venison and beef we'd relied on through the winter.

Her skin glowed dark pink, far hotter than the effort she expended on the slice of breast on her plate. The fact I knew she was with child was driving me mad. It was really none of my business, given the uncomfortableness regarding the lifting of the chastity restriction on our orders. It was merely a reminder another priestess could do something I couldn't, especially when Shi Hua hadn't confided in me.

"It would be nice if we were ahead of whatever the renegades planned for once," Brother Jeremy growled. He was Luc's second and had been assigned to Orrin just before Luc took over as high brother. The young priest was the only remaining clergy of Light from my grandfather Kam's reign as high brother.

Part of me wondered what Kam would have made of this mess. I liked him long before I knew of our familial relationship, and I missed him terribly. Losing him to an assassin's blade meant for me was one more sin of Gerd's, his own damn daughter.

"It would help if we had a true oracle at our disposal," Nicholas said quietly.

All of us paused eating and stared at Light's chief warden. Even my blind sisters turned their heads in the direction of his voice.

"Why, Chief Warden, did you just make a joke?" I grinned at him. The quiet man rarely offered his opinion unless he was asked directly, though he'd become more vocal over the last six months.

The corners of Nicholas's lips twitched beneath his turquoise facial hair. "It's been known to happen occasionally. However, I'm not jesting at the moment. Brother Jeremy is right. We can't keep chasing the renegades. It's as productive as a hound chasing its tail."

"So, what do you suggest?" Luc asked.

Nicholas shrugged. "We infiltrate them."

"But Thief has tried," Shi Hua said.

"They know Thief's practices too well as an offshoot of that Temple," Nicholas murmured. "It would have to be someone they'd normally be interested in turning to their cause."

"Then who? And how?" I waved my hand to indicate everyone at the table. "Anyone we truly trust is too well known to the renegades."

"We have two possibilities," Nicholas said. "Chief Justice Elizabeth or Brother Garbhan."

"Me?" Garbhan squeaked. The newest brother of Light was a winter younger than Jeremy. On the surface, he seemed terribly shy and unsure of himself. However, he'd been one of Reverend Father Farrell's primary aides. And after a couple of incidents Shi Hua and Jeremy mentioned involving the Reverend Father, Luc and I rather suspected everything we said in front of Garbhan was reported back to the Issuran home Temple of Light.

"Of course." Elizabeth leaned forward as if trying to peer into Nicholas's soul. "Garbhan could be extremely dissatisfied with his new posting since he's no longer directly advising the Reverend Father. In my case, we use the story that the renegades in Tandor succeeded in converting me."

"High Brother, I assure you I have no complaints about being assigned to your Temple," Garbhan protested with a wild look in Luc's direction.

However, Luc was staring at me. From the tight rein on his thoughts, he didn't like his chief warden's idea, but he wouldn't undermine the man in front of his peers. No doubt we would be discussing this matter later in private. Luc turned to Garbhan.

"Your loyalty isn't the issue, Brother." He smiled at the young priest. "However, most priests in your position would consider such a transfer an insult."

"B-but with Tandor gone, and the loss of most of your staff—" Garbhan blinked. "Oh!" His face shifted from orange-yellow to a red-orange. Maybe the naïve persona the young priest displayed was his true face. Few people could control their body heat to such a level.

"Can High Sister Mya or someone from her order create a sub-personality for us?" Elizabeth asked.

"You mean like what your seat of Child did with High Brother Aduba to gain the confidence of the renegades?" I asked.

She nodded.

"I'll make the inquiry, but between her and Talbert, I believe it's possible." I pushed back my own plate, my appetite gone despite Deborah's excellent roast duck. "I'm not sure putting you in that position is such a good idea."

"Nicholas is right." Elizabeth gestured in the general direction of Light's chief warden. "It wouldn't take much to make it appear as if the renegades broke me. Garbhan is too valuable to risk since we have so few Light talents in Orrin. I'll just need a little extra help to make the deception work."

I opened my mouth for my retort on the matter when someone knocked on the door of Balance's new dining room. "Come!"

Warden Gina pushed the door open, her skin orange-red and worry rolling off her psyche. "I beg your pardon for the interruption, Chief

Justice, but Peacekeeper Jaime is here. There's been an incident involving your squire."

Alarm jerked my body. "Nathan?"

She nodded. "Magistrate DiCook requests your presence along with a member of Light."

My heart sank. There was only one reason Malven DiCook would want me and one of the clergy from Light.

There had been a murder.

# Chapter 3

My worry over Nathan superseded my annoyance at Luc ordering Jeremy to accompany me. Things between Luc and me had been strained since the order came down lifting the chastity restrictions of our Temples. Because Balance and Light formed the backbone of the judicial proceedings, not only in Issura but the entire world, the original restriction was necessary to provide a semblance of impartiality in court proceedings.

Luc and I had broken that rule years ago. Our illicit affair hadn't really mattered because I couldn't conceive. But now . . .

Now, we needed as many children with Light and Balance talents as we could produce. Especially Light, because the demons were more vulnerable to their direct powers. The renegades allied with the demons had been targeting that particular order due to the demons' susceptibility.

And I could never bear any child, much less one with Luc's abilities. Which meant he needed to lay with other women to have those children.

As he'd been doing for the past three months with Sister Claudia.

A shiver ran through me. The large buildings were built closer together at this end of the city. They blocked the warmth of the summer sun from reaching the street despite the day being less than a candlemark past First Afternoon.

"A copper for your thoughts?" Jeremy murmured.

Nassa snorted and tossed her head as if affirming the priest's question. I patted her neck. However, the last thing I should discuss was my own envy.

We rode through the slums of Orrin on the southern edge of the harbor, well away from the duke's estate and the homes of the other nobles and prosperous merchants. The people here were much less afraid to speak aloud about the Red Justice. Therefore, I had an excuse to answer the younger priest without betraying my private musings.

"I'm thinking we should have brought more wardens," I said as I scanned the crowd. From the color of their exposed skin, few were happy to see me in their neighborhood. "Balance help us, I hope we don't have an incident beyond the one Magistrate DiCook called us to attend."

There was a time when I wouldn't have feared walking in any part of this city. However, we had six wardens escorting us today as well as two peacekeepers, but they may not be enough if the people staring at us and muttering decided to get ugly.

The first demons in a hundred years showed up when I covered the Duchy of Orrin as a circuit justice because my own Reverend Mother refused to name a replacement after Chief Justice Penelope passed. Since I'd been assigned as chief justice of Orrin, or sentenced rather, more demons appeared. And the citizens of the city and duchy blamed the justice with the red eyes for the demons' return.

Now, Orrin was crowded with refugees from Tandor. The resettling process was slow, and tempers frayed. In three months, everyone had forgotten we'd fought and destroyed a demon army along with Issura's southernmost city. No, they only remembered what they lost.

Or what they believed they were losing by helping our neighbors.

"Back this way, m'lady," Peacekeeper Jaime said, pointing to a narrow alley barely wide enough for two horses abreast between a warehouse and a ramshackle tenement. From the grim set of the peacekeeper's mouth, something more than the muttering crowd disturbed him. When I had asked about DiCook's summons, Jaime shook his head and said I would have to see for myself.

I didn't need my odd sight to find the body on the cobblestones, nor did I need the cluster of peacekeepers. The smell of death put the sweat of men and the stink of fish to shame. I dismounted, and Nathan surged past the crowd of DiCook's people and flung his arms about me.

My fingers met rough homespun clothing when I wrapped my arms around the boy. I eyed my head of household as she approached me. There wasn't any need to touch Sivan's clothing. She would have been dressed the same as Nathan and my stablemaster.

"Where's Hogarth?" I asked Sivan.

"With the magistrate." She gestured at the knot of peacekeepers.

Nathan peered up at me. Despite his efforts to maintain a stoic demeanor, salt crystals stained his cheeks. "You have ta find out who killed Yellow Fin."

"We'll do our best, young squire," Jeremy said. "Why don't you stay here with the wardens while the chief justice and I examine the site?"

The Light priest spoke gently to Nathan However, I could feel the sharp pricks of his psyche against mind. He lost his carefree attitude on the battlefield of Tandor. The loss of his bright outlook on life left a bad taste in my mouth.

Jeremy wasn't the only one affected by the aftermath of that battle. One of Shi Hua's nightmares accidentally set off the alarms of their Temple, and Elizabeth had resorted to warding her bedchambers each night to keep from disturbing the sleep of everyone else in Balance with her terrible dreams.

The peacekeepers parted when we reached them. The corpse had gone cold, but the size of it bothered me. It lay in a cool puddle that could have been water, but the sharp pungent stench said the liquid was something else. I knelt carefully beside the body and gently fingered the clothing at its shoulder. The weave of the cloth was rougher than even the clothing my three staff members currently wore. It felt like the roughspun used to carry grain. The flesh beneath was bone-thin.

I looked up at Jeremy.

"Throat's been slit." He frowned. "There should be more blood than this even for the boy's small size."

"Aye," DiCook said. "That was our conclusion as well."

"Why in the name of Child would someone bother with a street urchin?" I asked.

"Also, a good question," DiCook muttered. "And why leave him where he could be found? Why not burn the body themselves?"

I gently lifted the corpse's wrist. Its hand hung limp from my grasp. "Rigor has come and gone."

Something about this didn't feel right. Not even the people of the slums would leave a body lying around like this. There was too much danger of a demon possessing the corpse and wreaking havoc. Protocols regarding prevention of demon infestations had been slacking over the last century, but with the Battle of Tandor, those same protocols were being strictly enforced now. They could save Orrin from a similar fate as our sister city.

I looked up at the men. "Who found Yellow Fin?"

"Squire Nathan did, m'lady," Hogarth fingered the sailor's cap he wore as part of his disguise. He gestured at the warehouse. "The boy said this is one of the places he and his friends hid before he entered Temple service."

I examined our surroundings. After witnessing Shi Hua climb over impossible walls and dance along rooftops, I could make out the tiny hand and footholds those with appendages smaller than mine could use. Near the top of the building to my left, there was a single window with a broken shutter. I would question Nathan, but that attic was clearly one of the street children's nightly refuges.

However, I needed a better picture of events down at street level that resulted in Yellow Fin's body being left in the alley. A healthy layer of dirt and offal covered the cobblestones. The building to each side were contrived of wood, but their foundations were a mix of stone and brick.

"Would you give us some room, Magistrate and Peacekeepers?" I settled on the cobblestones and crossed my legs. "Let's see who left this poor unfortunate here." Despite the heat of the summer day, I pulled on my gloves. No sense in sticking my bare hands in the filth.

Resting one covered palm on the alley cobblestone and the other on the riverstone foundation of the tenement, I concentrated on the threads of time and pulled on them. A demon-black wad of nothingness shot toward me from the past. I tried to release the strings of time, but I couldn't stop the demon magic.

White light flashed around me, blinding me, and pain spiked through my mind. When I could see again, cobblestones dug into my spine and ribs.

Jeremy lay on top on me in the alleyway, his arms wrapped around my neck. Somehow, he kept my head from slamming into the stones or bricks around us. I glanced around the alley. The corpse still rested on the cobblestones in the same position it had been. However, all the peacekeepers and the magistrate had been knocked over by the . . . whatever that thing had been.

"What the demon was that?" I muttered.

"A trap spell of some kind," Jeremy said as he climbed to his feet. "I barely raised a ward in time. Otherwise, I fear we all would have journeyed with the boy to Death's realm."

Balance take whoever had done this to Nathan's friend. I needed to be more thorough in my examinations. I should have learned that lesson after the horrors that had been inflicted on Brother Jon of Light, not to mention Peacekeeper Dante and his family. But the damn spell had been so subtle.

No, not subtle. It had been placed on the corpse in the past. I accidentally yanked it forward to the moment of my rewind. So technically, it didn't exist when Jeremy and I approached the body.

I sighed and looked up at the priest. "Well, I think that answers why the body was left here."

# CHAPTER 4

Rather than take any more chances, I ordered the corpse to be salted before I allowed Master Devin and his apprentice to load the body into their cart when they pulled up a few moments later. The healers were accompanied by Sister Raven Claw and Warden Hitari of Death. I trusted the master healer to wait until I arrived at their guild house before beginning his examination. The clergy of Death here in Orrin did, too. However, the home Temples of Death still held a grudge over the schism between them and what became the Healers Guild, so one of Death's clergy were required to observe.

Jeremy insisted Master Devin examine me for any injuries before he left despite my protestations. Magistrate DiCook seconded Jeremy's request. The healer pronounced me as healthy, and as stubborn, as ever except for a bruised right shoulder. My joint had taken the brunt of Jeremy's weight when he dived to cover and ward me against the trap spell.

Magistrate DiCook stepped closer to me while the apprentice turned around the wagon to make their way to the center of Orrin. The healers' horses trotted at a steady, solemn clip, followed by Raven Claw and Hitari on their mounts. Even the formerly mumbling crowd showed the appropriate silence for the demise of someone so young as the wagon and its escort passed them.

"Can you still do the rewind?" DiCook murmured.

"I can try," I replied. "But let Brother Jeremy and I doublecheck the alley before we make another attempt. I doubt you'd want us to fry your peacekeepers' brains if we miss another trap spell."

DiCook shook his head. "I'm not talented, and I know you'll correct me if I'm wrong, but it was almost like the trap wasn't in the now. Like it came into existence when you started your spell."

"Because it existed in the past. When I rewound time, my spell yanked it to our moment," I said. "I pulled a similar stunt with the demons in the Tandoran tunnels." I shook my head. "Either someone survived who knew about my deed, or I wasn't as inventive as I thought."

DiCook snorted. "How many refugees did you and Luc bring back? It could be any one of them."

His observation only brought back my worry concerning Elizabeth. She'd been at the skinwalkers' mercies for nearly a year after they taken over our sister city. The same city we destroyed in order to kill the demon army. Every time I was sure Elizabeth was innocent of being under the renegades' influence, something like the trap spell on the boy's corpse made me wonder about her true loyalties. She, Luc, the Diné Reverend Father of Conflict, and Brother Bumblebee, a Diné Light priest, were the only ones who knew about my stunt placing the magical equivalent of a flashbang in the past of the Tandoran tunnel system.

No, the surviving demons in the tunnel knew about my trick as well. Were there more renegades among the survivors from Tandor than we realized? Had the demon disguised as Gray Sparrow the innkeeper spied on us and passed along the information before we killed her? Or had the Wildlings missed another disguised demon? If I continued rolling such questions and concerns through my mind, they would surely drive me mad.

"Despite my talents, I can only deal with one problem at a time," I answered. "We investigate Yellow Fin's death step-by-step as we would any other murder."

DiCook snorted at my attempt at levity, but he remained silent while Jeremy and I did a thorough check of the alley. When we were done, I settled on the cobblestones once again.

I hesitated before I reached for the timelines. I'd never had to worry about anyone being harmed directly by this spell before now.

I looked up at DiCook. "Magistrate, you and your peacekeepers should vacate the alley in case I missed something."

"You heard the chief justice, lads and lassies." He jerked his head in the direction of where we'd entered. "Out."

After a bit of grumbling and protests, the peacekeepers divided and walked back to the streets framing the alley. Our wardens were smart enough to stay out of our way unless one of them needed to witness for me if Jeremy or no other Light clergy were available.

"You, too, Malven," I murmured.

"Nah, I trust you." He spat on the cobblestones before he grinned at me. "And I trust Brother Jeremy here even more. The boy's faster than you."

"I'm not a boy," Jeremy growled.

DiCook looked startled at the priest's foul mood. Nor was it like Jeremy to snap at anyone, even if I had nearly gotten us killed. But he had been increasingly short with everyone since he returned home.

Maybe I needed to speak with Luc privately about sending Jeremy over to High Sister Mya of Child. Her talent would be far more useful to the young priest's peace of mind than a reprimand would at this time.

"Of course, you may stay, Magistrate," I said softly. "However, the risk to life and limb are your responsibility."

"Understood, Chief Justice." He glanced at Jeremy with a worried expression.

I didn't need to touch DiCook's mind. I had the same concerns about Jeremy, as did Shi Hua. She had continued her intimate relationship with Jeremy because they were ordered to, but she'd asked me for my advice when it came to the changes in his behavior since the Battle of Tandor.

"Let me know when you are ready, Brother," I said.

He inhaled deeply. The sharper edges of his psyche receded, but it still prickled against mine. A visit to Child was definitely in order before the week was out.

"I am ready to witness for you, Chief Justice," Jeremy murmured.

I reached into the memories of the surrounding cobblestones and bricks. The stones were steadier, but the bricks and wood paid more attention to the humans since they injured and transform the respective building materials. I yanked on the timelines from two days ago, half-expecting something to rush out of the past again. However, my spell worked as expected this time.

My odd eyesight marginally picked up the chill wisps of the past, but I still couldn't see them as clearly as anyone with normal human vision could. I still had to rely on a witness to relay the actions just like my blind sisters did.

Candlemarks slipped between my fingers, faster than the normal passage of time but slow enough for Jeremy to make out events. Sweat beaded along my hairline and trickled down my spine.

"Slower, m'lady," Jeremy said. "Four peacekeepers are passing through the alley. I can't estimate the time. Magistrate?"

"I've increased the number of personnel patrolling during the evening and night hours over the last few months," DiCook said.

"Has there been problems in this section of the city?" Jeremy shifted to view the time shadows as they continued up the alley.

"Not yet," DiCook grumbled. "Hoping to prevent it."

"Continue, Chief Justice," the priest murmured.

I sped the passage of hours. Jeremy noted the peacekeepers passed through this alley at least once per hour. However, the intervals were random. DiCook trained his people well.

"Hold!" Jeremy said. He took a few steps toward the west end of the alley and circled a spot of grayish mist. "The person appears to be dressed in a black cloak, leggings, and boots in the style of the Temples."

"Balance or Death?" I gritted my teeth at holding the time lines still.

"There's no insignia on the robes, and I can't see their face." Jeremy stepped back from the faint image. "Continue."

The time phantom stopped before me and dumped its bundle on the cobblestones and piss. My anger and sorrow at the treatment of the child's body nearly made me lose my grip on the threads of the past.

"From the angle of the shadows, the person arrived shortly after First

Morning." Jeremy crouched across from me. "They're unwrapping the child from a blanket." He gasped. "Hold!"

"Brother . . ." My entire body shook from the strain of holding time in one moment.

He pointed at something and looked up at DiCook. "Do you see this, Magistrate?"

DiCook's face paled to a dull yellow. He nodded and muttered a curse under his breath.

I couldn't hold the lines at one point any longer. My fingers burned as the moment slipped from my grasp, and time snapped back to the now. I leaned my elbows on my knees and tried to catch my breath. I hadn't lost control of a rewind spell like that since I was a novice.

A hand touched my left shoulder. "You all right, Anthea?" DiCook murmured.

I reached up and patted his hand. "Despite Brother Jeremy's efforts, that trap spell affected me more than I realized. It's nothing a little rest and some tea won't take care of."

"Perhaps Master Aaron should take another look at you before you continue this investigation," DiCook said. Both he and Jeremy took my hands and pulled me to my feet.

"First, tell me what you saw." My gaze flicked between the two men. The skin on Jeremy and DiCook heated to a brilliant red under my odd sight.

Jeremy exhaled. "The blanket held the insignia of Mother."

My stream of obscenities would have blistered the ears of the demons themselves.

# CHAPTER 5

I didn't dislike High Mother Bianca. At least, not the way I loathed clams. But Balance help me, I didn't trust the woman. Not after she accused me of misconduct at midwinter.

Granted, my birth mother Gerd had been the primary instigator in the false charges. But even after everything that had happened in Orrin, I still wasn't sure if Bianca was Gerd's accomplice or her gudgeon.

However, the boy's murder in the slums, the blanket both a clergy member and a civilian official witnessed in my rewind, and Dragonfly's news gave me more than enough reasons to make a formal visit to the Temple of Mother. And if I was making this a formal visit, I would take my chief warden.

Upon returning to the Temple of Balance, I dispatched Nathan with a note of apology regarding my tardiness to Master Healer Devin. The murdered boy was going nowhere, and catching Bianca off guard might be a more productive use of my time. After giving Little Bear a brief account of the events in the slums, my entourage and I headed for the Temple of Mother.

The architecture of each of the Temples represented their namesake deity. Balance's walls were stern, unyielding, with narrow horizontal windows high on the top edges. The only hint of softness was in its central dome.

Mother's structure seemed to be nothing but curves. Round towers marked its four corners. Scalloped carvings linked the slender turrets. More reliefs decorated the walls. While Balance was a fortress, Mother was a work of art that even my strange eyesight could appreciate. The craftsmanship of the Temple would be the only pleasantness of this visit.

Upon our arrival, one of the junior priestesses escorted my party to Mother's main receiving room. She left and closed the double doors behind her.

I sat on one of the cushioned armchairs and pushed back my hood. Jeremy and Little Bear took their stances at my shoulders while the other four wardens spaced themselves to keep eyes on the main doors, the windows, and the service door to the kitchen area.

Tapestries covered the marble walls. While I couldn't make out the individual designs, they were probably a blend of Chumash, Toscan, and Briton patterns, which had become the standard in Issura over the past three hundred years. Back when Luc and I traveled circuit in the east, he often let me look through his eyes to see what neither my blindness nor my odd sight could discern. While the lack of temperature differences meant I couldn't appreciate the artistry of the tapestries, I could detect the tiny spy holes in the walls of Mother.

None of my party said a word while we waited. We all knew we would be spied upon or listened to by the sisterhood. No sense giving Bianca any foreknowledge of the purpose of my visit.

Nearly a quarter of a candlemark passed before the double doors of the receiving room opened again. High Mother Bianca swept into the room with a flair of her robes and her hair piled high on her head. Two junior mothers accompanied her, their hoods raised and their eyes downcast, supposedly in the piety of service demanded of their order. Her chief warden, a dour-faced woman named Maebh, stationed herself at Bianca's right hand as the priestess claimed the chair on the opposite side of the rug from me. The two priestesses stood behind Bianca and Maebh, but spaced widely, a position from where they could launch spells at us while their chief warden could cover their high mother with steel.

Good to know no trust had developed between Bianca and me over the last six months.

I hadn't bothered to rise when she entered. It was a petty move on my part, but with the magic hangover headache centering itself between my eyes, I wasn't in the mood for niceties. But then, her staff hadn't served me any refreshment either.

Maybe I wasn't the only one acting in a petulant manner.

"To what do I owe this visit, Chief Justice?" Bianca drawled my title as if it were an insult.

"If I may remind you, High Mother, you voted to have me named as Chief Justice of Orrin at my trial last year," I said.

"You may not," she snapped. "State your business because we are both aware this isn't a social call. Or are you planning to illegally imprison me as you did High Father Jerrod?"

I didn't bother defending myself. Imprisoning Jerrod had been my way to protect him while I negotiated with demon dealers in my efforts to rescue Luc and capture or kill those same renegades. My efforts could have gotten both Jerrod and me executed if I let him be involved with the demon dealers.

Instead, I focused on the real purpose of my visit now. "A child who should have been under your care was found dead this morning in the south side slums."

Her skin color remained steady. "And you bring me this news rather than High Brother Xander because . . ."

"Upon superficial examination, the child's throat was slit." I shrugged. I wasn't about to give her any information regarding how we knew the boy's body had been dumped. "The Healers Guild will do a more thorough examination of the corpse to learn if there were any additional injuries."

Only Chief Warden Maebh reacted to my news, and even then, it was only a slight shift in her body color. She went from bright yellow to a burnt orange. None of the three priestesses showed any signs of distress at my statement.

The chief warden cleared her throat. "If I may, Chief Justice?" At my nod, she cleared her throat again. "The fault for this child's death is mine. I've been adamant the High Mother and our priestesses remain here given the recent attempts on your own life as well as the other seats in Orrin."

Maebh either wouldn't or couldn't meet my gaze, but then, that was my purpose in showing my own face. The color of my eyes disturbed people. Luc was the first person to tell me the truth. My attempted healing spell to give myself normal human sight had gone wrong and turned my eyes the color of blood.

I wasn't surprised Bianca would allow her chief warden to take the blame for her own inaction. As much as I wanted to truthspell the clergy and staff of Mother to find out what unspoken thing lay between them, I didn't have enough evidence to interrogate anyone here. Yet.

"While I appreciate your loyalty in protecting those clergy under your charge, Chief Warden, we all have our duties to the citizens of Orrin. We cannot allow our personal fear to interfere with our service."

My reprimand of Mother's chief warden finally elicited a reaction from Bianca. Her fury spiked against my own mental shield, and her face and hands glowed bright red.

"How dare you criticize my staff?" she hissed. "Each Temple deals with their own matters—"

"Unless terrible situations like this occur where our roles cross," I said coldly. "However, your chief warden may have her hands full already in attempting to keep you safe. If so, you need to petition your Reverend Mother for additional wardens."

Bianca sniffed. "Why would I need more?"

"Gerd escaped custody." I smiled. "While my death and High Sister Dragonfly's top her list for revenge, you, my dear High Mother, are running a very close third."

Color drained from Bianca skin until it was a dull greenish yellow. The priestesses accompanying her gasped. Maebh instinctively started to reach for her sword.

"She wouldn't dare," Bianca said. The disbelief in her voice said everything about her relationship with Gerd. As I suspected, Bianca was in deeper with my birth mother's misdeeds than anyone in Orrin realized.

"She had no problems attempting to kill her own child for the last thirty-one winters." I waved my hand in a nonchalant manner. "Everything from illegally terminating a Spring Ritual pregnancy to hiring the Assassins Guild. She had Sister Gretchen tortured and murdered for stealing a demon grimoire from her. She allowed renegades to torture and rape the priestesses of her own Temple while plotting with those same renegades to take over the city of Orrin." I leaned forward in my chair. "What makes you think she'd show *you* mercy?"

Bianca's nostrils flared as she considered my words. "Why are you warning me?"

This was what Luc would call a fishing expedition, but I didn't dare admit such at this time. Instead, I exhaled and met her gaze squarely. "We lost too many clergy in the Battle of Tandor. We cannot afford to lose anyone else. Not if we want to win this war."

"So, this is merely your concern for queen and nation?" Bianca's right eyebrow rose.

"No." I stood. "This is my concern for the survival of the human race. But if we stoop to slitting the throats of our children, I wonder if we deserve the lives the Twelve have bestowed on us. Maybe the demons truly have the moral high ground." I stalked out of Bianca's receiving room before I did or said anything idiotic.

Like trying to slap some sense into someone as self-obsessed as the high mother.

# CHAPTER 6

When we returned to Balance for our mounts, Little Bear insisted on accompanying me to my appointment at the Healers Guild with Warden Dezba and ordered Wardens Daniel and Tahoma to remain at our Temple. My chief warden revealed why he did so once we turned off the main thoroughfare.

"Our young squire is quite distraught over his discovery this afternoon." Little Bear eyed me as we rode. Neither he nor any of my wardens allowed me to walk further than the Temple District this days. Not without a heavy escort. Sometimes, not even then.

Otherwise, Little Bear insisted on horses. "Now that Sivan and Hogarth have been identified as Temple personnel by the south side citizens, we can't allow them to go back."

"And Nathan's friends will starve if they don't receive some assistance," I said. "A certain priestess refuses—"

"You can't continue taking on every other Temple's duties," he grumbled.

I couldn't help chuckling at the ludicrous nature of our situation. "I don't disagree with you, Chief Warden. I'm open to suggestions on how to get a certain priestess to perform her own damn job."

"If you hadn't already locked High Father Jerrod in the Temple of Balance, I would have suggested trying that with the certain priestess."

I turned to look at him. "Why, Chief Warden, between Nicholas of Light and you making jokes, I'd think the end times were here."

"Who said I was joking?"

Little Bear's quip made me wonder if I'd gone about my duties in the wrong way. I sighed. Of course, I had. Luc prodded me more than once that I should have taken a more diplomatic approach with the other seats. My own Reverend Mother used my illegal execution of a member of the royal family to force me to take the chief justice position in Orrin. I'd let my resentment toward my birth mother and my fury at the head of my Temple affect my relationships with the clergy here.

As always, it came back to Gerd. I'd given her the very tools she needed to attempt to remove me from my own Temple. If it weren't for the magistrate . . .

Balance help me. It was a wonder DiCook hadn't hung me out to dry after the way I treated him in the beginning of my tenure. So much had changed in the last year. I was used to the steady rhythm of riding circuit in the eastern foothills. The politics of the third largest city and second largest port of Issura would be my downfall.

When we arrived at the estate of the Healers Guild, the stablehands took our horses. An apprentice I didn't recognize bowed to us. Her long hair was bound in a bun in the Diné style.

"Chief Justice, Brother. Masters Aaron and Devin and High Brother Xander await you."

"And you are?" I prompted.

"Healer Apprentice Simi, m'lady." She smiled shyly. "I began my studies the day after the summer solstice."

I inclined my head. "A pleasure to meet you, Apprentice Simi."

"Will your wardens be joining us?"

"If you don't mind, we'll enjoy your herb garden. We know the way," Dezba said with a smile. The two Light wardens noticeably relaxed at her statement. I couldn't blame them. Observing Master Devin or Master Aaron's examination of a suspected victim of foul play wasn't my idea of an enjoyable time either. However, I often learned useful things by consulting with them.

"This way, Chief Justice, Brother." Simi pivoted and led Jeremy and me to the treatment building. Little Bear followed because he insisted a warden accompany me at all times. While I trusted the healers, he did not. Not after someone had poisoned the healers' almond oil stock and nearly killed me, Sivan, Nathan, and Devin. Dezba and the two Light wardens headed for the Healers' garden, though no doubt they'd finagle a snack and a drink from the guild's cook.

The Healers Guild estate consisted of two huge stone and wood manses. One was designated as living quarters for the guild members and their staff. The other was used for treating the sick and injured. All the lemon oil in the world couldn't totally eliminate the odors of decay and death, so I didn't blame guild personnel for the separation. Unfortunately, I'd spent too much time over the past year in the treatment building thanks to the Assassins Guild. Both my Reverend Mother and Ambassador Quan of Jing said I was too stubborn for Death to want to drag me to her realm.

We followed Simi to the treatment room Master Aaron had set aside for examining corpses. As the apprentice said, the guild leader was already there, which was an unusual occurrence. Normally, his second Master Devin handled these examinations. But it was the change in the insignia on Master Devin's assistant Bly that drew my attention first.

"You passed your examinations!" Even though I wasn't a physically demonstrative person, I wrapped my arms around her and hugged her tight. "Congratulations, Master Healer Bly!"

"Thank you, Chief Justice." She blushed at the compliment.

"You never hug me," the High Brother of Death protested.

Bly and I parted, and I eyed Xander.

"That's because we hear too much of each other these days." Still, I crossed to the priest and hugged him as well. Even though he'd become the seat of Death after the demise of High Sister Bertrice during the Battle of Tandor, he often took his morning and evening meals at Balance even when he did not spend the night with my junior justice. It relieved my mind he took an active interest in Yanaba and their child-to-come.

I leaned back and examined Xander's face. "Why isn't Sister Raven Claw observing?"

"I sent her to the south side because I was dealing with a Temple matter."

He sighed. "However, she also admitted she didn't think she could remain impartial given the circumstances."

I released my grip on the tall young man and turned to Aaron. "You rarely attend these post-mortem examinations anymore, Guild Master. What has piqued your interest in this matter?"

"I would like to say this was a mere formality in regards to Master Bly attaining her rank since this will be the first time she is the lead physician in such an examination." Aaron stroked his bare chin. Unlike so many other men in Issura, he remained clean-shaven instead of adapting the moustache and short chin-beard that had become popular among the civilians. "However, the apprentices noticed some problematic issues when they were removing the clothing from the body."

"Problematic issues?" I cocked my head. The guild master had a gift for understatement.

"Similar to the atrocities that were done to Sister Gretchen," he murmured. "And Squire Ming Wei."

Even though the time was approaching First Evening, well past our midday meal which I hadn't finished, my stomach rebelled at the memory of what had been done to the priestess before the renegades finally strangled her and stuffed her body in a barrel of Pana wine.

And if I thought too much about the horrors visited on Yanaba's squire before she came to Balance, I would definitely be sick.

"Twelve take them all," I spat.

"That's why I excused Sister Raven Claw," Xander murmured. So, this wasn't about any bias the priestess held toward the Healers Guild.

I almost wish the sister's dismissal was about the rift between the Temple of Death and the Healers Guild. Politics annoyed me, but it was nothing compared to the rage I felt toward the brutality inflicted on an innocent. Every person in the room glowed with the same fury. I sucked in a deep breath in an effort to calm myself. The best thing I could do for Yellow Fin was to discover who did this to him and bring the culprit to justice.

Jeremy and I joined Xander against the one bare wall and observed the proceedings. Little Bear squeezed himself between an apothecary cabinet and an equipment table in order to keep an eye on everything else.

Bly went to work with a brisk efficiency. Or maybe it was her desire to get a distasteful task over with as soon as possible. She had learned much from Devin over the last six months. The guild's clerk took notes for Bly with additional comments from Aaron and Devin, but for the most part, the older healers remained silent and stayed out of the way as the newly minted master catalogued the injuries inflicted on the boy.

On the other hand, poor Simi turned a pale green right before she fled the room. I looked up at Xander.

"Is it all right if I check on her?"

He nodded. "Brother Jeremy is here if there are any questions. I haven't met a healer apprentice or a Death novice who didn't empty their stomach over their first time with a situation such as this."

I stalked out of the examination room. Little Bear followed, but thankfully, he kept a discreet distance. The examination room was close to the main entrance into the manse, and the wide double doors were ajar. I didn't have to guess or reach out mentally for the young woman. Someone was definitely voiding their stomach in the garden. I jogged down the portico steps and followed the stone path to the mulch bed. The healer apprentice bent over the stone edging.

"Simi?" I placed my right hand on her shoulder. The girl straightened and burst into tears.

"I failed!" she wailed and flung her arms around my waist.

"You didn't fail at anything." I patted her back.

"Yes, I did." A sob shuddered through her body. "I was supposed to learn from Master Bly. She said it's an honor to assist the Temple of Balance. And I couldn't hold my stomach."

I guided her further along the winding garden path until we came to a wooden bench near the poppy beds. At the edge of my vision, I saw Dezba rush toward me, but Little Bear intercepted her. The two conferred quietly.

Once Simi and I sat on the bench, I wrapped my arm around her shoulders. She wiped her eyes and mouth on the edge of her apron.

"Do you really believe you're the first person to be affected by a dead body?" I said softly.

"I-I—" She licked her lips. "W-we are supposed to look at patients objectively."

"That's when you're trying to find the best way to treat someone's illness or injury," I said. "A healer needs to keep their head clear to find a solution. However, if you can look at the harm resulting in someone's death without feeling empathy for that person's suffering, then you shouldn't be any kind of caregiver."

Simi sniffed. "But the masters will send me home for running out on the examination."

"I can guarantee they will not," I said dryly.

"B-but—" More tears trickled down her face.

"Simi, the healing gift is exceedingly rare." I squeezed her shoulders. "Guild Master Aaron won't throw away such a talent. Besides, if vomiting got anyone out of their duties and responsibilities, I wouldn't be a justice."

"Y-you got sick?" She swiped her sleeves across her cheeks.

"My very first execution."

"But if justices can't see—"

"I can."

Her body stiffened beneath my arm. "I-I'm sorry. I forgot for a moment."

I chuckled. "Even for my blind sisters, it's not the view. We feel the condemneds' death, as we should since we are responsible for trying, convicting, and executing the person."

"Wh-what did the first person you had to execute do?"

Not even Luc had ever asked me that question. I sighed.

"The man I executed murdered his brother because he coveted his brother's wife."

Simi gasped. "What an awful thing to do!"

"Yes, and he regretted what he had done the instant after it happened, but it was too late." I shrugged. "My aim was quick and true, and he felt no pain, but the impression of Death taking a soul is not one you forget. I lost my morning meal all over the man's corpse in front of everyone, including the Reverend Mother of Balance. You are fortunate your gift allows you to help people."

Simi stared at the poppies before she looked back up at me. "I do not envy your position, Chief Justice."

"There are times I dislike my position as well, but hopefully, finding Yellow Fin's killer will appease Balance Herself." I squeezed the young apprentice's shoulders once again. "Master Bly chose you as her apprentice because she obviously sees potential in you. Are we ready to go back inside now that your stomach is empty?"

She nodded.

We rose and walked back to the examination room. I didn't envy Simi's position either. The young woman's innocence had been destroyed by witnessing the terrible acts inflicted on Yellow Fin, and like me, she'd probably have nightmares for quite a while after this.

# Chapter 7

Upon returning to the Temple district from the Healers Guild, the bells pealed First Evening. I turned to Dezba. "You're relieved for the evening, Warden. I need to relay our findings to High Brother Luc."

She glanced at Little Bear, who inclined his head.

"Very well, m'lady." She guided her mount toward the alley between Balance and Knowledge. The tiny passage was the closest to our own postern gate.

"You think I won't perform my duties adequately and inform my superior?" Jeremy bit out when she was far enough away not to overhear. The vehemence in the bright young priest's tone took me by surprise. The sharp shards of his psyche grated against my own mental walls again. It was almost painful.

Before I could formulate a response, Little Bear kneed his horse between ours. Nassa didn't respond, but Jeremy's mount skittered back a few steps. The two Light wardens escorting their priest exchanged looks, but thankfully, they didn't reach for any weapons.

"You will treat your superior with the respect she deserves." My chief warden's rebuke was far milder than the one I would have normally offered. But then, he was trying to save the priest a lashing for insubordination.

Jeremy drew a quick breath and looked ready to launch another scathing remark, but Little Bear's calm, steady demeanor reached the younger man far more effectively than harsher words would have. Jeremy exhaled, and the prickly edges of his mind receded. He faced me and bowed.

"My apologies for my ill manners, Chief Justice."

Both of the Light wardens relaxed at Jeremy's words.

"Accepted." I inclined my head in acknowledgement. "Today's events have disturbed all of us who were involved. And for the record, I would expect Justice Yanaba to report her findings to both me and the high brother of Light in the event of a murder investigation."

"Yes, m'lady."

Despite the young priest's confession of remorse, I definitely needed to have a quiet word with Luc about Jeremy's behavior. Over the last three months, his attitude had become increasingly distant, as were his ill temper over minor things. Enough so, that Shi Hua confided her worries to both me and Yanaba.

The five of us entered Light's postern gate. Their stablemaster Henry and two of his hands took our reins.

He bobbed his head. "Would you like one of my boys to return yours and the Chief Warden's horses to Hogarth, Chief Justice?"

"No, thank you, Henry." I smiled at the man. "Food and water will be enough. I have a feeling we will need them once I've spoken with the high brother."

"Was this about the boy that was found in the slums this afternoon?" Like my own Hogarth, Henry had been a warden for his Temple and kept an ear out for any fishwives' tales that might prove informative and useful.

"Have you learned anything I should know?"

"There's a rumor floating around the docks the body was dumped by someone in Temple robes."

A chill ran up my spine. No one but I, the magistrate, and Brother Jeremy knew that. The peacekeepers and wardens had been far enough away, they wouldn't have seen the ghost images clearly. However, the person who had actually left the boy's corpse in the alley knew what he or she wore. Unless there might be a witness who feared retribution if they came forward? Or had the rumor been started to cause us more grief?

If Jeremy was right and the person who dumped the corpse wore Balance robes, it would make my investigation a damn sight more difficult.

People in Orrin distrusted me thanks to the recent spate of demon incidents in our city alone.

"Do you have a source?" I asked.

"My brother heard it at the Seven Coins when he was delivering shellfish there around midday." Henry shrugged. "Mentioned it when he stopped here for our delivery."

The Seven Coins was a reputable inn. Luc and I often stayed there when we were on circuit and had to come to Orrin. Back then, I avoided the Temple of Balance itself like the plague unless duty forced me to go there.

"We should send someone through all the inns and taverns. See what other information we can find. If there was a witness who hasn't come forward, we need to find them before the person who is framing the Temples does," Jeremy said, giving voice to my own worries.

"I agree with the brother," Little Bear murmured.

"And I need some wine," I bit out. "Let's raid Light's stores and sort through the clues we do have. We'll proceed from there."

Much to my relief, we'd missed the First Evening services. When we entered the main sanctuary, the only people there other than Brother Garbhan, who was on ministerial duty, and Chief Warden Nicholas were two Love wardens. I needed an entire barrel of Pana red even more when I saw Sister Claudia of Love exit the hallway leading to the private chambers of the clergy. She may have been wearing her public veil over her face, but I'd recognize her even if she piled on several layers of Diné wool and Plains Nations buffalo robes until she was as round as a pig. Luc was with her, and he wore a huge smile.

My gut clenched. It was the same ridiculous smile Xander had been wearing for the past three months, and the same one Jeremy most likely would be wearing once Shi Hua told him she was with child. And if the smile weren't enough, the color of her skin from the extra heat a woman's body produced while growing a babe inside her womb confirmed the news.

That smile Luc wore made me want to draw my sword and chop Claudia into tiny pieces. Which wasn't fair to her. She was doing her duty. We needed more people with Light talent. But something deep and dark inside of me wanted to claim Luc as mine, even though I had no right to do so.

And frankly, I wasn't sure I could handle bearing a child if I were fertile. Not even Luc's babe, much less anyone else's. I feared I would be an even worse parent than my birth mother.

The pair spotted me from across the sanctuary. Luc matched the speed of Claudia's demure glide across the wood floor. He'd become quite adept with the specialized steel crutches Master Devin had designed for him since the loss of his left foot. He could move nearly as fast on them as he used to be able to run.

They halted before me, and Claudia glanced at Luc. He gave her an encouraging nod.

"May I speak with you privately, Chief Justice?" she said.

I didn't want to hear this news. I was the one who pointed out Luc couldn't disobey the edict handed down from our home Temples before the Spring Rituals. However, my heart still broke at the idea he had to lay with other women.

But to deny a minor request from a fellow priestess would be incredibly rude. I swallowed the lump threatening to choke me and nodded.

She led the way to one of the private consultation rooms adjoining the main sanctuary. Once we were inside, she murmured a word. Magic tingled across my skin, and I realized she'd lit the alabaster globe that indicated the room was in use.

She drew her veil back from her face. Braids cascaded down her back. Her skin color was a steady orange-yellow. "You have already deduced the news, haven't you?"

"Yes." I belatedly added, "Congratulations."

She sighed. "He loves you. He will always love you, Anthea. You have nothing to fear from me." Of course, she'd learned about his feelings for me. It was difficult to withhold thoughts and emotions from another talent during such an intimate act.

"I . . . know." I folded my arms across my chest. "I hope you can forgive me for my petty feelings. It isn't fair to you or your child." I inclined my head toward the globe. "Is that the reason Dragonfly suggested you to . . . Luc?"

Claudia nodded. The bells hanging from her braids chimed. "My mother was a Light talent, but of course, she could only register as a civilian practitioner. I inherited a small measure of her skills."

She stepped closer to me. "I hope you realize part of his joy in our conception is that his duty is done, and he can return to warming your bed."

My face heated at her obvious conclusion. "There's no point in my case."

"I am merely suggesting the two of you take advantage of the edict while it is practical." A wry smile crossed her face. "If you wish to be present for the birth, you are more than welcome, and I would be honored by your presence."

I laughed at the absurdity of her request. "Let's see how I handle Justice Yanaba's birthing before I answer your gracious offer. I'm not sure I would be much help."

"This child would have been yours if not for Gerd." Claudia's voice held so much bitterness, but I knew it had nothing to do with me personally.

"I'm sorry for what she did to you and your sisters."

Claudia snorted. "I don't hold her actions against you. I hope you can find it in your heart not to hold your feelings for me against Luc's child."

Her words drove home the truths I wanted to avoid. "I shall do my best."

"That's all the Twelve can ask of any of us." Claudia drew her veil back into place, the bells on it and her robes jingling, and extinguished the globe.

When we exited, the fear and worry on the men's faces was comical. The two female wardens appeared to be disgusted by the men.

I leaned toward the Love priestess and said, "I believe they expected us to duel at dawn."

"Crossbows at twenty paces?" Claudia's laughter chimed as delicately as her bells.

"You would bring a crossbow to a sword fight." I chuckled. The humor between us eased the ache in my heart a bit. Maybe, I could grow to accept the situation regarding her unborn child.

"If you two are finished mocking us, perhaps you and Brother Jeremy will enlighten us as to your findings," Luc said. The scowl he wore didn't disguise his joy. He was going to have a child.

And someone else lost a child in the last day. A child that should have been protected and cared for and cherished as much as Luc and Claudia would cherish the child she carried.

The swirl of emotions in my heart was too much. My eyes burned, and my nose clogged.

"Since you have business to discuss, I will take my leave of you, Chief Justice, High Brother." Claudia inclined her head before she swept out of the sanctuary in a whirl of silk and lace accented by the tinkle of bells. The two Love wardens quickly trotted after her.

"Well . . ." Luc drawled expectantly.

"May we have a couple of bottles of wine to get through this?" Jeremy muttered.

Luc looked askance at him before his eyes met mine. *What's going on?*

"Our brother misspoke." I shook my head. "We're going to need a barrel."

Sitting in the high brother's private dining room with the Light clergy, I calmly sipped from my goblet while Luc let loose a stream of Cantish invectives after our reports, including a couple of obscenities I hadn't heard before. His head of household Istaqa was right. The crisp white wine paired nicely with the baked fish, fresh asparagus, and wheat bread Light's staff served as the evening meal.

Jeremy had warded the room before we started our discussion. When Luc finally had to stop cursing in order to breathe, the younger priest also added the gossip from Henry's brother.

Luc rose from his chair, grabbed his crutches, and started pacing. "Three months? Three months of peace is all we get?"

"We knew it was merely the quiet before the next storm," I said softly.

"We also knew the renegades would try something here in Issura eventually," Shi Hua said. She hesitated a moment before she added, "There's something else you should know. The Temples in Jing have received no word from Reverend Father Chen regarding the other cache of demon eggs either."

Shi Hua's news added to the unease that had settled on my shoulders since Dragonfly shared her dispatch from the home Temple of Love this morning. Jing's Reverend Father Biming of Thief had traced part of a cache of demon eggs to this side of the Peaceful Sea. The hatching of those eggs resulted in the demon army we faced in Tandor.

From what Biming, Shi Hua, and Ambassador Quan said of Chen, Jing's Reverend Father of Conflict, he had issues with his ego and often let his pride get in his way. However, he was an accomplished warrior and adamant about his duties. He and members of his order chased the other half of the eggs. If neither the Jing Temples nor Emperor Chengwu had received any message from Chen over the last three months, Balance only knew whether he and his people were even still alive.

Or where those damn eggs were. Or even if they'd already hatched.

"With all due respect, High Brother, we need to focus on what we can control," Little Bear said before he turned to me. "Given your reaction to Henry's revelation in the stableyard, the rumor is true."

I nodded. "The news gets worse. The robes the person who dumped the corpse wore were either Balance or Death."

"There was no insignia though despite the style and color," Jeremy added.

Luc paused in his pacing. "Just like the renegades who abducted me wearing Light colors without symbols of rank or location."

I nodded again. "However, the blanket originally wrapped around Yellow Fin's body to carry it to the alley bore the insignia of Mother."

Luc dropped into his chair and leaned his crutches against the table. "Jeremy, did—"

"Of course, I had someone confirm it," the younger priest snapped. "The magistrate saw the same thing I did."

Everyone stared at Jeremy.

Realizing his poor manners, his face turned a brilliant crimson. "I apologize for my outburst, High Brother. This affair disturbs me more than I care to admit."

*Should I ask?* Luc whispered in my mind.

*Yes, there's additional information you should be aware of regarding your second*, I replied. *But now is not the time for that particular discussion.*

"It's disturbing to all of us." Shi Hua laid her hand over Jeremy's. He normally would have responded to her gesture with a smile or turning his palm to meet hers. He didn't respond, and the hurt in Shi Hua's expression was obvious even to me.

*Now, I know what part of our discussion will be about*, Luc said sourly.

"Have you spoken with High Mother Bianca about the dead boy?" he said aloud.

"Only as far as informing her about the death of one of her charges." I cut into the fish on my plate. "Neither she or the two other priestesses with her were surprised. Chief Warden Maebh was disturbed. She tried to take the blame for Yellow Fin's death by stating she had been restricting the clergy of Mother due to the recent spate of attempted assassinations on Temple seats in Orrin."

Luc snorted. "Like the High Mother would do anything someone else told her to do."

"Mother's chief warden may have been the one who dumped the body," Garbhan said quietly. "The act could be preying on her conscience."

Everyone at the table turned to stare at the newest Light priest. He so rarely offered an opinion.

"That's merely speculation at this point," Shi Hua murmured. She'd withdrawn her hand from Jeremy's and now poked at her dinner.

Little Bear tapped a galloping rhythm with his fingertips on the oak tabletop. "Nor do we have enough evidence to truthspell her." His drumming stopped. "What if Gina spoke with her, warden to warden?"

I pushed back my plate and leaned my elbows on the table. "Maebh's not likely to confide in a junior warden."

Little Bear shrugged. "Both High Sister Dragonfly and Justice Yanaba wanted to recruit Gina as their chief warden. She could say Chief Justice

Elizabeth has asked Gina to accompany her to her new assignment, and she wanted to speak to another chief warden before making a final decision."

"That's an excellent idea, Chief Warden." Luc leaned back in his chair.

"Why can't you talk to her peer-to-peer?" I asked.

This time, Little Bear's face glowed red. "Because, um, there was a confrontation between her and Sivan before Chief Justice Penelope passed."

"When?" I growled. "And what exactly happened?" The clergy of both Balance and Light had completely turned over in the last two years. If there were additional issues between the Orrin Temple personnel, Luc and I needed to know.

Little Bear took a long swig of water and cleared his throat. "It was the Spring Rituals three years ago. I swear Maebh and I were only discussing our duties—"

"But that wasn't how Sivan perceived your interactions," I said.

"No." He sighed. "Thankfully, Maebh chose not to file charges against Sivan though the magistrate urged her to."

I paused in taking another sip of wine. "DiCook wanted to throw Sivan in the gaol?"

"Given the situation with Chief Justice Penelope at the time, I think it was his way to get all of us to calm down." Little Bear smiled wryly. "She would have certainly have executed her own head of household in her mental state at the time."

"So," Luc drawled. "It's a matter of keeping the Balance household running smoothly rather than any personal issue between you and Maebh?"

"Yes, High Brother." The relief from Little Bear was a palpable thing.

I'd never seen my chief warden nonplussed before. But then, I'd been on the receiving end of Sivan's temper as well, though I'm sure her annoyance with me wasn't fueled by drink or lust.

Luc turned to me. "So, what's our next step?"

"High Brother Xander and I have instituted general inventories at our respective Temples." I shrugged. "Unfortunately, our culprit may have acquired their disguise elsewhere like the skinwalker and his minions did.

Otherwise, we'll stick with my chief warden's plan and see if Gina can shake some information loose from Maebh."

"There's another matter we need to address," Jeremy said.

"Yes, Brother?" Luc inclined his head to encourage the younger priest.

"The south side slums are turning into a giant flashbang with a very short fuse." Jeremy toyed with the condensation on the side of his goblet. "Is there anything we can do to encourage the queen to increase the pace of resettlement? It's been three months, and less than ten percent of the Tandorans sheltering in Orrin have been placed."

Little Bear shot me a wide-eyed look. "Should I have accompanied you this afternoon?"

I shook my head. "Tensions were high due to the murder of a child."

"There was also resentment of us, Chief Justice," Jeremy said. "They expected the Temples to save them."

"We did—" I started.

"At the cost of their lives and homes!" Jeremy gestured wildly in the direction of the south end of the city. "Now, they live in pest-infested tenements, eating what little scraps are given to them, when they would rather continue their trades."

"I'm not unsympathetic to their plight, Brother," I snapped. "But pray tell, where do we place them within our duchy that won't cause more resentment among our own populace?"

"What has the magistrate said about conditions on the south side?" Once again, Garbhan's quiet voice cut through the emotion in the room. Now, I was beginning to understand why Reverend Father Farrell of Light had chosen such a young priest as one of his personal advisors.

"Peacekeepers patrolling past the Temples of Death and Vintner do so in groups of three or four," Little Bear said.

I cocked my head and regarded him. "How did you learn this?"

"The magistrate mentioned it to all the chief wardens." Little Bear shrugged. "If tempers boil over, the Temples will be the next closest targets other than the butchers and the lower docks."

"Twelve take everyone," I muttered and rubbed my temples as a headache I couldn't blame on too much wine intruded. Despite my jest at wanting a whole barrel, I'd barely drank half of the white wine Istaqa had poured for me. "Then we need to speak with both the duke and the magistrate. The last thing we need is a human riot in the middle of a demon attack."

# CHAPTER 8

I eyed Luc across his dining table, everyone else waiting for orders from us. "Is there anything else we need to worry about?"

He shook his head. "I'll make the arrangements for us to meet with Duke Marco and Magistrate DiCook tomorrow evening about the tensions in the south side of the city."

I nodded before I turned to Little Bear. "Would you please send Daniel to the seaside taverns? He's good at listening for information."

"I'm not sending him alone," Little Bear said. "Would you mind if I ask Chief Warden Citana for a volunteer from her Temple?"

"Spreading the risk?" I asked.

A wry smile twisted my chief warden's mouth. "More like fostering good will since Love didn't have to share their information regarding Gerd."

"Understood." I nodded. He was absolutely right. I turned my attention back to Luc. "Anything in particular you want them to listen for?"

He shook his head. "I think we've covered everything we can for now." *Will you be coming back tonight for the other thing you wish to discuss?*

I nodded. "Very well." *Yes.*

Part of me was glad it was difficult for Luc to make his way through the Orrin tunnel system after the loss of his foot. I wanted the option to leave by my choice. Despite Claudia's reassurances, I couldn't see how things simply would go back to the way they were between Luc and me.

No matter how much I desired and needed them to.

"How do we keep an eye on the south side?" Shi Hua said. "Surely, you're not sending Sivan, Nathan, and Hogarth back now it has been revealed they're Temple?"

"No, we can't." Little Bear watched me as if he expected me to change my mind after our earlier talk.

"The peacekeepers can't do it by themselves when they're equal targets for the citizens' disgruntlement. We need to come up with an alternative," I said. "While you arrange a meeting with the duke and the magistrate, High Brother, I'll confer with High Brother Talbert. He may have some ideas."

"Very well then." Luc exhaled. "We have a plan for moving forward."

Once I officially retired to my bedchambers for the night, I locked the entrance before I shed my sword and robes. It took a moment to strap on the arm sheaths for two more knives in addition to the ones in my boots. There was a time when I didn't feel the need to visit Luc while armed, but the Assassins Guild and the demons convinced me it was best to use the chamber pot with weapons on my person.

Crouching on the far side of my wardrobe, I laid my palm against the cool green-blue block that formed the secret passageway to the Orrin tunnel system. I threw my senses past the marble, but no one was nearby. No one but Temple personnel used the tunnels these days.

The sisters of Love had sealed the entrance to the tunnels from the Green Lady Inn. While they'd tried to cater to their worshippers' desire for privacy, their need for security took precedence, especially after what Gerd and her renegade allies had done to the priestesses and wardens. Shi Hua and I had collapsed the exit outside of Death's Gate in our efforts to destroy a demon. Temple clergy and wardens guarded the three remaining exits from sunrise to sunrise. We couldn't afford for renegades to infiltrate Orrin.

Not again, anyway. The cost the last time had been far too high.

I said the appropriate spell. The marble floor vibrated slightly beneath the soles of my boots as the block folded itself out of the way. I slipped through the passage and into the side tunnel that connected Balance to the main tunnel. With a second spell, the block folded back into place. The third spell was an alarm spell that would sound, warning my wardens, if anyone tampered with the entrance to my Temple while I was gone.

The soft lavender glow coming from the bedrock walls reassured me. Tiny creatures lived on stone and earth underground. Creatures so tiny that anyone else with normal vision couldn't perceive them. But like any other creature, they had body heat, and when they gathered en masse, like in the tunnels, with no other living things to compete with them, they gave me sufficient illumination to make my way to the side tunnel leading to the Temple of Light.

There was a time when I would have simply opened the passageway into Luc's bedchambers. But the last thing I needed was to get shot by the crossbow he kept at his bedside while I disabled the wards and alarm spells placed on the block guarding the entry.

*Luc?*

*One moment.* The familiar touch of his mind was unnerving and missed at the same time. This conversation would be harder than I thought.

The marble folded itself to the side. I ducked and entered the high brother's bedchambers. Luc stood by the wall, perched on his crutches. Like me, he had stripped down to his silk tunic and leather leggings. I ignored the affectionate look he gave me, marched over to his desk, and sat in one of the visitor's chairs.

"We have an issue with Brother Jeremy."

"All right," Luc drawled. "I see we're getting down to business immediately." He closed the passage before he crossed to his desk, leaned his crutches against the wall and sat in his chair.

I clasped my hands in my lap. As much as I rehearsed what I needed to say about the young priest, the reality made me quite uncomfortable. "He lost his temper more than once today during the investigation into Yellow Fin's death."

"Any normal person should be disturbed after a child has been wantonly abused in a perverse manner and his throat slit." Luc folded his arms over his chest.

"His behavior this afternoon went beyond mere uncomfortableness." I gestured helplessly. "It was bad enough Little Bear stepped in."

"A chief warden has no right to discipline any member of the clergy—"

"This wasn't just discipline. A chief warden will interfere when he thinks his seat's life is in danger," I snapped.

Luc raised an eyebrow. "Did Jeremy draw on you, or Little Bear on him?"

"No, thank Balance," I admitted. "And both of your wardens who accompanied us kept their heads as well. However, Yanaba and Xander have noticed changes in Jeremy's temperament since he returned from Tandor."

"Are you saying you want him lashed for insubordination?" Luc asked.

"No!" I stood and slammed my palms on the wooden surface of his desk. "I'm saying I think something happened in Tandor. Something bad enough he needs treatment at Child."

"Has Shi Hua said anything to you?" Luc said softly.

"About Jeremy's behavior toward her, or about her pregnancy?"

"Either."

I sighed and resumed my seat. "She has mentioned she's worried regarding his recent change in attitude. But this was after Yanaba and Xander mentioned their concerns to me. But even with my odd sight, I can see he's not treating her as he used to before the Battle of Tandor. As for her pregnancy, no, she hasn't told me."

"But you know?"

I gestured at my eyes. "I can't help the fact I can see the changes in her body." I cocked my head at the tone of Luc's question. "I haven't said a word to anybody until you tonight. Are you saying Jeremy's uncomfortable as to the reality of impregnating her?"

"I presumed that was part of the problem." Luc rubbed his chin and stared at a scratch on his desk. "I'm a little disappointed Xander didn't come to me himself with his observations."

"He never expected to attain a Temple seat this soon," I murmured. "He's still feeling his way through his duties. And in this case, he's more concerned about someone he considers a friend. He's not trying to offend your sensibilities as an equal by talking to me if that's what you think."

"So, you're going to totally ignore the fact I know Shi Hua's pregnant, too," Luc teased.

"I'm more worried she informed you before she told Jeremy because she was afraid to tell him," I muttered.

"Ouch." Luc winced. "I hadn't considered that."

"Well, you need to consider it." I shook my head. "However, Jeremy was acting oddly before they conceived. The last thing you need is only Garbhan to depend on. The trading season has finally gotten back to relative normalcy."

"You don't think . . ." Heat and suspicion mixed on Luc's face.

"That Jeremy has been replaced by a demon." I shook my head again. "No. Definitely not. Unless . . ." I realized what terrible thought had occurred to Luc.

I could see whether a skinwalker wore a human skin or if a demon had merely changed their shape. However, demons were more skilled at wearing human skins than their sorcerer apprentices. So much so, even I with my peculiar sight couldn't detect the difference. However, we discovered the Wildlings could detect the demons' scent, regardless if the damn creatures wore a human skin or not, now that they knew how to discern it. High Sister Reby and the surviving Tandoran Wildlings had checked all the refugees by smell to ensure a demon wearing a human skin didn't sneak past us when the civilians disembarked in Orrin.

Despite my initial fear High Brother Jax of Orrin's Wildling Temple had been corrupted or replaced by a demon, Reby and her cohorts checked everyone in the Orrin Temples. Thankfully, Sisquoc from Tandor had been reassigned to Orrin while Reby and the rest of her people took samples of things contaminated with demon scent on a trip through Issura so the rest of our queendom's Wildlings knew what to smell for.

But our efforts meant nothing if Jeremy had been replaced after he'd been checked.

"Do you want me to fetch Jax or Sisquoc?" I asked softly.

Luc shook his head. "I'll send Jax an invitation to the midday meal. If it truly is Jeremy, then I'll make arrangements for his treatment with Mya.

While Jeremy's faced demons before, watching the slaughter of your comrades on the scale of a battle can affect anyone's emotions, and the boy does wear his publicly."

I glared at Luc. "Can I suggest you not start your discussion with Jeremy by calling the father of Shi Hua's child a boy?"

"Forgive me." He inclined his head before he frowned. "I just hope Ambassador Quan and Reverend Father Farrell don't get into a pissing match over Shi Hua's son."

"And will your Reverend Father care if it's a girl?"

"Are you suggesting Quan will take her back to Jing if the babe is a girl?" Luc's tone wasn't accompanied by a sneer, though his inflection indicated his personal feelings toward the ambassador.

I stared at Luc's bedchamber ceiling for a moment to gather my patience. Just because Quan attempted to pursue a romantic relationship with me, it didn't mean I was interested in one with him. Whereas Luc had actually lain with Claudia, even if he was ordered to do so. I quashed the image of them together in my mind.

However, when I looked at Luc again, a thread of irritation still ran through me. "First of all, Quan is not stupid enough to violate an international treaty. If the child is born here, Issura still has first claim.

"Second, if the child is a girl, Reverend Father Farrell may not have a choice about accepting her into your order. Issura has to change when it comes to admitting women to Light. Especially at the rate the renegades are targeting your order. Dragonfly did not choose Claudia for you at random. Claudia and her mother would have been in Light if not for our stupid rules."

"You were the one who insisted I follow the damn edict—"

"This isn't about the blasted edict!"

"Then what in Light's name crawled up your arse?" Luc spat.

"Claudia knows about us."

"With the new edict from the home Temples, it doesn't matter if she knows!" Luc clenched his fists on the top of his desk in his effort not to totally lose his temper with me.

However, fury already spat from my own spirit. "Of course, it doesn't matter to you. You can legally sleep with whoever you want now, but you have the continued gall of accusing me of fornicating with the ambassador of Jing!"

I abruptly stood and stalked toward the tunnel entrance before I said or did something truly idiotic.

"Where are you going?" Luc snapped.

I whirled to face him. "Since nothing I say is of import to you, it's best I leave. However, you damn well better do something about your second's attitude. Otherwise, the next time he fails to show me the proper respect, I can and will have him lashed."

I turned back to the wall, muttered the spell, and slipped into the tunnel system while Luc continued to splutter behind me.

# Chapter 9

I barely slept that night, and when I did, it was full of horrible night-mares. A mélange of demons, dead children with their throats cut, and Luc laughing at me while he had intimate relations with Claudia in my own bed. I didn't need the expertise of Child to know the dreams came from my own insecurities. I finally gave up trying to rest and went to my office well before the rest of my staff woke to review the disposition of Yanaba's cases and write my own reports to the home Temple.

As the warden in charge of the night's watch, Ahiga checked to see if I needed anything. Otherwise, he and the other two wardens on duty left me alone.

Shortly after First Morning, I sent Warden Gina to the Jing Embassy with an invitation to the midday meal here at Balance. It was a task beneath her, but I didn't dare send Ming Wei. The embassy would trigger terrible memories for the child since she was cared for by Ambassador Quan's personal healer after the noble who purchased her from her parents tried to burn her alive.

I was equally reluctant to send Nathan after Little Bear's mention of how yesterday's discovery had affected the boy. However, the point became moot when my squire suffered some sort of breathing attack during his dawn chores. Little Bear rushed him to the Healers Guild, but Master Bly assured my chief warden it was a case of nerves after she thoroughly examined my squire. She suggested someone from the Temple of Child talk with Nathan about yesterday's events in the south side slums. Finding Yellow Fin's body had disturbed my squire much more than any of us realized.

Little Bear came to my office to relay Master Bly's advice upon his return to Balance. I wondered how parents dealt with these kinds of problems with their own children. If it weren't for my staff, I'd be lost when it came to the squires' care.

There was a knock on my office door just as Little Bear finished his report. He opened it.

Gina was grinning when she entered.

I leaned back in my chair and groaned. "What did Quan say or do?"

"It's not that bad." She chuckled. "He has requested you and Sister Shi Hua join him and his concubine for a late midday meal if a candlemark after First Afternoon is acceptable. There are several matters he wishes to discuss with you."

"Did he list any of these matters?" I said sourly.

"Only that his concubine is concerned about the sister's welfare given the recent edict from the Temple of Light. And that it might be helpful to the sister to talk to one of her own who has experienced childbirth."

Of course, Yin Li was concerned. No one outside of a select few from Balance, Light, and Thief knew the alleged concubine was a sister of Love and Shi Hua's maternal aunt. From what little Shi Hua said of her past, she was closer with her aunt than with her own mother, but it had more to do with Yin Li being only seven years older than Shi Hua.

"All right." I nodded. "Would you please relay the invitation to Sister Shi Hua?"

Gina turned to go, but I realized I'd forgotten something very important I'd meant to do yesterday.

"Wait, Warden."

She turned to face me again.

"After speaking with the sister, would you please go to Thief and request an audience between me and the High Brother for Third Afternoon?"

"Shall I tell him this pertains to the child's murder?" Gina's posture stiffened, and I winced at the reminder of yesterday's event.

"I'm sure he will already know." I sighed, not wanting to deal with the matter after the ugly dreams from last night. But I couldn't shirk my duties.

Not after the way, High Mother Bianca had shirked hers. "However, you may confirm the subject with him or his staff if they ask."

"Will there be anything else, m'lady?"

I shook my head. "Make sure you break your fast before court starts."

That comment loosened her bearing, and she smiled again. "Yes, m'lady."

After she departed, closing the door behind her, Little Bear shook his head. "I really must object to you using our wardens as routine messengers."

"I trust *my* wardens to take care of themselves on the streets of Orrin if they are accosted," I snapped.

"May I speak freely, Chief Justice?" he asked.

I squelched another groan. Whenever Little Bear addressed me in such a formal manner, he was about to say something I wouldn't like, but that I needed to hear. I waved my right hand.

"Go ahead."

"I'm assuming you spoke with the high brother of Light about Brother Jeremy's behavior."

I nodded.

"Did you and High Brother Luc argue over Brother Jeremy's behavior or over a personal matter?"

I leaned my elbows on my desk. "First, why such a question?"

Little Bear crossed his arms over his chest. "Because if the high brother isn't considering your . . . grievance with the merit it's due, I will make sure either Gina or I accompany you in any excursions involving Brother Jeremy."

"And if it's the other situation?"

"I'll warn Sivan and the rest of the Balance staff to tiptoe around you for the next fortnight." He grinned to lessen the bite of his words.

It wasn't fair to take my bad moods out on my staff. I knew it, and part of me was grateful Little Bear had the guts to point it out without fearing any reprisal from me.

"You have my bad moods timed?" I cocked my head.

He shrugged. "Give or take a few days." He waved at one of the visitor's chairs. "May I?"

I nodded, and he lowered himself into the seat.

"What exactly happened with you two?" Little Bear asked. "I'm assuming it has something to do with Sister Claudia being with child?"

"It's all mixed together." I sighed again and leaned back in my chair. "I brought up the situation that happened yesterday with Jeremy. Luc said Shi Hua was also with child, which I already knew."

Little Bear smirked at that comment.

"Next thing I knew our discussion devolved over his anger about Ambassador Quan making advances toward me, which he hasn't since our voyage to Tandor. Luc accused me of jealously concerning Claudia—"

"But the edict—" Little Bear waved his right hand in the general direction of Standora.

"He accused me of pushing him away with the edict, and I lost my temper."

"And?"

My blood burned with the shame of my behavior last night. "I told him if he didn't get Jeremy under control, I would have him lashed for insubordination."

Little Bear was silent for so long I expected him to rise and walk out of my office. After a few heartbeats, he merely said, "Oh."

I waited a few heartbeats more before I said, "You're not going to lecture me about stepping beyond my place?"

He exhaled a deep breath and leaned back in his chair. "You already know you did. Me lecturing you isn't going to rectify the situation. However, I am worried about Brother Jeremy. He was on the verge of violence last night. I don't think the wardens with him would have acted fast enough." He hesitated for a moment before he added, "I hope you don't take this the wrong way, Anthea, but I already spoke with Nicholas. Fortunately, the Light wardens had reported the incident to him before I did."

"And?" I prompted.

"All the Light wardens have seen the same problems with Brother Jeremy we have." He shook his head. "Nicholas has his own issues keeping

Mateqai from doing anything stupid to the brother for his treatment of Sister Shi Hua."

"Balance!" I swore. "We have more love triangles in this city than Kemet has pyramids."

Little Bear snorted in an effort to retain his humor. It didn't work. After a moment, I chuckled along with him.

A knock on my office door interrupted our rare light moment.

"Enter!" I yelled as Little Bear rose from his chair.

Nathan pushed the door open and bowed. "High Sister Dragonfly is here for your morning appointment, Lady Justice."

"Thank you, Squire." I nodded. "Will you please inform the high sister I will be just a moment more with the chief warden?"

"Yes, m'lady." Nathan pulled the door shut behind him.

I looked up at Little Bear. "Are there any other domestic squabbles about to blow up in my face like a damn flashbang?"

"Not that I'm aware of, m'lady." He smiled. "I shall endeavor to inform you before they do."

I hoped to Balance he did because I wasn't sure how much more of the domestic squabbling among the Temples I could take.

# CHAPTER 10

Every time I met with Dragonfly, we discovered more wrong-doing by my birth mother Gerd. The possession and attempt to sell the demon grimoire should have been sufficient to remove her head months ago. But no, she stole from the other sisters. She stole form the Temple of Love itself. She blackmailed worshippers. It explained why she'd dismissed her head of household a decade before I was sentenced to Orrin's Balance seat and never replaced him.

However, there was a small ledger Dragonfly found we hadn't deciphered yet. My gut said this was more important than the other falsified ledgers. Whatever it contained made Gerd paranoid about being caught. She hadn't bothered encoding her real Temple ledgers showing her theft. Could it be a manifest of additional demon artifacts she'd bought and sold? A listing of her contacts within the Assassins Guild? Neither Dragonfly nor I could find the key to the code Gerd used in today's attempts to decipher the small book, so I tucked it back in the safe hole in my office wall. Since the safe holes in the wall of the Temple itself could only be opened by members of that order, it was the most secure place in the world.

Assuming I totally trusted Yanaba and Elizabeth.

I sent a carefully worded inquiry as to Gerd's escape, along with the latest list of incriminating acts we'd discovered, to the home Temple in Standora via courier. If I received an actual reply from the Reverend Mother, it wouldn't be for another four days at the soonest. But I didn't want to be lashed for insubordination any more than I really wanted to punish Jeremy for the same offence. I had sufficient scars on my back from my one and only lashing sixteen years ago.

I could have used Shi Hua to distance speak with the Reverend Mother, but I didn't want to drag the young priestess into my Temple's issues. The poor girl was already caught between the Jing and Issuran Temples of Light.

Dragonfly and I finished a little early, or rather, we gave up because we both felt like we'd been running the same path over and over again. Once the high sister took her leave, I slipped into Balance's courtroom from the public doors. I was supposed to be evaluating Justice Yanaba's performance behind the podium after all. Warden Jonata nodded at me before returning her attention to the citizens perched on the new gallery benches.

Most of the people here didn't even look at me as I took a seat in the back row. Only Magistrate DiCook and one of his peacekeepers noticed my entrance from where they sat near my senior clerk Donella, but both men turned back to the tableau before them. The rest of the attendees' attention was fixed on Justice Yanaba propped on her stool behind the podium. The statue of Balance Herself loomed over the younger woman like an overprotective mother.

I squinted and examined the front dais again. No, not an overprotective mother. More like the young justice's shadow.

She questioned the witness, a woman, working through the standard inquiries establishing the witness's identity and her relationship to the case. The energy of Sister Shi Hua's truthspell crackled against my skin. Was the intensity of the spell due to her pregnancy or simply that she was practicing her native skills more in the time she'd been assigned to Orrin's Temple of Light than she had while acting as Ambassador Quan's concubine/bodyguard?

Her place in Orrin was only supposed to be a temporary assignment while all the Reverend Fathers conducted their audits of Light after we'd discovered Luc's former second, Brother Mat, was really a renegade named Micah. The conspiracy to attain control of the Temples was only the tip of our problems. The demon army in Tandor had delayed the audits. All of which contributed to Reverend Father Farrell's paranoia regarding the sister and the child she carried.

I recognized the man in the rebuilt accused's box as one of the volunteers who had guarded Tandor's walls during the siege. He was a silversmith named Govind if I remembered rightly. Did the duke miss this former citizen of Tandor when he said all the skilled craftspeople had been reassigned?

I didn't like thinking Marco may have lied to me. After his mother tried to have both of us murdered by her pet sorcerer and the demons the sorcerer had summoned, I thought the duke and I were beyond such things. It was something more to add to my list of topics to discuss with him later tonight.

Assuming Luc and I were still meeting with the duke. After last night's argument, I didn't relish having to apologize to Luc, but it needed to be done. Not for our personal relationship, but since Balance and Light were both necessary to the queendom's legal system.

Justice Elizabeth sat to the right side of the podium, listening to the proceedings. Her frown cut an ugly slash across her face. It wasn't like her to show her emotions. She had too much experience to be so obvious.

Yanaba appeared to look at the witness. Few justices developed that particular pose. Considering every priestess in our order was blind but me, it was a particularly useful skill when questioning someone. Especially when this witness was nervous as the color of her skin indicated to my peculiar sight.

"Ela, according to Peacekeeper Leyti, you said Govind stole a sack of flour from you. Is that correct?"

"Yes, m'lady," Ela said.

"Did you see him steal this bag of flour?" Yanaba asked.

"No, m'lady."

"Then how do you know it was Govind who stole your flour?"

"I-I—" Like most citizens who'd never had a truthspell laid on them, Ela miscalculated the effect on her. When a person resists a truthspell, a mild abdominal discomfort starts. The longer the person fails to tell the truth the more pain the spell inflicts until it feels as if their entire body is on fire.

Part of my training included attempting to resist a truthspell. Few could keep their mouths shut. Those that did passed out from the agony in their gut. Some had even died.

Ela clutched at her midsection and gasped. Finally, she blurted, "He didn't steal the flour!"

A murmur ran through the citizens in the gallery. Elizabeth's frown deepened. The majority of Yanaba's face was covered by the cowl of her robes so I could only see her lower lip and her chin. However, her posture didn't change.

"Why did you falsely accuse Govind of theft?" my junior justice asked calmly.

"Because he's a minion of the Red Justice and she's stealing our children," Ela shrieked. She clung to the railing and panted. A louder wave of exclamations came from the gallery. DiCook shot me the briefest of glances, and his frown now matched Elizabeth's.

Icy fingers crawled up my spine at her proclamation. A truthspell was ineffective if the person under it truly believed what they said. The fact that she was sure in her heart I was behind the missing children unnerved me.

I reached out with my mind. *Jonata, may I see through your eyes for a moment?*

*Yes, m'lady.*

I touched the warden's hand. Looking through another's eyes disconcerted me. There was far more detail, but the colors were muted and odd to me. Everyone's skin was a shade of brown instead of the bright yellows and oranges I saw. On the other hand, their clothing and accessories were far more brilliant than the greens and blues in my sight.

Focusing on the witness Ela, I examined her. Her dress lacked any adornment. The fabric was clean, but it had been repaired more than once. Her feet were bare with the heat of summer beginning. She probably lived on the south side.

Govind, on the other hand, wore the roughspun shift every prisoner wore during a trial. It was probably in better shape than his own clothes, but I knew from first-hand experience the gaol tunics were itchier than a bed of fleas.

*Thank you*, I silently said to Jonata as I released her hand.

While I had examined Ela through my warden's eyes, Yanaba lectured the witness on the penalties for false testimony.

"Now, let us start again." Yanaba tapped her left index finger on the podium before her. "I'm giving you one, and only one, opportunity to amend your original statement, Ela. And I remind you, you are still under a truthspell. Do you understand?"

Ela audibly gulped before she muttered, "Yes, Lady Justice."

"Did Govind take any possession of yours?"

"No, m'lady."

"Did you falsely accuse Govind of taking your bag of flour?"

"Yes, m'lady."

Ela was no longer fighting the truthspell. Perhaps, she'd learned her lesson about specious accusations.

"Claiming anyone is abducting children is a very serious charge, Ela," Yanaba said. "Do you wish to recant that statement?"

"No," she snapped.

"Did you see Govind kidnap any child?"

"No," Ela said.

"Do you know anyone who saw any child's abduction first hand?"

"I heard someone had while I was at the fountain in Dancer's Square."

Yanaba stilled her index finger from its tapping. "I cannot take hearsay as a legitimate charge."

"Everyone knows the Red Justice is in league with the demons!" Ela's voice rose. "She kidnaps the children from the streets and drinks their blood!"

Well, *that* was a new twist on the rumors about me.

Yanaba's index finger resumed its tapping on the podium's wooden surface. "First, let us establish meaning. When you say 'the Red Justice' to whom are you referring?"

"The chief justice."

"Who is . . . ?" Yanaba prompted.

"Chief Justice Anthea of Orrin," Ela bit out.

"Thank you." Yanaba's lower lip curved beneath her hood. "Demon dealing is an offense punishable by death. Do you offer evidence of Chief Justice Anthea dealing with demons?"

"She brought demons inside the city walls," Ela insisted.

"Did you witness this act?"

Ela stuttered a few times before she said, "No, but—"

"Let me guess," Yanaba remarked dryly. "Everyone knows."

"Yes."

"That is still hearsay, citizen." The edges of Yanaba's hood fluttered when she exhaled heavily. "Do you have knowledge of any first hand witness to any demon dealing by Chief Justice Anthea?"

"Why don't you ask the chief justice yourself?"

I didn't need to see Ela's face to visualize the sneer that followed her words.

"An excellent suggestion, Ela. Shall we settle this, once and for all?" Yanaba's head tilted in my general direction. "Chief Justice Anthea, accusations have been made against you in this very court."

For the third time, a wave of excitement swept through the people in the gallery. They all twisted in their seats to look at me. Ela pivoted and her jaw dropped.

"Do you submit yourself to the jurisdiction of the Temple of Balance of Orrin?" Yanaba continued.

I rose to my feet. "I do."

"Given that Chief Justice Anthea is our superior in this court, we recuse ourselves in favor of our sister, the honorable Chief Justice Elizabeth, formerly of the city of Tandor." Yanaba banged her sword pommel on the podium before she sheathed it and gracefully slid from her stool.

Warden Tahoma crossed the dais to take her arm and lead her to Elizabeth's chair. Elizabeth rose, Yanaba settled herself in the vacant chair, and Tahoma escorted Elizabeth to the podium.

Upon sitting on the stool, Elizabeth drew her own sword and banged the pommel on the podium with a loud *crack*. I prayed to Balance she hadn't just broken my brand-new podium. It had taken us nearly three months to restore the furniture Yanaba had destroyed by activating the Temple's defense spells when demons snuck into Orrin. Elizabeth set her sword across the top of the podium.

"Clerk, please note for the record Justice Yanaba has recused herself in the matter of the Crown versus Govind, and I, Elizabeth DiBalance, formerly Chief Justice of Tandor, now preside. Citizen Ela, do you have any objection to the substitution?"

Ela inhaled, but before she could speak, Elizabeth held up her hand.

"A reminder before you say anything, Ela." Elizabeth lowered her hand, and the witness remained silent. "If you attempt to lie again under our sister of Light's truthspell, I will not be as forgiving as Justice Yanaba. Do you understand?"

"Yes, Lady Justice." For the first time since I entered the court, Ela sounded subdued.

"And Govind?"

The silversmith straightened in the accused's box. "Yes, m'lady."

"I find you innocent in the matter of the alleged theft of flour from Ela." Elizabeth smiled at the man. "However, I ask that you stay in order for restitution to be made under that charge and to answer questions regarding the inquiry into demon dealing by Chief Justice Anthea."

"Yes, m'lady." He bowed. "Thank you."

"Back to my question to you, Ela." Elizabeth's smile disappeared. "Do you have any objection to me presiding over the case? If you do, I'm happy to recuse myself, but we will have to wait until a justice can be spared from another city, which we have no way of knowing how soon that could happen, or until Justice Erato passes through the city of Orrin in two months on her circuit."

"But-but you—" Ela waved at Govind, whom Warden Gina was releasing from the accused's box.

"You brought additional allegations that Govind assisted Chief Justice Anthea abduct children." Elizabeth waved her right hand in Yanaba's general direction. "As our sister justice has pointed out, we take these allegations quite seriously. We cannot tolerate any justice whose ethical or moral qualities have been called into question, and that question must be answered immediately and with extreme prejudice.

"Now, do you agree to me presiding over this case?"

Ela was obviously flabbergasted by the abrupt turn of events. She looked back at me before she turned to Yanaba, then finally Elizabeth. "I agree to you presiding over this case, Lady Justice."

Maybe she realized how deep of a pit she'd dug for herself. She'd already irritated Yanaba by attempting to lie while under a truthspell. She'd flung allegations against me that I knew damn well were fraudulent, and by her own admission, she'd falsely accused a man of theft.

The last time a justice had been charged with wrongdoing, the Reverend Mother of Balance herself had ridden down to Orrin to preside over the trial. And Alara DiBalance was definitely the least sympathetic jurist in the queendom. Since I had been the justice on trial, I could attest to that fact. The Reverend Mother would have already lashed Ela for trying to lie in her presence.

So, I wasn't a bit surprised Ela decided to take her chances with Elizabeth.

"I shall remind you once again you are under Sister Shi Hua's truthspell, Ela." Elizabeth leaned forward on the podium. Her hood slid back a bit, and her sightless eyes seemed to bore into Ela. "You have made allegations Chief Justice Anthea and Govind have abducted children in the city of Orrin for nefarious purposes. And the first time you answer one of my questions with 'everyone knows', Balance help me, I'll put you in the gaol for thirty days for contempt of court. Do you understand me?"

Ela bowed her head and whispered, "Yes, m'lady." The acoustics in the Temple of Balance's central dome were designed so even those sitting high in the galleries could hear the testimony from those on the floor.

"Anthea?" Elizabeth waved her hand in my direction. "If you and Govind will have a seat on the witnesses' bench, we will get started."

The lack of properly addressing my rank wasn't a mistake on Elizabeth's part. This had become a formal inquiry into whether charges would be filed against me for a capital crime. Therefore, rank had no bearing before a justice hearing the case.

Even mine in my own damn court.

I strode down to the floor where Gina met me. I unbuckled my harness and gave her my sword. It took a few moments to release the straps on my forearms and remove the steel from my boot sheaths. There were a few titters at the number of weapons I turned over to the warden.

"The witness has relinquished all arms, Lady Justice," Gina announced as I sat down next to Govind.

"Very well," Elizabeth announced. "We shall begin." She ran through the introductory questions to establish Ela's identity, trade, and current residence, which was the south side as I suspected, and her reason for being here. I rather had the impression my sister justice did it to see if she could get a rise out of the other woman over the repetition.

"Prior to me taking over this case, you gave testimony Govind was working with Anthea to abduct children. Did you actually see them together perform such an act?"

"No, m'lady."

"Did you witness Govind act alone in abducting any child?"

"No, m'lady."

"Did you witness Anthea act alone in abducting any child?"

"No, m'lady."

"Do you have personal knowledge of anyone who was a first-hand witness in seeing Govind and Anthea abduct any child whether together or separately?"

"No, m'lady."

"Then how did you come by this information."

"Every—" Ela stopped herself and sucked in a deep breath. "I was at the fountain in Dancer's Square to fetch water for cooking, and I heard people there talking about the dead boy in the alley between Maiden Street and the Duke's Road."

"When was this?"

"Shortly after the First Morning bells rang yesterday, m'lady."

I wanted to wring someone's neck. People knew about Yellow Fin and never bothered to find a peacekeeper to report it. How could anyone be so callous toward a dead child? And with demons on the loose, how could anyone be that careless? Possessing the dead was how the isles of Britannia were lost.

"Are you saying everyone in your neighborhood was aware a dead boy lay in an alley and none of you reported it?" Elizabeth repeated my very thought. She was much calmer and matter-of-fact about the situation than I would have been. Maybe it was a good thing Ela implicated me. It saved her from me ordering a lashing, even though it was quite possible Elizabeth might order it anyway.

"I didn't see him, but Robin the butcher said he did. I was afraid to go look." Ela hunched her shoulders at the memory. "None of us wanted the peacekeepers' attention."

"Did Robin the butcher see who left the body in the alley?"

"No, m'lady. According to him, Old Anne saw what happened."

"Who is Old Anne?" Elizabeth said.

"She lives in a room at the top of the apartments on the corner of Maiden Street and Sailor's Way. She had the wasting limb disease as a child, but it only affected her right leg. She was a seamstress until her joints became too swollen from age to work. So, she sits at her window and watches the comings and goings of people on the street."

That's how the rumor was started. This Anne could be the key to my investigation.

Unfortunately, I was stuck here until Elizabeth cleared me.

"Did Anne see the face of the person who left the boy's body in the alley?" Elizabeth continued.

"I don't know, Lady Justice."

"Did Anne claim the person in the alley was Anthea?"

"I don't know, m'lady."

"Why did the people at the fountain think it was Anthea?"

"B-because Old Anne supposedly told Robin the person who left the corpse in the ally wore black Temple robes."

Elizabeth turned her sword over in her hands as she considered her next move. "Sister Shi Hua, would you place truthspells on both Govind and Anthea?"

"Yes, Chief Justice." The Jing priestess rose from her bench and approached us. The corners of her mouth twitched as if the proceedings were for her personal amusement, but thankfully, she didn't break out into a full smile.

She murmured the words to counter the truthspell blocker we discovered the Temple of Love had developed to protect their worshippers' secrets before she laid the actual truthspells themselves. The tingle of Light magic surrounded me and sank into my flesh.

"Govind, we will start with you since you didn't have a chance to offer testimony earlier."

The silversmith froze. I elbowed him and indicated he needed to stand with Ela in front of the podium. However, it took Gina's hissed order before he scrambled to his bare feet and stood before Elizabeth.

"Yes, Lady Justice," he said belatedly.

Elizabeth repeated the process of establishing his identity, trade, and residence like she had with Ela. The justice ended by saying, "How do you know Ela?"

"She lives in the same tenement on Siren Street my family and I do," he answered.

"Have you stolen anything in the three months since you arrived in Orrin?"

"No."

"Have you borrowed or taken anything without permission?"

Govind bowed his head. "I ate the last almond pastry my wife brought home from her job at the bakery and blamed it on the children."

I bit my tongue to keep from laughing at the contrite tone of his voice. Elizabeth smiled at his admission. Giggles and guffaws came from the gallery.

"Do you know why Ela made a false statement about you to the peacekeepers?" Elizabeth continued.

"Justice, please don't—" Govind groaned as the truthspell did its work.

"Answer me," Elizabeth demanded.

"She was offended I refused her advances." He panted at the sudden disappearance of pain. Damn, even under a truthspell, he tried to be gracious.

"Is this true, Ela?" Elizabeth said.

"Yes," the woman whispered.

Elizabeth stroked her left temple with her left index finger as if her head ached. "Did Old Anne say Govind was the person she saw wearing Temple robes who left the child's body in the alley?"

"I don't know, m'lady."

"Did Old Anne say Anthea was the person she saw wearing Temple robes who left the child's body in the alley?"

"I don't know, m'lady." A sob escaped Ela's throat.

"If you don't know anything, why did you accuse Govind and Anthea of kidnapping children?" Once again, Elizabeth was far calmer than I would have been in the same circumstances.

"Because I was angry Govind spurned my advances." Now, Ela wept openly. "And I believed the gossip I heard at the fountain about the chief justice drinking the missing children's blood. For Light's sake, look at her eyes!"

Elizabeth didn't comment on that ridiculous statement. She stopped rubbing her temple and said, "Anthea."

I stood and joined the other two before the former Tandoran chief justice. The last time I was in this position, I faced the Reverend Mother of Balance and the other eleven seats of Orrin for the illegal execution of Samael DiRoy, a cousin of the queen and the idiotic sorcerer who had summoned demons, thinking they served him.

Ela shuffled a half-step away from me, and I had to force down my humor once again.

"Yes, Lady Justice," I said.

For the third time, Elizabeth ran through the standard questions to establish my identity, trade, and residence.

"Are you currently leading the investigation into the murder of the boy found in the south side alley?" These were questions to which Elizabeth already knew the answers. However, I was aware why she asked them. She hoped Ela would gossip about her experience at Balance with her neighbors as well.

"Yes, m'lady."

"Who discovered the body?"

"My squire Nathan."

"When was this?"

"Shortly after First Afternoon yesterday."

"When did you find out about the boy's body?"

"I learned of Yellow Fin's death when Magistrate Malven DiCook sent Peacekeeper Jaime to fetch me and a member of Light to investigate the scene less than a candlemark later. The magistrate in turn learned about the matter when my squire reported Yellow Fin's body to a patrolling peacekeeper." It was my turn to emphasize the boy's name. That he had been a living, breathing human.

Elizabeth's deep frown returned. "And yet, Ela knew three hours before you received the peacekeeper's report." Not a question, but a statement driving home the point she found Ela's lack of compassion disturbing.

And since it was a statement, I said nothing.

"Which member of Light accompanied you to the site of the body?" Elizabeth continued.

"Brother Jeremy."

"Do you know who deposited Yellow Fin's body in the alley?"

"No, m'lady. I rewound time, but the person kept their hood pulled down far enough neither Brother Jeremy or Magistrate DiCook could see their face."

"Was the culprit wearing Temple robes?"

"Yes, the person was wearing what appeared to be black Temple robes."

"Do you know where the robes came from?"

"No, m'lady. Both I and High Brother Xander of Death ordered inventories in our respective Temples. No robes were missing, and the person witnessed in my rewind of time had no insignia on their robes for us to identify them."

"Did anyone in the south side come forward with knowledge of the child's body?"

"No, Lady Justice." I let a thread of my fury wrap around my tone. "Everyone the peacekeepers and our wardens spoke with denied any knowledge of Yellow Fin's body."

"Did you abduct Yellow Fin?"

"No m'lady."

"Did you kill Yellow Fin?"

"No, m'lady."

"Have you abducted anyone under the age of majority?"

"No, m'lady."

"Have you ever directly harmed any person under the age of majority?

"Only through inaction. My squire Nathan was poisoned by the Assassins Guild in their attempt to kill me at midwinter."

"Very well. I declare this inquiry into Govind and Anthea allegedly abducting and killing children closed." Without missing a beat, Elizabeth added, "There's still the matter of Ela's restitution for falsely accusing Govind of stealing a bag of flour."

Ela's weeping had gradually died during my testimony, but now it returned in full measure.

"I don't like reversing another justice's order, and you are quite lucky Justice Yanaba granted you a second chance as far as changing your statement goes." Elizabeth shook her head. "But then, you compounded that error by additional false charges against Govind and Chief Justice Anthea of much more serious crimes. The punishment for those is thirty days in the gaol, five lashes, and a three-crown fine."

Ela's face went from orange-red to a sickly greenish yellow. "I-I don't have that kind of money."

Odd how that was her primary worry. Thirty days in the gaol could be the difference between eating and begging, for without any means of earning a living during their imprisonment such a sentence could leave a prisoner destitute. Why didn't she feel comfortable having her family go to the Temple of Mother for assistance?

For the same reason Nathan and the other street children didn't trust the priestesses. I wasn't happy about Ela's accusations of me, but I wouldn't put her family at Bianca's mercy either.

I stepped forward. "If I may, Chief Justice?"

"The court recognizes our sister Chief Justice Anthea," Elizabeth said.

"Ela has given us the name of a possible witness in Yellow Fin's death. I ask that she be allowed to accompany me now to visit with Old Anne to make restitution to me. And in the case of Govind, she will provide almond pastries every Rest Day for the remainder of summer, one each for Govind, his wife, and their four children."

I glanced at Ela, who didn't look entirely pleased by my suggestion.

"However, the prerogative is, of course, yours, Chief Justice," I added. Ela looked as if she were about to faint.

"I think we'll need to have a warden accompany her to purchase the treats," Elizabeth said. "I'd hate for any of Govind's family to become ill from them. Ela, do you agree to Chief Justice Anthea's proposed terms, or would you rather spend a month in the gaol?"

Ela swiped her face with her sleeves and sniffed loudly. "I accept the terms, Lady Justice." Maybe there was hope for her after all.

"Sister Shi Hua, if you will dissolve the truthspells on all three of our witnesses?" Elizabeth gestured toward us.

"Yes, Lady Justice," the priestess responded. The tingle of her magic disappeared from my muscles.

"I hereby declare this court adjourned." Elizabeth banged her sword pommel on the podium once again.

The spectators filed out of the courtroom, but four ladies hung back, shooting me ugly scowls. Probably friends of Ela.

"You'll need a member of Light," Shi Hua murmured beside me.

I glanced at the four women in the gallery before I looked at Shi Hua again. "Do you fear the fishwives will attack me?"

"No." She grinned up at me. "Someone needs to protect them from you."

# CHAPTER 11

Once all the civilians had departed except Govind and Ela, Warden Mateqai pulled Sister Shi Hua aside. Elizabeth, Yanaba, and I pretended to ignore them. I knew he attempted to convince her to let one of the brothers of Light accompany me to the south side slums. I also knew who would win that argument.

The bells tolled Third Morning before Shi Hua loudly said, "Your advice has been heard and answered, Warden. Don't make me charge you with insubordination, too."

Mateqai's face flamed to bright pink. Despite his anger, he kept a calm expression and curtly nodded. "As you wish, Sister."

"Are we ready?" I asked.

"Yes, Chief Justice." Shi Hua's scowl said she wasn't letting go of the warden's overprotectiveness any time soon. For once, I was smart enough not to address it either. The personnel of Light usually reflected their high brother's mood. No doubt, the fight last night between Luc and me probably was partly responsible for Shi Hua and Mateqai's bickering.

I led the group through our Temple and garden to the stableyard. Warden Yar of Light had returned with mounts for Shi Hua, Mateqai, and himself. I was rather glad to have the huge man with us. He was as flexible as the grass on the Old Continent's northern steppes where his family was from and as solid as their winters. I trusted him to knock some sense in Mateqai if he started picking at Shi Hua again.

Ela didn't look at any of us. The horse Hogarth held for her consumed her attention. Her eyes were wide.

"Ya never been astride a horse before?" Hogarth asked.

She shook her head and took a step back in mute horror.

"This 'ere's Blossom." He patted the old mare's neck. "She's as gentle as they come. Our squires are both learning to ride on her."

"B-but Temple horses are trained to kill." Her voice took the tone of a whispered wail.

I squelched my own exasperated sigh. "Ela, our steeds are trained to protect their riders. If we get into trouble, even in Orrin, Blossom's first act will be to get you clear of any danger."

"If there's trouble, jus' hang on ta the pommel." At Ela's confused look, Hogarth touched that part of the saddle. "Blossom'll bring you straight back here."

"And if you fall off, stay perfectly still," Shi Hua added. "Blossom will keep anyone meaning harm away from you." She shook her head. "When I was a novice, a tiger escaped from the emperor's zoo. It was the Temple horses, not any of the people who herded the cat back to its paddock."

Ela blinked. "Why's a tiger dangerous if it's just a cat?"

"It's not just a cat." Hogarth chuckled. "They're about twice the size of our mountain panthers. Now, up you go."

He showed her which foot to put in the stirrup. After a couple of fumbles, Ela was more or less settled on Blossom's back.

Gina and Jonata took the lead out of our postern gate while the Light wardens took the rear. I motioned for Govind to ride beside me. Behind us, Shi Hua spoke softly with Ela.

"How are things with you and your family?" I asked Govind.

"Besides losing my shop and all my tools?" A wry smile tilted his mouth, and he shook his head. "My wife found some work as you heard in court. We have a roof when it rains thanks to the crown's stipend, but . . ." He shrugged.

"What about the Smiths Guild?"

"No tools," he said again. "The whole point of an apprenticeship is to earn the money to buy or to make your own tools. I would have to start all over again, and I have a family I can't even support now."

"Demons take them," I muttered. "The whole point of the guilds was for you to support each other."

"You've seen the resentment towards those of us from Tandor first hand," he said softly. "I thank Child every day High Sister Mya is treating my youngest without expecting a donation. However, I am open to suggestions on how to change our circumstances."

The threads of a plan to help the silversmith wove through my mind, but I'd have to tread very lightly. And maybe, just maybe, I could call in a few favors in the process.

"I have meetings the rest of the day, but come see me at Third Afternoon tomorrow." I held up my hand when Govind opened his mouth. "I cannot guarantee anything at this point, so don't raise your hopes just yet."

"Yes, Chief Justice." He grinned, showing bright red teeth. "Thank you for your effort. That's more than I can get from the guild."

The street traffic cleared a bit once we were past the Temples. The sharp acidic odor of the tanners mixed with the offal and copper of the butcher shops and the bitterness from Vintner's outdoor simmering cauldrons. Most of Orrin simply didn't have the right soil for grapes or hops, so our Vintner processed many of the herbs and seeds we could grow for medicines and salves. It meant keeping the huge cooking pots well away from the Temple itself, or every worshipper and all the clergy would be intoxicated from the fumes.

Pedestrians grew more numerous as we entered the south side. Tenements rose above our heads. Once again, we were getting ugly looks and murmurs from passersby about the Red Justice coming down to this section of the city twice in as many days. But everyone stayed clear of our horses. Perhaps it was because Ela rode with us.

We reached the tenement on Maiden Street Ela had said contained Old Anne's room. While Jonata and Yar checked the exterior of the building for problems, I looked up the side of the tenement, then at the warehouse down the street next to where Nathan found the body, and calculated the angles in my head. Yes, someone in the corner apartment on the top floor could definitely see into the alley. And Old Anne may have caught a glimpse of a face when our culprit exited onto the street.

When the silversmith followed us into the tenement, I said, "Govind, you can go home now."

He shrugged again. "Since I was accused of this Yellow Fin's abduction and murder, I would like to see it through if you don't mind, Chief Justice."

We all looked at Ela, who found a knothole on the wooden floor very interesting.

I turned back to Govind. "I don't mind in the least. Master Silversmith."

We climbed the four flights of stairs. The place reeked of unwashed bodies, even less frequently washed clothes, and stale foods. Ela led us down a narrow corridor on the top floor.

"No exterior exits," Gina mumbled. "One stairwell up the center of the building that will act as a chimney. This entire place is nothing more than a bonfire waiting for a spark."

I coughed, and my warden glanced back with a contrite expression.

Ela stopped at the end of the hallway and froze at a bang from inside the room. Instead of swords, Gina and Jonata drew their daggers and edged in front of Ela. At a nod from me, Gina knocked on the door.

"Anne," I called. "This is Chief Justice Anthea of Balance. I need to speak with you."

Silence reigned in the corridor and from the room. I extended my senses before I looked at Shi Hua.

*A man*, she confirmed silently.

I nodded again. Gina raised her right knee to her chest. Her boot shot out and landed on the edge of the door squarely at waist level. The inside latch splintered like the dry kindling it was, and the door crashed into the wall. I followed the two wardens into the room.

The shutters of both windows were wide open. A plump man stood over an open trunk at the foot of a tiny bed, a shocked expression on his face. He held up a beaded dress over his tunic and leggings. At the sight of us, he dropped the fabric, showing an apron stained with old, dry blood. The beadwork clattered as it fell back into the trunk. The man's head whipped around as he took in both skinny windows of the single room. He slumped as he realized there was no way he'd be able to squeeze out of them even if there were a way to climb down the exterior of the building.

Ela pushed past me. "What are you doing, Robin?"

"I-I—"

Gina crossed to the bed, pulled back a blanket, and spat an obscenity. Her face was greenish-yellow when she looked up at me. "You'd better take a look at this, Justice."

I strode the few steps to Gina's side. What I'd initially taken as a pile of clothing was a body under a thin blanket. The old woman's corpse was already cold, but that didn't disguise the gaping slice across her throat or the blood soaking the pallet on which she lay.

Ela squealed. I looked up to find her hands clasped over her mouth as if to contain more screams threatening to erupt.

Gina took a step to her left. "There's a crutch lying on the floor. It looks like it was knocked from the peg." She gestured at the rack fastened to the wall between the chair in the corner and the bed. The same rack held a dress from another peg. "There's knitting in the basket as well."

I pulled back the blanket over the corpse's right leg. It was shriveled as Ela described in court. "I take it this is Anne?"

Ela nodded. From her expression, I doubted she'd seen this level of violence.

Gina blew out a deep breath. "Not to step on your toes, Chief Justice, but I'd say she died from talking to one too many people."

# Chapter 12

With the chill in my spine, I wanted to go back to my own bedchambers and crawl under the blankets despite the heat of summer. This day was shaping to be even more disturbing than yesterday had been.

"Warden Mateqai, please inform Master Healers Devin and Bly we will need their assistance," Shi Hua ordered. "After that, please inform Magistrate DiCook of what we found."

"Shall I also inform High Brothers Luc and Xander of this matter?" Mateqai said. Whatever irritation he felt about Shi Hua refusing his advice earlier was gone from his voice.

"Yes, please."

Mateqai shot a look at Yar who cocked his head. No word passed between the two men, but the message about the sister's safety and well-being was clear. Mateqai slipped out of the room. Yar filled the doorway. Robin the butcher wasn't going anywhere soon.

"Sit on the floor, Robin," I ordered.

The butcher immediately dropped to the floor. The scent of his fear penetrated the odors of the tenement and the reek of the old woman's loosened bowels.

Movement from Govind caught my eye. I recognized his gesture as a Cantan sign to ward off evil. Luc had made the sign after the first one of the very few murders we'd dealt with while on circuit. I didn't like that gruesome murders were becoming our norm in Orrin.

"Govind, go home," I said. There's nothing more you can do here."

The silversmith shook his head, but I wasn't sure if he were refusing my suggestion or refusing the evidence of his vision. He dragged his attention from Anne's body.

"I swear demons make more sense to me, Lady Justice." He swallowed hard. "For someone to do this . . ."

Shi Hua crouched next to the bed and gently turned over the corpse's right hand. "Rigor hasn't set in, nor has the blood on the pallet completely dried." She looked up at me. "I estimate First Morning was when she died."

"Probably just before," I murmured. "Kill her while the entire building slept. No noise. No attracting of attention."

Our attention shifted to the butcher who quivered in a heap next to the open chest.

"I-I didn't kill her," Robin blurted.

"I don't recall asking you if you did," I said mildly.

"There looks to be blood and skin in three of her nails," Shi Hua added.

"Hers?" I asked.

"Angle's wrong," Gina commented. She reached over and raised the corpse's left hand. "And there aren't any wounds on her hands."

"The debris may be irrelevant," Jonata said. "She may have gotten carried away with scratching her ass in her sleep."

"Warden!" I snapped.

"No offense meant, Justice." Jonata waved at the pallet. "Surely, you can see the fleas in her bed."

I let out an exasperated sigh.

"I'll cover her hand," Gina volunteered. She removed a kerchief from her pocket, cut a length of yarn from one of the balls in Old Anne's basket, and sheathed her dagger. If we were lucky, we could use the scrapings from the dead woman's nails for a tracking spell.

Shi Hua tried to rise to get out of the warden's way, but she lost her balance. Gina kept the sister from falling face-first into the bed.

"Thank you, Warden." Shi Hua's laugh was self-deprecating. "My center of gravity is changing on an hourly basis these days."

"Would you truthspell Ela again, Sister?" I examined the civilian whose skin took a decidedly greenish cast. "I'd like to clear her before the magistrate arrives."

My statement startled Ela out of the horror she was caught in. Her hands dropped from her mouth.

"You can't possibly think—"

I held up a hand. "I have to follow all leads. You could have killed Old Anne before you came to the Temple of Balance this morning. Are you objecting to being truthspelled here and now?"

She hesitated. Her glance darted from person to person in the room.

"You have already developed a reputation for lying to or about the justices in Orrin," I said softly. "I would hope you'd want to rectify that impression by cooperating with us now."

A wash of orange flooded across her cheeks. At least, she no longer appeared like she was about to vomit or pass out.

She swallowed hard and nodded. "I'll answer your questions under truthspell, Lady Justice."

Shi Hua stepped forward and murmured the words of her two spells again.

Once I felt it settle over Ela, I said, "Ela, is the dead woman in the bed the same person you know as Old Anne?"

"Yes, m'lady."

"Did you kill Old Anne?"

"No, m'lady."

"Do you know who killed Old Anne?"

Ela's attention shot to Robin, but she'd learned her lesson from the hearing at Balance. "No, m'lady."

"Do you know of anyone who wished to harm Old Anne?"

She hesitated a moment before she said, "I only know the landlord was irate because no one had paid Old Anne's rent since the Queen's Army marched south."

Suspicion buzzed in my head like flies. "Who was paying Old Anne's way?"

"I don't know," Ela said. "You would have to ask the landlord."

"Who is the landlord for this building?"

"His name's Gregorius." Ela shrugged. "He doesn't live here though."

"Where does he live?" My cynicism had already answered that question, but I wanted to hear Ela's answer.

"Somewhere in the Merchant District," she said. "I'm not sure where exactly, but he's a city representative for the district."

"When does he come here to collect the rents?" I asked.

"First Morning on Rest Day." For the first time, a hint of a rueful smile curved Ela's lips. "He knows everyone is sleeping late while they can."

"Very well." I nodded to Shi Hua who dismissed the truthspell. "Thank you for your cooperation, Ela. You may go."

"And don't forget, Gregorius won't be your only visitor on Rest Day," Gina called out as Ela turned to go.

She looked back over her shoulder at my warden. "I won't." Maybe it had sunk through Ela's brain how lightly she'd gotten off after her missteps today. A few almond pastries were a small price to pay. She left the room, her bare feet padding against the dry unvarnished wooden floor.

"Aren't you going to question me?" Robin squeaked.

"Don't worry." I pushed back my hood and smiled at him. "You'll get your turn."

When Mateqai returned with DiCook and a handful of his peacekeepers, I met the magistrate down on the street.

"Do you mind if I have Robin sit in the Balance gaol overnight?" I murmured.

DiCook spat to the side before he said, "You can do whatever you want with him as far as I'm concerned. Mateqai said you caught him rifling through Old Anne's belongings."

I nodded.

"What the demon has this world come to?" DiCook muttered. "Why would anyone slit an elder's throat?"

"The people in this neighborhood already knew Yellow Fin's body had been dumped in the alley long before Nathan found him," I said. "And according to one person, Old Anne allegedly claimed to see the culprit in the black Temple robes."

DiCook stared at me for a long moment. "Well, you finally learned not to go anywhere in Orrin by yourself, so it makes sense they'd try something new."

I stared back at him. "You really suspect this is solely about me?"

"The Assassins Guild haven't been able to kill you, and they've been trying for nearly a year." DiCook watched people pass on Maiden Street while he stroked his short beard. The citizens gave the peacekeepers a wide berth while staring with suspicion or curiosity. "Destroying your reputation would accomplish the task where poisoning or stabbing you failed."

"I have a reputation?" I splayed my right hand over my chest in mock dismay.

He looked at me with a wry smile. "I'm assuming the problems on the south side are the reason we're dining at the duke's estate tonight."

"Yes." A sick feeling spread through me. I wasn't sure how I'd deal with Luc after last night's fight.

Thumping bootsteps on the inside stairs drew our attention to the main doorway. Sister Raven Claw stepped outside alone and approached us.

"I don't believe there's much in the way of injuries or the cause of death for Master Bly to catalog," the Death priestess said.

"It's not just Anne's injuries." I waved at the building. "I want Master Bly to remove some blood and skin that may not be Anne's from her nails."

Raven Claw nodded. "I see. The covered right hand. A tracking spell for her assailant. I'll inform High Brother Xander. Also, he asked I pass a message to you. Last rites for Yellow Fin will be at First Evening. The high brother mentioned your squire was a friend of the boy."

My stomach churned some more at that thought. I'd been to too many funerals in the last year. At least, I wouldn't be expected to say anything about the deceased this time.

"We will be there." I bowed to the sister. "Give your high brother my thanks."

She bowed in return.

More footsteps came from the interior stairs. Master Bly had commandeered the six wardens and Govind to carry the pallet with the shrouded body to her wagon and load it. She and Simi both nodded politely to me before they climbed onto the high seats of the vehicle and guided their team of horses toward the Healers Guild estate. I'd already informed her I'd come straight to the examination after my meeting with Ambassador Quan. Sister Raven Claw and her two wardens mounted their own steeds to escort the wagon to their destination.

I frowned as I pivoted and examined the street and buildings. I knew what I wanted to do. Could I use the two-dimensional framework of the street to widen my reach—

The idea exploded in my head, and I grinned like a fool.

"Anthea, you look like a madwoman," DiCook chided. "Someone was just murdered—"

"Because she saw something she shouldn't have." I grabbed his shoulders. "And I think I know how to recreate her view."

I released the magistrate, raced into the building, and climbed the steps two at a time. Behind me, DiCook's boots thudded on the wood planks.

I entered Anne's room. It didn't feel any bigger after her corpse had been removed. I strode to the window that looked down into the alley and placed my palms on the sill. Ribbons hung from the edges of the shutters and were tied to pegs on each side of the window. Such a clever idea for someone whose reach or strength were faltering on their later years. However, clever uses for ribbons couldn't be my priority right now.

*Yanaba?*

The solid touch of her mind met mine. *I'm here. How can I help you?*

*I need to do a rewind so I can see what a dead witness saw from her window.*

Yanaba swore a series of colorful oaths inside my head. *Old Anne?*

*Yes. Someone wanted to silence her.* I tried to tamp down my excitement. *What if we used your bond with Orrin itself to rewind a four-block section of the south side? We only need two days at the most.*

Yanaba was silent for a long time. *It would be theoretically possible.*

*As theoretically possible as you latching onto High Sister Mya's tracking spell in order to kill the demons hidden inside the city and funneling Balance's defensive spells through yourself,* I responded lightly. However, Yanaba nearly killed herself in the process. After three months, she still couldn't walk outside any of Orrin's gates or tunnel exits without experiencing excruciating pain. Almost as if her very soul was being torn apart. She'd literally become a part of the city of Orrin to stop the demons.

*I seem to recall several lectures from you since then about casting such risky magic,* Yanaba said, but I could hear her laughter in the back of my mind.

*If you can think of a better idea of trying to discover our body dumper's identity—*

After another long pause, I could feel the tickle of a third person.

*Are you insane?* Elizabeth shouted inside my head.

A warm callused palm covered the back of my left hand. Shi Hua entered our link, her child a faint presence in the background. *What the demon are you three arguing about?*

I quickly outlined my plan. Elizabeth objected again.

We waited for Shi Hua's opinion. *I'm in, but Yanaba, you'd better not make me unravel your spirit from another spell.*

*Twelve, help me,* Yanaba swore vehemently. *I don't want to go through that again. But if my bond can help us solve two murders, then I'm willing to take the risk.*

"I'll be downstairs to watch what happens in the alley," Shi Hua said out loud. "Do you need Warden Yar to guard the prisoner?"

I shook my head. "I believe Magistrate DiCook's peacekeepers can handle escorting the butcher back to the Balance gaol."

"But I didn't do anything!" Robin protested.

"Really?" Yar rumbled. "I thought you would look quite lovely in a dead woman's wedding dress."

The butcher's skin glowed a deep crimson, but he was smart enough to keep silent.

Once the peacekeepers escorted Robin out of the room, DiCook looked at me. "He didn't actually try to put Anne's dress on, did he?"

"No." I grimaced. "It wouldn't have fit anyway."

"Either way, it's damn disrespectful." DiCook stared at the ceiling for a moment before his attention returned to me. "Where do you want me?"

"Go to the alley entrance with Sister Shi Hua." My smile was not humorous in the slightest. "You might recognize our body dumper if our trick works."

The magistrate nodded, and he followed Shi Hua and the two Light wardens out of the room.

I looked around Old Anne's quarters to find something to use as a focal point. If I could establish one, Yanaba could build on it for our rewind of the last two days.

The wood of the room was useless. The dead rarely tell tales.

A twisting set of lead pipes sat to my left. Steam running through them would heat the entire building in the winter, but in the summer, they were cold. Lead didn't like to give up its secrets anyway.

I pivoted and crossed to the opposite side of the room. A copper spigot protruded from the opposite wall of the window where I stood. A copper basin was attached to the wall below the spigot. Another copper pipe drained the basin and re-entered the wall. I turned the lever of the spigot.

No water came out. Not even a single drop. When was the last time the residents of this building had running water? The copper might be useful, but the metal needed to be used consistently to have any awareness of time.

I stepped to my left, opened the cupboard, and smiled to myself. A small iron cookpot sat on the bottom shelf. I pulled out the pot and ran the fingers of my left hand around the inside. It was clean with no dust. This would be my focal point.

I settled on the relatively clean floor and crossed my legs with the pot in my lap. All the dirt on the wood planks had been tracked in by other people over the last few hours. I sent a silent prayer to Death, asking Her to watch over Anne as She guided her to Light.

Closing my eyes, I reached for Yanaba. Elizabeth was still with her. I had the impression they were kneeling before the statue of Balance in our courtroom. If my junior justice extended herself too far, Elizabeth would be there to reel her back.

*We're ready*, I said to Shi Hua.

*The magistrate and I are, too*, she replied.

I inhaled deeply and slowly, and released the air just as deliberately. I grasped the strings of time. It almost felt as if Yanaba's hands covered mine. Together, we pulled the strands for a four-block radius of the south side slums around me back for two days.

We let the time flow forward little-by-little. I felt more than heard Shi Hua's gasp. Alarm filled the air as the people around our perimeter saw past versions of their friends, neighbors, and themselves flit about the apartments, shops, and streets.

*He's unrolled the blanket with the boy*, Shi Hua reported. *Yes, definitely a man. We can see his face when he turns north on Maiden Street. Old Anne would have seen his face when he looked up at the tenement.* Another pause before she added, *The magistrate recognizes him.*

All of us working together to keep the rewind steady was far less taxing than doing such a spell alone. If only we had more people with these gifts.

Shi Hua muttered a silent oath. *He disappears at Siren Street.*

Of course, he did. Siren Street was the north edge of our spell. Yanaba and I released the time strings. Everything snapped back into now. Voices from the street below drifted through the windows. People marveled at the ghostly figures they'd just seen. Others recognized they'd viewed the past superimposed over their reality.

My neck and shoulders ached, and I blinked at the sweat dripping down my face. Using the hem of my robes, I wiped away the salty droplets before I rolled my head and each shoulder to loosen my muscles.

*You heard?* I asked.

*Yes*, Yanaba and Elizabeth said at the same time.

*Send Nathan across the street to let Luc know the latest*, I said. *I need to go talk to the magistrate.*

*What about the rewind of Anne's room?* Yanaba asked.

*I'll do it next, but I have a bad feeling it will be the same man Shi Hua and DiCook saw.*

Before I could set aside the iron pot, running bootsteps thundered in our direction. Both Jonata and Gina drew their swords.

Shi Hua whipped around the doorframe and skidded to a halt. A contrite expression crossed her face as the wardens sheathed their swords.

"I beg forgiveness, ladies." Shi Hua bowed to them. "I hurried back since Chief Justice Anthea needs a witness for the rewind of the room itself."

"Don't call us 'ladies,'" Gina said sourly. "We work for a living."

More thundering bootsteps warned us before Mateqai and Yar caught up with their sister. DiCook jogged up to the doorway, huffing and puffing like he was about to have a heart seizure.

"Then the working wardens and the magistrate need to leave the room," I ordered. "The sister and I need some free space in here."

Everyone but Shi Hua retreated to the hallway. I stretched my arms and waggled my fingers before I grasped the sides of the pot again.

"Ready?"

Shi Hua nodded and moved to the corner with the lead pipes to give her a thorough view of the room.

I grabbed the strings of time and yanked them back to yesterday evening.

"Anne is sitting in her chair," Shi Hua reported. "Her feet are propped on her foot stool. She's knitting by the last rays of the sun."

It was summer. The days were longer, and everyone took advantage of every moment of the light.

"She stands, grabs her crutch, and shuffles over to the chamber pot." Thankfully, Shi Hua didn't go into detail about that. "She latches her door. She returns to the pegs and removes her dress. She puts on a shift, the same one we found her in. She hangs up both her dress and the crutch on the pegs. Warden Gina was correct."

Shi Hua took a step toward the middle of the room "Anne uses the bed frame to work her way to the side of the bed. She pulls the blanket over her as she lays down. She's now asleep."

I let the threads of time slip faster through my fingers until Shi Hua said, "Slow down."

I gritted my teeth against the strain. More than one justice definitely made a rewind easier, even though we'd done a much larger area. Sweat trickled down my back and dampened my armpits.

"Someone slips a blade between the door and the jamb," Shi Hua continued. "They flip the latch up to unlock the door. Our man from the alley opens the door just enough to enter. His hood is up, but I can see his face. He crosses to the bed with the same blade in his hand."

The sister's voice hitched. "He grabs her hair with his left hand, yanks her head back, and slashes her throat. She wakes and claws at his hand in her hair. She's trying to scream. He jerks back and hits the crutch with his shoulder. It falls to the floor. The crutch must have made a noise. He quickly wipes his blade on her shift and hurries from the room, pulling the door shut behind him."

Tears filled Shi Hua's voice. "She's gone. It's First Morning."

I let the strings speed through my fingers and counted silently to myself before I slowed them again.

Shi Hua sniffed before she continued. "The door opens. It's Robin. He sees the body and starts to leave. He pauses and re-enters the room. He closes and latches the door. He crosses to the bed and covers Anne's body with her blanket."

Anger filtered through Shi Hua's voice. "He checks the basket and the cupboard before he opens the chest. He finds a small bag."

She Hua stepped closer to the bedframe to see what Robin was doing. "He dumps the contents into his palm. It's coins. A gold crown, three silvers, and multiple coppers. He puts them back in the bag and places it inside his apron pocket. He picks up the dress and holds it to the window. His attention jerks toward the door. The latch snaps, and the door flies open. Wardens Gina and Jonata rush into the room."

I released the timelines. Instead of a sharp snap, current time slid into place with a gentle click.

"Did you hear the sister, Magistrate?" I called out as I worked to get my cramped fingers to let go of the iron pot.

"Yes," he yelled back from the hallway. "We've got the jackass on theft."

I sighed while I clenched and stretched my hands. Even though Yanaba and Elizabeth assisted me with the first rewind, I would be paying through achy muscles for performing three such spells in less than a day, more so for two over the last candlemark.

Outside, the Temple bells rang First Afternoon. My belly rumbled in response. I hoped to Balance Ambassador Quan served a very large midday meal.

I set aside the iron pot and tried to stretch out the rest of my tight muscles. DiCook stepped into the room. Even if he wasn't scowling, his deep orange color would have given away his displeasure.

"Who is he?" I asked as I climbed to my feet.

"A Briton by the name of Drest," DiCook said. "Came here as a child with several other families a little over thirty winters ago, all refugees from the pirate attacks of the time. One of my predecessors as magistrate hired him as a peacekeeper."

"Let me guess." I crossed my arms. "One of the idiots taking bribes at the gates?" DiCook hadn't been happy I'd discovered that problem, but he'd cleaned up the mess under his nose.

The magistrate shook his head. "Worse. In my first month in office, I caught him extorting protection in the form of money, goods, and intimate favors here in the south side."

I groaned. "Please tell me Justice Penelope didn't release him." My own predecessor as chief justice had been going senile at the time, and the Reverend Mother hadn't done a damn thing to curb Penelope's excesses despite repeated pleas from the Balance staff.

"No." Disgust fill the magistrate's voice. "One of his friends in the peacekeepers warned him I was coming to arrest him. This is the first time I'm aware that he's been seen in Orrin since then."

My thoughts swirled as I paced around Old Anne's room. As long as she had lived in this room, she may have recognized Drest when he left the alley yesterday. I stopped and faced DiCook again.

"What happened to the friend that warned him?"

DiCook grinned. "I dismissed him. He's now a butcher."

"Please tell me you are joking."

"Believe me, I wish I was." DiCook gestured in the general direction of the Temples. "That's why I was pleased you asked he be kept in the Balance gaol. It would be too tempting for him to have an accident in his cell at Government House."

# CHAPTER 13

It was almost a relief when Shi Hua and I finally left the south side slums and headed for the Embassy District for our meeting with Ambassador Quan. Jonata and Mateqai packed Old Anne's belongings into the trunk with room to spare. I hired Govind to haul the trunk to Balance. I sincerely doubted Anne had filed a statement of last wishes with Death, but one of the Death clergy would have to confirm it. If that were the case, I would need to try to find her closest relatives.

If they still lived in the city, which I also doubted. Otherwise, Anne would have been living with them, not by herself.

I really missed Bertrice at the moment. Nothing against Xander, but his predecessor had been the high sister of Death in Orrin for two decades. She knew the politics and idiosyncrasies of the city and its populace. Her advice had been invaluable, and I failed to make better use of it for the short time we'd been colleagues. I wished she were here to talk to. She was probably the closest I ever had to a mother-figure.

*Are you that worried Ambassador Quan may do something untoward during this meeting?* Shi Hua asked silently.

I laughed and shook my head, a little glad she knocked me out of my wallowing. *He's been behaving himself since our trip to Tandor. My guess is your Reverend Father of Thief and your aunt have something to do with it.*

*More like his experience at the hands of the renegades. Despite the issues within the imperial court, he's never truly suffered before.*

Perhaps Shi Hua was correct about the reason for Quan's mellowing. However, my concern lay on the fact two people from the most vulnerable in our community had been murdered for no reason other than someone's sick pleasure. But I couldn't burden the mother-to-be with my worries.

"Aren't you even going to comment on our link earlier?" Shi Hua asked out loud.

"Most people don't like it when I know something before they do." I could feel her staring at me. "Especially Lady Katarina. I've learned to wait until the person addresses the subject with me, like Justice Yanaba or Sister Claudia have."

"I simply thought the high brother would have told you since I informed him yesterday morning."

As much as the petty part of me wanted to make trouble for Luc, I couldn't put Shi Hua in the middle of our fight. Instead, I said, "Give him a little credit. Besides, he probably thought I already knew."

Shi Hua giggled. "Well, if your etiquette failed when it came to the duke's wife . . ."

"How did Jeremy handle the news?" I said softly.

The sister didn't look at me, but she blinked rapidly before she took a deep breath. "He's happy and angry at the same time. I tried to talk to the high brother about Jeremy's mood swings . . ."

"Didn't he take your observations seriously?"

"He said none of us were comfortable dealing with the new edict. But now the wardens won't let Jeremy near me, and he's taking it quite personally."

*You mean Mateqai won't let Jeremy near you, right?* I shook my head, resisting the urge to look at him over my shoulder. If that particular warden overstepped propriety, Luc would have no choice about having him lashed.

"None of the wardens will." Shi Hua switched back to silent speech. *Jeremy almost stabbed Tadhg while in the throes of a nightmare three nights ago. And he threatened to drown Istaqa for bothering me in the bath.*

Things were worse than I knew. Was Luc that clueless about what was going on within his own Temple? Or was he too ashamed about his lack of control over his people?

"*Was* Istaqa bothering you?" I asked.

Shi Hua shook her head. "For once, our head of household was innocent. Istaqa has been very considerate lately. That day at the bath, he had brought me some peppermint tea because my digestion was upset."

"If you don't feel safe at Light—"

"No," she said sharply. "I know Yanaba wants to share this experience of having a child—"

"This isn't Yanaba talking, Sister." I gave Shi Hua a stern look. "Because of the apprehension I have for the brother's sanity, your safety is my top worry."

"You mean you don't want a diplomatic incident with Jing," she said bitterly.

"I'd be saying the same thing if you were Issuran," I said.

"You sure it's not your guilt over the deaths of Yellow Fin and Old Anne? Do you view me as helpless as them?"

It wasn't guilt. I was genuinely concerned about Shi Hua's security. The renegades had been actively targeting Light priests here in Issura. It only made sense they would target the women carrying possible Light children next. I realized if Claudia were in possible danger from Luc, I'd do the same for her. It eased the little knot of jealousy inside me.

We made the left turn onto Embassy Row, and I understood frightening Shi Hua wasn't the best idea. Maybe I would have a chance to speak with Yin Li or Quan privately about the situation.

"How about we table this discussion until after our meeting with your ambassador?" I forced a smile.

It didn't fool Shi Hua one bit. However, she merely nodded and said, "Of course, Chief Justice."

When we reined to a halt before the Jing embassy, two imperial guards stood at attention before the gates. They were accompanied by fierce marble dragons in front of the wall pillars. The two humans saluted us. The statues showed the same indifference they displayed every other time I visited the estate Ambassador Quan called home.

One of the guards stepped forward and addressed Shi Hua in their language. She answered in kind and inclined her head.

He turned to me. "Welcome, Chief Justice Anthea. Ambassador Quan and the Lady Yin Li await you in the garden. Do you wish us to care for your horses, or will one of your wardens be entrusted with them?"

I blinked in surprise. The guard had spoken flawless Issuran. In the past, I had resorted to the Peaceful Sea trade tongue to communicate with the embassy staff. Shi Hua was trying to teach Yanaba and me the Jing language, but my efforts left something to be desired.

"Warden Mateqai will stay with our horses," Shi Hua said.

Gina and Jonata exchanged glances. Mateqai's skin turned a dark pink though his expression remained impassive. Yar said nothing. He dismounted and handed his reins to Mateqai before he moved to Shi Hua to assist her in dismounting.

I would have thrown a fit if a warden treated me as helpless. In fact, I had done so on more than one occasion.

On the other hand, I had also envied Shi Hua's excellent balance. With the babe growing in her womb, her center of gravity was changing as she said earlier. We couldn't afford her falling off a roof. Or a horse. Sometimes, our wardens had to save us from our own stubbornness.

A servant came out of the guardhouse as the man who had spoken opened the right gate to let us pass. The servant bowed to us and escorted Shi Hua, me, and our three wardens along a stone path to our right.

"I hope my flower garden has been kept up," Shi Hua mused.

"It has, Sister," the servant said in the Peaceful Sea trade tongue. "Mistress Yin Li was quite adamant that nothing be changed. She was very complimentary of your design."

Shi Hua's cheeks flooded with red at the compliment.

Late spring flowers bloomed in concentric circles around a gazebo. Dragon heads decorated the corners of the square wooden structure. Wind chimes of fired clay hung from the edges of the roof, their noise a pleasant music in the slight breeze of the afternoon.

A table had been set in the gazebo. Quan stood at the top of the steps. The woman with him looked enough like Shi Hua they could have been sisters. However, it was the young boy standing next to Yin Li who drew my attention.

He stood ramrod straight, like a warden or one of the Conflict clergy, though he carried a hint of a toddler's baby fat. His aquamarine hair was pulled back in a formal topknot, similar to Quan's.

Surprisingly, it was Yin Li who made the introductions. "Chief Justice, Sister, this is my son, Shang. Shang, this is Chief Justice Anthea of Orrin and your first cousin Sister Shi Hua of Light."

The boy bowed deeply to both of us. "Greetings, honored guests," he said in perfect Issuran.

We retuned his bow. When I straightened, Quan's gaze met mine.

"Quit giving me that look, Anthea. He's not mine."

"Of course not, Ambassador," I said dryly. "When would you have had time with all your other extracurricular activities, such as being demon bait?"

Yin Li tittered prettily behind her hand, as a good concubine would have. "Po, you did not tell me the lady justice was so clever."

"You have no idea, my dear." Quan said, matching my tone. He raised Yin Li's hand to his lips. "But if there is to be a battle of wits, my coin is on you."

This time, Yin Li's smile was genuine. "I welcome any friend who can keep you on your toes."

Quan waved behind him. "We have another table for your wardens, Chief Justice. I know you don't trust me, but I can assure you a Temple member watched the preparation of food quite closely."

"That doesn't mean you didn't slip an aphrodisiac in my wardens' cups between here and the kitchen," I shot back.

"And I am not so foolish to fail to politely ask a woman, especially one who knows how to wield a blade with expert skill, for any favor," he responded.

My stomach rumbled quite loudly. "Can we continue our verbal sparring over our already late midday meal?"

Quan laughed. "Considering you're an even more dangerous opponent when hungry, by all means." He waved toward the table.

I turned to the wardens and tilted my head. They circled the gazebo while Shi Hua and I climbed the steps. As Quan had said, a table in white linen had been set up roughly ten yards away. The wardens sat so none of them had their backs to us. I doubted any of them would touch the food or drink either.

Wicker chairs with embroidered cushions surrounded the table covered in cloth-of-gold. Individual dishes of fine ceramic had already been placed on our table along with silver utensils. A selection of first of the summer vegetables and fruits with fresh-from-the-oven breads made my mouth water. Steamed clams sat in their shells on a bed of ice. A ceramic pitcher sat in a bucket also full of ice.

"Mother, may I dine with the wardens in order to practice my languages?" Little Shang looked up at Yin Li with a pleading expression.

However, a frown marred her beautiful face. "What about your cousin?"

The boy turned to Shi Hua and bowed. "I meant no insult, Sister."

She laughed. "None taken. Why don't you entertain our wardens? We will talk later, my cousin."

"Thank you, Sister." Shang bowed to her again before he raced down the steps and across the riverstone path to the wardens' table.

Yin Li shot her niece a glare. "You are as much of a brat now as you were at his age."

"That's an impolite thing to say in front of a foreign dignitary," Shi Hua chided.

"Besides, I already know how much of a brat your niece is," I said in a conspiratorial whisper.

Yin Li's mood lightened, and she laughed. "I wasn't sure what to expect, but I definitely like you, Chief Justice."

"It's Anthea, Sister." I grinned. "And yes, I believe we will be great friends."

◇

We ate and made small talk. I was delighted to find the pitchers contained sweetened, diluted lemon juice.

I saluted Quan with my goblet. "Where did you get the fresh lemons? It's nearly impossible to bring them from the Middle Sea without them rotting before they reach this side of the world."

"The Tehas tribes have been experimenting with growing citrus trees." He shrugged. "It seemed a good investment. The Lucayans tried a couple of decades ago, but their islands sit too low. One typhoon wiped out all the groves."

He took a sip from his goblet and smiled. "We both know you don't make social calls, Anthea. What may I do for you?"

I hesitated for a moment. Bless her, Yin Li rose and nudged Shi Hua's shoulder.

"Come with me. I'd like your opinion on some herbal beds I'd like to put on the west side of the estate."

"But I really should—"

"Go spend some time with your family, Sister." I smiled. "You haven't seen your aunt in six years, and it would be good to know your cousin. I promise to keep you apprised of anything the ambassador and I discuss."

For a moment, Shi Hua seemed torn between duty and her own needs. Finally, she pushed to her feet and faced Quan. "If you even think an inappropriate thought about the chief justice, it's not her blade unmanning you that you need to worry about."

His right eyebrow rose. "Are you threatening a member of the imperial family, Sister?"

"No, I'm making a promise," she hissed. "And by Light, I keep my promises."

Alarm filled Yin Li's expression. She muttered something in Jing and tugged on Shi Hua's arm. The sister of Light glared at the ambassador for a long moment before she wrapped her hand around her aunt's elbow.

Together, they followed a path around the rear of the manse. Yar rose from the other table as did little Shang. The two males followed the priestesses at a discreet distance.

Quan grunted. "It seems I'm no longer the child's favorite."

"Really, Po?" I mocked. "You're jealous of a warden?"

"No." He toyed with the gold beads at the ends of his chin-length moustache. "The boy needs as much love and support as he can receive. What I fear is Shi Hua's reaction to the fate of the boy's father."

"She knows him?" I was curious. Shi Hua rarely talked about Jing. I knew part of it was her specialized training, but the other part was homesickness. Part of her feared she'd never see her homeland again.

"Brother Shang is, was, the advanced training master for the Temple of Conflict in Chengzhou. He trained both women. Shi Hua has a deep respect for him, but Yin Li fell in love with him, and he with her." Quan released a deep sigh. "He accompanied Reverend Father Chen eastward, chasing after those blasted demon eggs."

"Shi Hua mentioned there has been no word from them in the last three months," I said softly.

"My brother fears the worst. The last communication from Chen said they were about to enter the Gobi Desert." Quan gulped the rest of his lemon juice. "Not even the Wildlings could pick up their trail after a few leagues into the desert. It's like the sand itself swallowed them."

I didn't know what to say. The Gobi was the largest desert on the Old Continent. So much larger than the Valley of the Lost between Issura and Diné. Out in such an isolated area, demons could be breeding like guinea pigs, and we'd never know.

Not until it was too late.

Quan shook his head as if to free himself from equally depressing thoughts. "As I asked before, what do you need, Anthea?"

"First, to pass on a warning. Gerd has escaped from the Balance gaol in Standora."

If the situation wasn't so concerning, I would have enjoyed the expression of shock on Quan's face.

"How could your Reverend Mother be that careless?" he shouted. His volume drew the attention of Gina and Jonata as well as his own guards.

My wardens started to rise, but I gestured for them to take their seats. Quan waved at his guards to return to their stations.

I pushed back my plate, leaned my elbows on the table, and lowered my own voice. "I need you to be honest with me. Who's handling the trade in children with Gerd no longer in Orrin?"

He leaned back in his chair and regarded me. "This is about the dead boy your squire found yesterday."

"Yes." I waited. While I wished I could truthspell Quan, he was the Jing emperor's half-brother as well as the ambassador to Issura. I had to put my faith in his code of honor. Despite his perverse and insatiable sexual appetites, he had no interest in children. Ming Wei ended up under his care because he stopped a Jing noble from abusing her.

Or rather the noble immolated himself and his slaves when he learned Quan was coming for him. Ming Wei had been the only survivor of the fire.

Quan exhaled. "A disgraced peacekeeper named Robin conducts the deals on the south side. I think you already know who he works for."

In other words, I merely needed to truthspell the butcher. If he hadn't stooped to stealing a dead woman's property, I wouldn't have the link I needed.

"What about a Briton named Drest?"

"If it's the man I used to know, he also was dismissed from the peacekeepers but for extortion." Quan smirked. "Last I heard, he fled to Cant without his ill-gotten coin."

"He tried to extort you?"

Quan shrugged. "Who do you think informed DiCook of Drest's extra income?"

"Then I'd watch my back if I were you, Your Excellency." I leaned back in my chair as well. "He's back in Orrin."

Quan's nostrils flared, and his expression grew somber as he considered the news. "That makes no sense. Does the magistrate know?"

"Yes." This time, it was my turn to smirk. "And he's still peeved about Drest's escape from three years ago."

"You're sure about this?"

"As sure as I can be without having him in my grasp." I took a sip of my lemon juice. "He murdered the woman who saw him dump Yellow Fin's body in the ally."

Quan watched me for a long moment before he said, "Don't underestimate Drest or Bianca, Anthea. They're both far more calculating than Gerd ever was."

"You're not even going to ask me how she escaped?"

"Only a naïve fool would believe their Temple hasn't been infiltrated by the renegades," he said dryly.

"I guess it's a good thing I'm not naïve, then," I replied.

He shifted as if he were uncomfortable. I've never seen Quan Po emotionally uncomfortable, not even after he'd been tortured by the renegades in Tandor.

"I hate to mention this, but are you sure Elizabeth—"

"No, I'm not." I stared at a bumblebee zipping amongst the flowers. "For all I know, you're a demon who stole Quan Po's skin." I snorted. "For all I know, I might be a demon."

"I doubt that."

I faced Quan again. "Look at who my birth mother is."

"Do you really believe Gerd lay with a demon?"

"No, I think my father did."

Quan roared with laughter. So loud several of his guards jogged toward the gazebo, intent on protecting their prince from the terrible Red Justice. He waved them back as he wiped away the red tears that rolled down his face and hung from his blue beard.

"Is there anything else you wanted to ask me?" he said once his mirth was under control.

I sighed. "I was hoping you and Yin Li could convince Shi Hua to move into the Temple of Balance until she delivers her babe." I hesitated a moment before I added, "Or even move back to the Jing embassy until she gives birth."

Quan quickly sobered. "Why?"

"I fear the renegades will start targeting the women pregnant by Light priests."

He shook his head and crossed his arms. "First of all, she can't come here, and you know it. The only thing I could do that would be more detrimental to our nations' relations would be to toss her on the next ship departing for Jing. What's really going on at Light? You can't tell me Luc has lost control of his people."

"You're right. I can't tell you that." For all the times, Quan had played diplomatic games with me, I now understood why. Sweet Balance, I never thought I'd be in this position.

He muttered a few choice words in the Jing language. They were the few I remembered from Shi Hua's lessons. None of them should be said in polite company.

Quan paused for a breath before he added in Issuran, "That's why Yar is with her. He's a good man." He looked at me. "She can't go to Balance without everyone calling into question Luc's leadership."

"I know, but I'm not sure I want to take the chance of losing Shi Hua," I said.

"Or her babe," he prompted.

"I truly wish I had foresight," I muttered. "If I'd known this edict was coming, I never would have suggested her transfer to Orrin's Temple of Light."

"What's done is done." Quan waved a dismissive hand, but then he cocked his head as he regarded me. "You could blame me for insisting Shi Hua move to Balance. If the south side boils into violence—"

"What have you heard?" I demanded.

"Besides the story that you've been stealing children and drinking their blood?" Quan cocked an eyebrow. "You do know someone was seen in black Temple robes near the boy whose throat was slit, don't you?"

"Yes."

"It's good to know you followed my advice on not underestimating your opponents." The ambassador smiled. "And that you're paying more attention to what happens around you."

I ignored his jab at my ego. "Are there any other previous associates of Drest's he might be recruiting?"

"None I can name at the moment. I can make inquiries, but it may take some time." Another smile. This one didn't have the leering quality from before our trip to Tandor, but it was definitely one of male interest. Any information he acquired would require another meeting between us.

"Do you really want to put Shi Hua's promise to the test, Po?" I said softly.

He sighed. "Given the edict, you can't blame me for trying—"

Yin Li and Shi Hua strolled around the corner of the manse, still arm-in-arm. Yar and Shang followed. A wave of grief came from the two women despite their placid expressions. Yar kept Yin Li's son back by pointing at various flowers, obviously asking questions of the child.

When the two women climbed the steps of the gazebo, Yin Li bowed to Quan. "Your Excellency, your father is requesting your presence."

I'd only met Quan's father once. He'd been a master of the Jing School of the Dragon and the Phoenix, one of the many institutions that mixed magic and philosophy for those whose talents didn't quite mesh with the Temples. Master Quan had served the empress at court until her consort feared Master Quan would try to place his own son on the throne instead of the rightful heir, the ambassador's half-brother. It sounded more like the imperial consort was jealous another man had caught the empress's eye, though the senior Quan and the empress's relationship supposedly ended upon her marriage.

These days, Master Quan appeared to be suffering from the disease known as the Child's Curse when I met him. However, the ambassador believed his father suffered from some sort of hex designed to mimic the illness.

The ambassador rose from his chair. "I apologize for cutting our talk short, Chief Justice. I do enjoy your visits. And I'll relay any additional information I learn to you or the magistrate as soon as I can."

"That's all I can ask, Your Excellency."

He lifted my left hand and kissed the back of it. "Until then. Yin Li would you be kind enough to escort our guests to the gates."

The ambassador jogged down the steps of the gazebo and strode to the manse. Once he entered a side door, I looked up at Yin Li.

"Has he had the Healers Guild here examine his father?"

She nodded. "And High Sister Bertrice before we lost her. It's definitely not the Child's Curse. Reverend Father Biming and I have tried to do what we can as well as Sister Shi Hua, but—" She shrugged and looked over her shoulder at the manse before her attention returned to me. "We are all at a loss."

I rose from my chair. At my action, my wardens stood as well and walked over to the gazebo.

"Thank you for entertaining us this afternoon, Mistress Yin Li." I smiled. "It has been a pleasure."

She inclined her head. "For me as well, Anthea." She lowered her voice. "Did he give you the answers you needed?"

"And then some."

In fact, Ambassador Quan had given me quite a bit to chew on. I'd have to tread carefully in building a case against Bianca. She'd made sure to keep her hands clean in the abduction and assaults on Orrin's street children as well as anything else she had been up to with Gerd.

The question was whether I could unseat her before she framed me for something even more heinous than slitting a boy's throat.

# CHAPTER 14

Once I returned to Balance, I told Nathan about Yellow Fin's last rites. He insisted he wished to go as I suspected he would. Sivan said she wanted to attend as well. I had a feeling that most of Balance would accompany us. At least, someone would be there besides the clergy and staff of Death.

My next task pleased me even less than dealing with a child's funeral. Gina accompanied me to the Healers Guild for the examination of Old Anne's body. This time, Sister Raven Claw of Death met us there with their chief warden Axton. The four of us watched as Master Devin, Master Bly, and Bly's apprentice Simi performed their tasks.

First thing they did was to retrieve the blood and skin from under the fingernails of the corpse's right hand. Simi handed me the vial, and I placed it in my cloak's left pocket.

"The amount of blood soaked into her pallet corresponds to her dying from blood loss due to the major arteries and veins cut on each side of the throat," Master Devin announced.

"Is there any way to determine if the same person or weapon slit both of our victims' throats," I asked.

"Normally, I'd say no, but young Simi here came up with a marvelous idea." Devin smiled. A feeling of pride by association came from him, probably because he'd been Bly's primary instructor.

"It really wasn't—" Simi stammered.

"Yes, it was." Bly crossed to the large piece of slate handing on the wall. "She figured out that the angle of a cut using a repetitive motion is always the same no matter the length of the cut."

"So, what you're saying is?" Raven Claw prompted.

"We can mathematically prove the same person who cut Yellow Fin's throat also cut Anne's," Devin exclaimed.

"Using the same weapon?" I asked.

"We believe so," Bly said. "But not with the same precision as who." She shot a nervous look at Raven Claw. "I swear we've been buying piglets, lambs, and rabbits from the market to test our theories." She turned back to me. "After the death of Sister Gretchen and the attack on you outside of the Temple of Light last winter, we notice the difference between the cuts."

I rubbed my forehead. Midwinter was a nightmare I'd rather forget. "You mean a slice on my arm versus what was done to poor Gretchen?"

"We've been experimenting with different weapons—" Bly started.

"Or everyday things that could be used as weapons," Simi blurted.

Bly didn't correct her apprentice. She was probably trying to subtly encourage the girl after she'd gotten sick over the examination of Yellow Fin's body.

"And catalog the descriptions and other information. We'll have a record for comparisons whenever Balance needs us to examine a body," Bly finished.

"However, we pray to the Twelve this is the last time we have to do this," Devin said fervently.

While I wanted the same thing as Devin, I also knew Balance wouldn't deign to grant my selfish wish. I had enough to execute Drest if I could get my hands on him, but I needed to find the evidence linking him to Bianca.

Otherwise, no child in Orrin would be safe again.

# CHAPTER 15

Alone inside my quarters after returning from the Healers Guild, I reviewed reports for the half candlemark before my next meeting. I sent a silent prayer to Balance my conversation with Talbert went as well as the one with Ambassador Quan had. Thief generally kept an eye on everyone and everything in Orrin, but Talbert never offered me any information unless I asked him directly.

And in private.

Shortly before Third Afternoon, I opened the passage and entered the tunnel system. Publicly, Talbert and I were awkwardly cordial with each other. However, I'd found his advice quite useful when it came to the renegades. The times we met to discuss Orrin's problem were rarely official.

I approached the entrance to Thief and felt the wards guarding it. Their magic was subtle, more of a vibration like that of a hummingbird's wings than the prickle of my own. Like with the entrance to Light, I didn't dare open the passageway into Thief. I'd nearly gotten myself run through with a warden's sword the last time I acted that idiotic. Nor did I reach out for Talbert's mind. Like a few of the clergy of Thief, he was a quicksilver, someone who was nearly impossible to read because they didn't seem to exist mentally. I had to trust he remembered our appointment and was close enough to feel his wards.

Marble groaned and rolled back into the Temple of Thief's entrance. I ducked and peered into the room.

"I'm alone," Talbert said, bent over to look through the passageway. His features were average. He kept his hair cut only as long as a fingertip at most. While I was tall for a woman, he barely came to my height.

"Just checking." I entered his bedchambers and straightened. The delicate scent of Jing black tea filled the room. "Your wardens tend to be a little overenthusiastic when it comes to protecting their seat."

"And yours aren't?" he said wryly. "Gina said this was about Yellow Fin."

"Actually, I have a list of subjects I need to discuss with you," I said as he reached down for the stone and murmured the spell to close the opening. The marble folded itself back into place, showing its face to the room once again.

"Then it's a good thing I ordered some refreshments for your visit." He straightened and gestured toward a small table in the corner. In the middle sat a ceramic pot with a spout, hot from its pink color, along with last season's apples and a selection of cheeses and breads.

"Twelve bless you," I murmured as we crossed the room.

"Go ahead and pour yourself a cup," he said while I sat at the table. His bedchambers were clad in dark blue and green marble as mine were, but engraved carvings in the stone were filled with various metals, such as gold, silver, and copper.

With a swirl of his robes, Talbert walked to his door, touched one of the symbols on the wall, and murmured a spell. All the metal embedded in the walls, ceiling, and floor glowed from the energy of his magic.

"Mind if I ask how you see my room?" He crossed to the table and took the seat opposite of me.

"Do you mean as in your decorating tastes?" I pretended to misunderstand as I poured myself tea. I didn't like talking about my differences.

"No." He chuckled as he poured his own cup of tea. "When I activate my wards, you get the same delighted expression as my youngest sister had when we watched fireflies in the summer as children. Most people don't even notice the designs."

Would things have been different for me if my parents weren't Temple? If I'd grown up with siblings like Talbert or Luc? Was there any harm to answering Talbert's question?

I feared the renegades would figure out the weaknesses to my odd sight. On the other hand, this was a chance to bond with a fellow seat.

"The marble is dark blues and greens to me." I took a sip of my tea and relished the slight bitterness after all the sweet lemon juice I had at the Jing embassy. "The metals are paler tracings of blue and green on the stone until you activate the spells." I couldn't help smiling. "Then the sigils glow with pinks and reds and purples. They truly do look quite lovely against the stone."

He looked around the room, taking in the symbols carved into the marble, before he turned back to me and raised his cup. "To our differences, Lady Justice."

I saluted him with my cup. "I'm trying to find a former peacekeeper by the name of Drest."

"Drest?" Talbert set down his cup. "Now, that's a name I haven't heard in a long while."

"He's back in Orrin."

Talbert pursed his lips. "This is the first we've learned of it." His eyes widened as he worked through the logic of why I asked about Drest. "He's the one who killed Anne?"

"Was she one of your watchers?" I said softly.

He nodded. A red tear trailed down his left cheek, the most emotion I'd ever seen from the priest. He wiped the liquid away and said, "She was also my aunt."

I leaned back in my chair, a little surprised by his admission. "And here I was afraid I'd never find any of her family. Why did she live in the slums?"

He shrugged, and a wry smile crossed his face. "That's where we both were born."

Another surprising admission, but it did explain the lack of personal décor in his bedchambers.

"What about her children? Grandchildren? Nieces? Other nephews?"

"A plague swept through Issura fifty years ago. Anne's husband and children died." A wistful smile crossed his face. "When I was about five winters, we moved to Standora. My mother tried to convince her to come with us, but she refused and she never married again. However, when I was assigned here, we renewed our relationship."

"Surely, you could have moved her closer to you, even find her a place in the Temple of Thief, if you're her only family." I waved helplessly with my left hand.

Talbert shrugged. "She refused to leave the south side. Her friends were there. And she was everybody's Aunt Anne, not just mine."

"You were the one paying her rent, then?"

He shook his head, then paused. "Well, not directly. I convinced her to work for me as one of my watchers, and I reimbursed her. Anne refused any gifts from me. She could be quite stubborn about such things." He smiled. "I know you didn't come to listen to me reminisce."

"No." I sucked in a deep breath. Repeating this story was starting to get to me. "Gerd escaped from Standora."

His own gasp startled me as much as him.

"Anthea, please tell me this is a sick joke."

"I wish." I took another sip of tea before I continued. "The Reverend Mother of Love believes she is heading south."

"What has your own Reverend Mother said about the matter?"

"Not a damn thing to me yet."

His eyebrows drew together. "Neither has my Reverend Father. To learn of this through Love is quite disturbing."

I snorted. "Really? With my Reverend Mother, it seems to be normal practice to leave me ignorant on important matters." I shrugged. "In this case, someone within Balance assisted Gerd. One of the wardens was found in her cell's bed, dead. The other warden disappeared about the same time. Knowing my Reverend Mother, she's embarrassed, and she's working to keep the news as quiet as possible."

Talbert shook his head, his expression mirroring my disgust. "I'll see what I can learn for you. What else?"

"What can you tell me about Robin, a butcher on the south side?" I leaned my elbows on the table and cradled my chin in my palms. "We caught him going through Anne's belongings."

Talbert looked away for a moment. "We have reason to believe he's been behind a handful of child kidnappings on that end of the city."

"More than the orphans?" Alarm trilled through me.

"Unfortunately, yes." His expression turned grim. "It's not Robin himself. Someone far thinner dressed in black Temple robes from the few descriptions—"

I started laughing. I couldn't help it. Once again, Talbert and I were stumbling around in the dark, each of us with one end of a thread, but unable to find the other side without assistance.

"Perverse child assaults and murder are not a laughing matter, Chief Justice," he said crossly.

He was right. I swallowed my dark mirth at the situation.

"One of the men in Temple robes running around the south side is Drest."

Talbert blinked as he put together the facts. "Aunt Anne saw him leave Yellow Fin's body in the alley?"

"And somehow, word got out that she had." I poured us both some more tea as I spoke. "We think that's why he killed her."

Talbert shook his head. "No, Anne wasn't that foolish to endanger herself. She would have reported anything like that to me."

"It was nearly an entire day between Drest leaving Yellow Fin's body in the alley and Anne's death." I frowned. "How often did she send you information?"

"Someone from Thief passes through the south side every day." Talbert waved his left hand. "If there's a green ribbon tied to her shutters, everything is fine. If there's a yellow ribbon—" He stared at me. "Was there a ribbon, and what color—"

I point at my eyes. "For a clever man, Talbert, you can be quite dense."

He held up his right index finger. "Let me inquire before you call out to Sister Shi Hua."

I shouldn't have been surprised he knew who accompanied me to the south side this morning. It wasn't like we were subtle when we rode down the main thoroughfare of Orrin, including right past the Temple of Thief.

Talbert rose, crossed to his door, and deactivated his wards and protection spells before he opened the door and called out for the warden on duty. The woman who appeared in the doorway was the same warden who nearly ran me through on a previous visit.

"Who checked on Old Anne in the south side for the last two days?" he demanded

She flicked a glance at me before looking at Talbert again. "Sister Cedar Grove did. Do you wish to speak directly with her?"

"Yes, please," Talbert said.

Another odd glance at me from the warden set my nerves on fire. She leaned close to Talbert's right ear so I couldn't see her mouth and whispered something to him.

Talbert looked at me over his shoulder, an amused expression on his face before he turned back to the warden. "Send them both in."

That wasn't the answer the warden was expecting. She took an uncertain step back before she pivoted and marched smartly down the corridor. Talbert closed the door, his amusement still plain as he returned to his seat at the table.

"Who is here I'm not supposed to know about?" I smirked.

"You'll see," he teased.

"Is it a good thing I still have my sword with me?" I asked dryly.

"May I suggest you listen to my people before you start whacking off their heads?" Talbert reached for a piece of cheese and popped it into his mouth.

So, we sat like that, staring at each other, for three hundred beats of my heart before there was a knock on his bedchamber door.

Sister Cedar Grove entered first. Her long hair hung loose down her back and she dressed as a civilian, linen skirt and tunic with shell necklaces and a bone nose ring. Like everyone else in the summer, she went barefoot. It was the man behind her who made my jaw drop.

"Forgive my tardiness, High Brother. It's getting harder to leave Light even with the new edict as an excuse—" Brother Garbhan realized I was sitting at the table with Talbert. The young Light priest's own jaws snapped closed with a distinct *snap* of his teeth.

I frowned at Garbhan and crossed my arms. "We knew you were spying on us, Brother. We just had the wrong Temple."

# CHAPTER 16

I turned to Talbert while the warden, with a smirk on her face, pulled the door closed behind Sister Cedar Grove and a stunned Brother Garbhan.

"So, it's not just Jing's Temple of Thief who recruits from the other eleven Temples," I ground out. Garbhan's stunned face would be amusing if I weren't dealing with two murder victims.

"No, we all do," Talbert said mildly. "It's not just the aristocracy and the civilian leaders we need to keep an eye on."

"But who decides which people are a danger to the human race and which aren't?" I snapped.

"The heads of the Temples around the world decide together," Talbert said. "No individual should make that decision."

I tried to release my anger at his pointed jibe, but it sizzled in the back of my mind like a fresh hog on a spit. "Let's deal with Old Anne first, and then my questions will be answered." I glared at the two men in turn.

"Understood," Talbert said.

After reactivating the high brother's wards, the sister had no trouble sitting next to me. Garbhan appeared as if he feared I would tear him apart with my bare hands.

I honestly considered it. However, Talbert patted the younger priest on the back and inclined his head toward the table. Both men took their seats, Garbhan sat closer to Talbert than me.

"Sister," Talbert started, but Cedar Grove held out her hand. A slip of parchment was between her fingers.

"This was in her hiding place for messages, High Brother. She didn't get a look at the face of the person who left the boy's body in the alley. Forgive me for not bringing this to your attention earlier, but since she merely confirmed it was a man wearing black Temple robes, I didn't believe it added anything to our evidence." Cedar Grove looked at me. "Since the yellow ribbons were still up, I checked this morning, but there was nothing else."

"That's because she was already dead," I murmured. What the hell had happened? Did the gossip get out of hand in Anne's neighborhood and people embellish on a tale? Or did Anne lie in her message to Talbert? But why would she do that?

Cedar Grove bowed her head. "So I heard on my way back from the market this afternoon."

Talbert crumpled the parchment and flung it across his bedchamber. "The fool!" His face glowed a brilliant red.

"Balance, help her," I murmured as I caught up with Talbert's deduction. "She deliberately started the rumor, hoping to draw out Drest."

"Of all the idiotic moves—" Talbert violently shoved back from the table, knocking his chair over as he jumped to his feet. He started pacing while mumbling obscenities.

My anger disappeared under a miasma of sympathy for Talbert and my own grief. My grandfather Kam had jumped in the way of a poisoned blade meant for me. The best of intentions had terrible consequences in both cases.

"Her sacrifice wasn't in vain," I said. "She did lead us to the culprit."

Talbert whirled to glare at me. "She was my family!"

"I know," I said softly. "Nor do I discount your grief, High Brother. All I'm asking is that you not to let that grief overwhelm you to the point where Anne's death was for nothing."

His shoulders sagged. "As always, your logic is impeccable, Chief Justice."

I breathed a little sigh in relief. I had enough problems between Bianca and Luc. I didn't need any with Talbert as well.

"My clerk Lailani should have sketches completed this evening from Sister Shi Hua and Magistrate DiCook's descriptions of Drest," I said. "Can you circulate them among your Temple personnel and your watchers, High Brother?"

"It would help if we had more people in the south side," Cedar Grove said. "The abductions have centered there."

"I have someone who may be able to assist you in keeping an eye on things." At Talbert's curious look, I added, "If you wish an introduction?"

He nodded. "That would be acceptable. Was there anything else you wished to discuss with me from your list?"

"The unrest on the south side was a palpable thing the last two days I've been down there." I relaxed a bit and reached for my tea. "Any idea what's flaming it besides the Tandoran refugees?"

"Mainly people losing their children," Cedar Grove said.

"I don't understand. Why wasn't any of this reported to the peacekeepers?" I said before I took a sip.

"Lingering resentment over the extortion from three years ago." Talbert's left eyebrow rose. "I'm assuming if you know about Drest, you know why he was dismissed from the peacekeepers."

I nodded.

"And I'm sorry to say this," Talbert continued. "But Chief Justice Penelope's excessive punishments didn't help. DiCook's done a damn good job cleaning up the peacekeepers, as you have the Temple of Balance, but there's still a lot of work to be done. Improving reputations is much harder than correcting behaviors."

"High Brother Luc and I are having a meeting with the duke and the magistrate tonight about the troubles on the south side." I turned to glare at Garbhan. "But I'm sure you've already been told that."

Garbhan met my gaze squarely. "You're right. I am here to tell High Brother Talbert about your meeting. You have every right to be angry about the situation, but I'm not going to apologize for my actions."

"Well, thank you for giving up the shy, unassuming mask you've been wearing," I said. Keeping my hands on my cup kept me from throttling the boy. "Does Reverend Father Farrell know about your extracurricular allegiance?"

Once again, Garbhan looked at Talbert.

The high brother shrugged. "It's your choice, but I wouldn't put it past Anthea to slap a truthspell on you if you don't. And trust me, if you try to resist her, the spell will kill you. The Reverend Father of Thief would prefer to keep you intact."

"Everything?" Garbhan asked.

Talbert shrugged for a second time, but he remained silent.

Garbhan turned to me. "I was assigned to Reverend Father Farrell's personal staff a year ago. Thief noticed peculiarities in all the Temples over the past three years. My task was to keep an eye on Light."

"So, you were spying on Reverend Father Farrell for Thief?" I said.

"Yes."

I narrowed my eyes. "Who is watching Balance?"

"Justice Melanippe."

That answer took me by surprise. "She was in my novice class," I murmured. Melanippe wasn't simply my classmate. She was the top of our class. Everyone doted on her, students and teachers alike. And our novice trainer Justice Rose often held Melanippe up as someone I should emulate.

Which made me dislike her intensely. I wouldn't go so far as hate because the word implied a personal connection. We barely spoke to each other.

"Why did Reverend Father Farrell really assign you to Orrin?" I asked.

"To spy on you and High Brother Luc," Garbhan said matter-of-factly. "In your case, he believes Reverend Mother Alara is far too lenient, and she should have beheaded you over the Samael DiRoy incident."

Normally, I would have repeated the refrain about the cousin of the queen summoning demons, but I gritted my teeth and kept silent.

"And in Luc's case . . ." Garbhan shook his head. "Farrell is jealous. Luc is a popular priest. He's been instrumental in your fights with demons. He hasn't let the loss of his foot get in the way of his duties. And after the events in Tandor, there's been talk of him succeeding Farrell as reverend father."

I looked at Talbert. "Is this talk being spurred on by your Temple?"

"No." He shook his head. "This is solely Farrell and the rest of the Light order. Farrell definitely believes Luc wants the Standora seat. Before Luc, there was some speculation within the Standoran Light Temple that Brother Jon might succeed Farrell."

"And when Brother Jon disappeared, you feared Farrell had him killed?" I said.

Talbert blew out a heavy breath. "It was a possibility we considered, but the little information we could ferret out when Jon went missing didn't lead to Farrell. However, the renegades' infiltration of Light along with you and Jax finding Jon's body while searching for Luc last winter did spur questions about Farrell's competence within the Light order."

I set down my cup. "Can you contact Melanippe?" Talbert opened his mouth, but I held up my hand. "I know you can't do it directly, but we need as much information as we can about Gerd's escape." I looked at Garbhan and grinned. "Beat you to revealing that tidbit of information, didn't I?"

"This isn't a contest, Chief Justice," Garbhan said. "And frankly, I find it refreshing that you and High Brother Luc have some integrity and honor despite your warped senses of humor. Or I did until your spat last night."

I glared at the young priest while Talbert smirked and Cedar Grove chuckled. Garbhan, however, merely watched me. Of course, Talbert wanted to one up me for learning something before he did. He prided himself on knowing every happening in Orrin even though he rarely acted directly on that knowledge, which irritated me to no end.

"And how are we supposed to trust you?" I snapped. "You admitted you are spying on us."

"I have to earn it." Garbhan turned to Talbert. "What did you think of her idea of using my recent demotion to infiltrate the renegades?"

Both Talbert and Cedar Grove stared at me as if I'd grown a second head.

I took another sip of tea before I said, "We hadn't gotten to that portion of the conversation when he sprung you on me."

"Y-you want to what?" Talbert spluttered.

I shrugged. "I told you up front I had a list of topics."

Cedar Grove leaned back in her seat and regarded me. "I've never met anyone who could elicit such a reaction from my senior priest before."

"Reverend Father Biming said the same thing about Ambassador Quan." I smiled over the edge of my cup.

"And what exactly in this plan?" Talbert asked.

I laid out how the seats of Thief and Child in Tandor had created a subpersonality for High Brother Aduba of Conflict in order to infiltrate the renegades. I then shared Elizabeth's idea of doing the same to her or Garbhan for the same reason. When I finished, Talbert folded his hands together with his index fingers resting against his lips.

"Well?" I prompted.

He lowered his arms to rest on the tabletop. "I see one problem with your plan. Gerd."

"She doesn't know Elizabeth or Garbhan," I said.

"But she knows you." He shook his head. "Any of the Orrin clergy would be suspect after what happened in last winter's convocation. And if she's on her way south as the Reverend Mother of Love suspects, she will rejoin the renegades in her efforts to kill you."

He was right. Deep in my heart, I knew he was right. When Gerd reunited with her allies, no one near me would be safe. Luc wouldn't be able to trick any of them again. Elizabeth could have worse done to her than the skinwalkers' efforts to break her during that awful year in Tandor. Poor Garbhan would be guilty merely from association. They'd torture him before they killed him and set a trap spell on his corpse like they did with Brother Jon.

And the renegades would make a point of killing Yanaba, Shi Hua, and their unborn children out of their sheer delight in bloodshed rather than any part of Gerd's revenge.

"I disagree, sir," Garbhan said. "Chief Justice Anthea is right—"

"They'd kill you before you could make any inroads—" Talbert started to protest, but the younger priest held up a hand.

"With all due respect, High Brother, this is exactly the opportunity we've been waiting for." Garbhan gesticulated wildly. "Anyone from Thief is automatically suspect, but they've been actively recruiting disgruntled clergy from the other Temples. My recent alleged demotion is the perfect opportunity." He grinned. "I could even spin my story by saying the Reverend Father wants to join them, and this is the only way he could make contact without arousing suspicions in Standora."

"It would be a suicide mission," Talbert snapped.

"Maybe not," Cedar Grove murmured.

"Wait a moment," I cut in. "Talbert's right to dismiss such a mad idea. I was wrong to even think of risking someone with Light talents given our current circumstances."

Talbert leaned back in his seat. "And what are our current circumstances, Anthea?"

"Another demon attack is coming," I said sharply. "You know it. I know it. Anyone who thinks otherwise is only fooling themselves. It's merely a question of when and where. And in the meantime, the renegades will do their damnedest to whittle away as many people with Light talent as they can."

Talbert rubbed the skin beneath his lower lip with the side of his forefinger. Garbhan, Cedar Grove, and I waited for . . . something to come out of his mouth.

"All Twelve Temples need to work together," he finally said. "If anything, the demon attacks in Tandor and Orrin proved that. No one Temple is solely responsible for our defense."

"You're reciting the same lines every teaching clergy has recited since the formation of the Temples," Garbhan said.

"Repetition doesn't deny the basic truth," Talbert said quietly. "Balance and Death worked together to take out a demon army in Tandor. Justice Yanaba used High Sister Mya's tracking spell to locate and kill the demons who snuck into the city—"

"We lost a good chunk of clergy and civilians setting that trap in Tandor," I snapped. "Not to mention, we nearly lost both Yanaba and Mya with the damn stunt they pulled."

"Maybe we need to be taking more chances," Cedar Grove said. "Even start more thorough training with the registered talents for additional assistance to the Temples."

"Let me think about this overnight—" Talbert started when outside, the Temple bells tolled First Evening.

"I'm sorry, High Brother." I stood. "You're right. We can discuss this further tomorrow. I'm already late to another appointment. Besides . . ." I smiled at Garbhan. "I'm probably not the only one who will be missed."

He scrambled to his feet, and the other two rose as well.

"After court tomorrow since I'm scheduled for duty at Balance?" Garbhan said.

Talbert nodded. "Cedar Grove, would you escort our young priest out?" A wry smile crossed his face. "And make sure you're seen in public."

"Yes, sir." The priestess circled the table and looped her arm around Garbhan's elbow. "Let's go to my bedchamber first so I can change. We want to make sure I'm seen wearing something more appropriate."

Garbhan's face glowed with her insinuation. Once Cedar Grove deactivated the wards and they left Talbert's bedchambers, he crossed to the entrance to the tunnels.

"It's not that I want to dismiss your idea out of hand—" he said softly.

I held up a hand. "I admit I often jump without knowing how deep the water is. Besides, it's not my ego you need to worry about. It's Elizabeth's. She won't take your dismissal of her idea as well as I would."

Talbert's laughter followed me through the tunnels and back to Balance.

# Chapter 17

Shortly after I returned to my chambers, the entire clergy, staff, and the wardens of Balance escorted Nathan to Yellow Fin's funeral. Everyone except Hogarth and Little Bear, who were completing a special task I'd assigned them. Other than the members of Death, we were the only ones to attend the funeral. No one from Mother bothered to come.

Ming Wei held Nathan's hand tightly on the walk over to the Temple of Death and through the service. For once, it wasn't because she was afraid. Nathan needed the support of someone who understood what it was like to be vulnerable to the whims of people who should have protected them.

Since this wasn't a ceremony of state but a personal one, the pyre had been built in a special courtyard Death used for the normal funerals. It chilled me that my thoughts divided deaths between "normal" and "abnormal".

White sparks rose into the dark sky. Usually, there was a sense of acceptance for the cycle of life from the clergy of Death. Their attitude helped the grief-stricken to deal with their pain.

But not tonight. Emotions ranged along frustration and anger. Xander's voice carried a burr of unease as he sang the final liturgy. Almost as if he feared there would be more victims like Yellow Fin.

As much as I wished I could guarantee I'd bring him no more mutilated children's bodies, I couldn't. I hoped keeping Robin in the gaol overnight and stewing in his fear would shake loose more information than a truthspell would. The renegades I'd encountered so far hadn't stooped to petty theft. His behavior stank of greed and lack of morals, not righteous zealotry.

Maybe I needed more of a prod when I questioned him, and given how Gerd treated Dragonfly and the other sisters of Love, the new high sister might be willing to help me with the interrogation.

When we returned to Balance, Hogarth met us at the entrance. I dismissed everyone to dinner. However, Sivan stayed by my side. Her worried expression tore at my heart.

Hogarth merely smiled. "Don ya fret, Sivan. Little Bear and I confirmed your numbers."

She sagged, but I wasn't quite so relieved. Especially after Xander's news that his inventory of Death also showed nothing had been taken.

I don't know why I hoped we'd find one of our Temples were missing robes. It meant someone within our respective domains was allied with the renegades, but it also meant someone associated with Drest was within our reach. However, I should have known he had access to other Temples' regalia after so many of the renegades pretended to be from Light. But that knowledge still didn't connect directly to Bianca. I was missing something important, but I didn't know what.

Ming Wei raced up to me and curtsied. "Chief Warden Little Bear sent me to tell you High Brother Luc is here for your meeting with the duke."

Dread curled in my stomach. I'd already had a bad day, but I'd been busy enough not to think too much about the fight Luc and I had last night. However, I could no longer avoid him.

"Thank you, Ming Wei," I said. "Please tell the chief warden I will be there momentarily."

After another curtsey, she raced down the hallway toward the back of the Temple.

Hogarth eyed me. "How long are ya gonna punish the boy for doing what he was ordered to do?"

Sivan gasped, but I wasn't sure if it were Hogarth's brazenness or the fact he beat her to the question that elicited her reaction.

"That's not really any of your business," I bit out.

Hogarth crossed his arms, and his bushy eyebrows scrunched into one long turquoise caterpillar over his eyes. "It is when you're grumping around the Temple and everybody has to tiptoe around your bad mood."

"I haven't been here most of the day," I protested. Why was I acting like a petulant child instead of ending this conversation?

"Thank Balance for small favors," he said.

"That is quite enough, Stablemaster." I pivoted on the toe of my left boot and started to march down the corridor.

"Apologize to him," Hogarth called out behind me.

I whirled to face him again. "I have nothing to apologize for!"

"It doesna matter." Hogarth shook his head. "You two sniping at each other is only doing the work of the renegades for them."

I spun and charged for the stables before I said something to the old man I'd truly regret.

In the yard, Little Bear and Warden Noko waited with their own horses and Nassa. I mounted my girl without a word to them. I didn't trust myself.

It was only after we followed Little Bear and his steed out the postern gate I noticed no one from Light had been in our stableyard. Was Luc that fearful of entering the Temple of Balance walls, or was he equally as angry over last night's argument?

When we reached the main thoroughfare, Luc, Nicholas, and Yar waited for us. Luc inclined his head with a wary expression.

"Chief Justice."

I inclined my head as well. "High Brother." If he was going to be terribly formal, then I could be, too.

Little Bear and Nicholas took the lead. Luc nudged his horse to fall in step with Nassa. I watched him from the corner of my eye, but he didn't so much as look at me.

We were passing the Smiths Guild when Luc said, "I heard an interesting rumor today."

"Oh." I tried to keep my tone neutral, but I was fairly certain I failed.

"Apparently, the Chief Justice of Orrin has been abducting and eating children."

The tension flowed out of me at his amused tone. "I expected Shi Hua to make a full report to you, but that's all you took from her recounting of the day's business?"

"Actually, I first heard it from High Brother Jax during the midday meal. Well before the sister reported your findings on the south side."

"Was your meeting with the high brother of Wildling productive?" I asked.

"He confirmed we have nothing to worry about," Luc murmured.

The part of me on edge about Jeremy was relieved a demon hadn't replaced the young priest. However, it meant High Sister Mya would have her hands full in treating his emotional disturbance.

"And what did you think about the rumor?" I said.

"Well, I've known for the last eleven winters you'll eat nearly anything in reach." Luc turn toward me and grinned. "But eating children is a new one even for you."

My lips curved of their own volition. "If you're going to harass me about my perverse proclivities, please get the rumors correct. I sleep with demons, and I drink children's blood. I don't eat their flesh."

Luc chuckled. "Please forgive me, Chief Justice." *Can we please talk later?* he added silently.

"Of course," I murmured in answer to both requests.

I didn't want to be angry with him. Hogarth was correct. I shouldn't be punishing Luc for the edict. We were both damn lucky no one cared about our affair before the edict came down. And it wasn't his fault I couldn't bear children.

I only had to get through this blasted dinner and hope we could find a solution to the problems on the south side of Orrin.

And without the duke's heir spitting up on my robes again.

# Chapter 18

Magistrate DiCook and two of his peacekeepers waited for Luc, me, and our escort in front of Government House.

"My wife is accusing me of having an affair with one or both of you." DiCook shook his head as his horse fell in step with ours. "I can count on one hand the nights I've made it home in time for dinner since midwinter."

"Well, if she knows of a way to eliminate the demons, I'm willing to put her in charge of the city defenses," I teased.

DiCook merely grunted.

"You need to tell your lovely wife the truth, Magistrate," Luc said.

"Oh, and what truth is that, High Brother?"

"You dislike her cooking."

I laughed. The wardens and peacekeepers snickered. DiCook made an obscene comment regarding Luc's mother and her choice of barnyard animals as sexual partners.

However, as we rode through the business district, I knew the rest of the evening wouldn't be as jovial.

"I've been pleading with the crown for assistance!" Duke Marco slammed his palm against the top of his cedar dining table, making most of the silver plates and utensils jump. His wife Lady Katarina and his sister Lady Alessa exchanged worried glances.

"And what answer has the queen given you?" I asked.

"Her Majesty understands Orrin, Pana Valley, and Standora have taken the brunt of refugees." Marco dropped his sarcasm and shook his head. "She claims she's still trying to find places for those in Standora since the capital ended up with the majority, plus she's looking at the expenses of sending the royal army to Tandor." He waved a hand dismissively. "She doesn't want to raise taxes, but—"

"She may not have a choice," Alessa interjected. The lady would have been a marvelous merchant in her own right. She managed her own holdings with aplomb, the bulk of which she inherited from her lover Sister Gretchen of Love, as well as assisting her brother in running the family shipping business.

"Why do you say that, m'lady?" Luc asked.

"One of our own ships, the *Mars Cognitum*, wintered in the Wari Empire," Alessa said. "The crew of a merchant we do business with in Cant found floating wreckage with the DiMara crest on a piece on their way north. We believe it is debris from the *Mars Cognitum* and was one of the ships the renegades sunk off the coast of Tandor." She shrugged. "Our family alone is looking at major losses with a lost cargo and the deaths of an experienced crew, not to mention the ship itself. Then there were the delays thanks to the abnormally severe winter weather, both in the Peaceful Sea and throughout the Gray Mountains. Multiply that by all the trade that passes through Issura, and the queendom's looking at a heavy dip in revenue for this year in addition to the extra expenditures for the Tandoran refugees."

I swore under my breath. It was obvious where this was going. The renegade take-over of Tandor was costing us more than just lives.

"The call to arms—" I started.

"The crown princess has had to release a good chunk of men and women, or we're not going to have a damn thing to eat," Marco said. "And it took several of us on the royal council to convince her of that."

I wanted to kick myself. The duke had far more on his plate than I realized.

"The other problem is that a good number of the folks from Tandor are unskilled labor or merchants," Katarina added. "We've had no problem placing the skilled labor. Some of them have been willing to go to farms or apprentice with the Mine or Lumber Guilds."

"That's not entirely true," I interjected. "I had a falsely accused Tandoran silversmith in court this morning." I turned to Luc. "Do you remember Govind? He was one of the volunteers on the Queen's Gate."

Luc nodded. "His wife Nala was a huge help in keeping the children calm during the evacuation." He chuckled. "She put their oldest three to work loading the smaller ones onto the boats. What on earth was he in court for?"

"False accusation by an Orrin woman who wanted poor Nala out of the way." I grimaced. "According to Govind, our own Smiths Guild is refusing to help the Tandoran smiths, demanding they become apprentices again."

"They what?" DiCook exclaimed.

The duke leaned his face into his palms. He inhaled quite audibly, raised his head, and clenched his fists. The same expression was on Talbert's face this afternoon.

Right before he knocked over his chair.

"So, the guild masters lied to me," he bit out.

"I'm sorry, Marco," I said softly. "I came here looking for a solution together, not to add more burdens on your shoulders."

He exhaled and reached for his goblet. "If I wanted ease, Katarina and I would have run away to Cant last year." He smiled at his wife, and she blushed at his loving expression.

I glanced at Luc and wondered if we shouldn't have done the same thing after everything that had been happening lately.

"Maybe we can force the guild masters to care about their members." Luc's concerned expression mirrored my own feelings. "But the rest of the Tandorans? If things are as bad in Standora as you're saying, Your Grace, sooner rather than later, the Queen's stipend will run out, and we'll have even bigger problems."

"Our problems are already worse than you think, High Brother. The Tandorans want their old way of life back." Katarina shook her head. "And there's no way to give them that. At least once a day, Marco receives a petition to go back to Tandor and restore their homes."

The aftermath of the Death spells still lay over the remnants of the city. Even though the Balance spells kept the effects within the city walls, anyone or anything living would perish the instant they crossed that barrier. The islands of Britannia were uninhabitable though it had been centuries since the queens had ordered the launch of the last resort magic of Death.

"I can understand their sentiment." I pushed back my empty plate and rested my cheek on my fist. Part of me often wished Luc and I still rode circuit in eastern Orrin. Life was so much easier back then. "They're mad as whitetail bucks during mating season, but I understand it. However, wishful thinking, on their part or ours, isn't going to ease the tensions in the south side."

"A bigger peacekeeper presence will make things worse, too," DiCook added. "Last night, there were some threats and intimidation from a couple of gangs. My people were lucky. Jaime's a good man. Kept his head. But I don't know what's going to keep things in check for much longer."

"Anthea, what if the Temples could hire some of them?" Katarina leaned forward. "Washer women or groomers or, or—"

"Are you trying to give all twelve chief wardens brain storms?" Luc said. I could envision Little Bear wearing the same incredulous expression as Luc. Except my chief warden would have followed with some very creative epithets.

"She has a point," I murmured. "We are the Twelve Temples. The soul of humanity. We need to lead by example."

Luc groaned and scrubbed his face before he looked at me again. "I recognize that gleam in your eyes. Under normal circumstances, I'd agree with you and Lady Katarina, but these are not normal times."

"No, they aren't. Which is why I would personally truthspell every person seeking a place in one of the Temples." I reached for the decanter. I would have preferred Jing tea, and no doubt the duke and his wife would have had their servants fetch some for me if I requested it, but their talk of resources made me realize just how blessed I was by my position.

"And what if you accidentally kill someone again?" DiCook glared at me while I poured the wine into my goblet.

"I've never killed anyone by accident, Magistrate." I set aside the decanter and raised my cup. "Now, if they're a renegade and chose to commit suicide via my truthspell, well, then, that's one less enemy we need to worry about, isn't it?"

In the end, we decided Duke Marco would address the city leaders at Government House tomorrow evening. That included the nobles within a day's ride, the guild masters and the Temple seats. I hoped the duke's passion would convince them it was in their best interest to find positions for the Tandorans.

The meeting would also give me a chance to meet this Gregorius, who owned the tenement where Old Anne had lived. Ela had already misspoken several times. She could be wrong about Anne not paying her rent. But if she were correct, I needed to find out why. While I doubted Drest had any connection to Gregorius, I still couldn't make assumptions. That meant following every trail, not just the ones I wanted because I was angry over one group's misdeeds.

At the end of the evening, I even managed to make the appropriate approving noises over my godson Kam DiMara, and for once, he managed not to spit up all over my robes. I would take whatever success I could get at this point.

"Truthspelling all the refugees from Tandor is still a lot of work for one Temple," Luc said as we rode down the bluff road from the duke's estate. With the green fog rolling in from the sea, even our horses' shoes sounded muffled against the cobblestones.

"As I said at dinner, I do have a couple of spare justices these days." I glanced at him. "What is it you're really worried about?"

"Don't you think it's suspicious matters are coming to a head in the south side just after we learn Gerd has escaped from custody?"

"Definitely," I answered. "Why do you think I volunteered to do the truthspells on the people from Tandor?"

"If it were me you were truthspelling, I'd know why you were doing it," he said sourly.

*Is this how you want to start our evening discussion?* I asked silently.

*You're the one holding the past three months over my head.*

There were so many things I could say, like his constant jealousy of Ambassador Quan. But if I did, they would only hurt Luc and make things worse between us. Instead I said, *I don't want to fight with you. Not again.*

*Then truthspell me and be done with it,* he snapped.

*I don't want to know what you did with Claudia!* My eyes burned.

*Why do I feel like nothing I could do will please you?*

*Because you're not the problem.* My throat ached. I didn't want to deal with this. Not with so many other things that needed my attention. Not when it was ripping us apart at the worst possible time. *You did what you were ordered to do—*

*You were the one that insisted I fulfill my obligation—*

"I know!"

Nassa jumped at my shout and galloped down the road. Her shoes struck the cobblestones and threw yellow-white sparks into the night. Little Bear and Noko spurred their horses after mine.

I couldn't help but notice the men from Light didn't speed up to catch us.

# CHAPTER 19

Upon my return to my bedchambers, I cursed myself as I undressed. The vial with the possible skin and blood of Anne's killer was still in my pocket. I immediately negated the idea of going to Luc for the tracking spell. I couldn't deal with him right now.

Instead, I marched over to Elizabeth's bedchambers and knocked.

"Yes?" she called.

I opened the door and looked inside. She sat at her desk, reading from the way her fingertips rested on the thick page of a book with the raised symbols of our Temple.

"It's me," I murmured as I entered. "I know it's late, but can I ask your assistance on something?"

"Of course." She smiled in my general direction.

"I need to perform a tracking spell."

"And you don't want to ask anyone at Light for their help after yours and Luc's tiff tonight?"

"How did you hear about that?"

Elizabeth waved toward the door. "Little Bear told Sivan. None too quietly I might add. People seem to think since I'm blind, I'm also deaf."

I groaned. I remembered that feeling. Every time I stepped out of the Temple of Balance in Standora during my novice years, people reminded me I was different than them.

"However," Elizabeth added. "I suggest we ask Warden Noko to attend us."

"Why Noko?" I asked.

"She's the head of this evening's night watch."

Once I got over my embarrassment at forgetting my own people's schedules, I summoned Noko. She followed us to the courtroom.

"May I ask why you are doing this so late, Chief Justice?" she said.

"Because in my racing around Orrin to save the populace from their own idiocy, I forgot I had the lead to our murderer in my pocket," I said dryly. "Hopefully, our culprit is snug in his bed, and I can arrest him." I made a sign for good luck.

Noko moved the podium and stool out of our way and set them by the south wall. Elizabeth and I sat cross-legged and facing each other in front of the basalt statue of our patroness. I removed the cork stopper from the vial and set it between us.

Taking a deep breath, I cleared my mind. Beneath me, I felt the steady, reassuring rhythm of the universe. Elizabeth and I tapped the stone, matching the world's heartbeat before breaking into different sub-rhythms. Energy whirled around us and lifted the strands of my hair that had escaped their braids.

A ribbon flared to life from inside the vial, something felt rather than seen. It sinuously flowed toward the main doors of the Temple.

Another beat entered our spell. This one discordant. Off. Unnatural.

Despite our pooled strength, Elizabeth and I couldn't keep the ribbon intact. It frayed and ripped under the counter beat until nothing was left. The energy wind faded, and the rank smell of burning blood stung my nose.

"What the demon was that?" I whispered.

Elizabeth frowned. "Some kind of counterspell." She shook her head. "Not even a concealment spell. More like something to eat the connection between body parts and the person they belong to. I've never even heard of such a thing."

I muttered a dozen obscenities as I rose and stretched. Noko assisted Elizabeth to her feet.

"I thought your rewind showed who killed Old Anne," my warden said.

"It did, but I can't convict him if I can't arrest him. And I can't arrest him if I don't know where he is." I picked up the still warm vial, but the skin and blood were charred. Unusable.

Now, where in Balance's name did a disgraced peacekeeper and extortionist obtain that kind of protection spell?

# Chapter 20

Once again, I had a difficult time falling asleep and when I did, a new nightmare plagued me. This time, Luc and I were immobilized by an invisible force in a cavern while Gerd slit the throats of Nathan, Ming Wei, and little Kam and drank their blood. My birth mother had possession of the demon grimoire she'd intended to sell last winter before Sister Gretchen stole it. Gerd used the incantations in the grimoire to summon the beasts of the demons' realm, and they started eating Luc alive.

A scream tore through my vocal cords, and I jerked upright in my bed. The door to my bedchambers slammed open, and white light blinded me. I shielded my face with my hands.

"Justice!" Noko's voice. "Are you all right?"

When she approached my bed, her body blocked the light. Her hand gripped her sword, and she looked around wildly for a foe to stab.

"I'm all right," I said. "Just a bad dream." Sweat drenched my night shift and hair. My body ached as if I'd really been fighting to free myself from unseen bonds.

She exhaled and sheathed her sword. "We're sorry for disturbing you, m'lady."

"I think I did the disturbing tonight," I said with a bit of disgust.

"Is there anything we can get you, Chief Justice?" Ahiga asked.

Noko stepped back, and I winced at the light from the lamp Ahiga carried.

"No, thank you." I waved a hand. "Please carry on."

"Yes, m'lady," Noko said.

The two wardens departed, closing my bedchamber door behind them and locking it again. I flung back the light blanket I used in the summer and rose. After stripping off the damp shift, I considered retrieving a clean one from my wardrobe, but it seemed like too much effort if I was going to have nasty dreams for a second night in a row.

Instead, I climbed back on my bed. I lay on my back and stared at the green pattern that swirled through the dark blue stone overhead. It almost resembled a seawolf with its tall dorsal fin slicing through the surface of the water, its head raised to bite into unwary prey.

Nightmares were hardly a rare occurrence for me, especially during the past year of running into, or rather from, demons. Was this dream a continuation of my insecurities? It made sense after Yellow Fin's funeral and my second fight with Luc.

But something about this dream was different. It felt too . . . real. I could smell the children's blood, hear the crunch of Luc's bones, feel an alien magic holding me helpless as people I loved died.

The deactivation of my ward on the passage to the tunnels disturbed my thoughts, and the scrape of stone on stone had me reaching for the dagger I kept beneath my pallet. As the marble of the secret passage folded back onto itself, I rolled off my bed and crept on bare feet to my wardrobe. The cold marble against my soles added to my gooseflesh. I raised the dagger, half-expecting a renegade.

Light magic tingled against my skin. A familiar grunt came through the passage before Luc pulled himself through on his back.

"Balance take you!" I swore as I stepped forward. "That's an excellent way to get yourself killed!"

"I thought you *were* being killed," he shot back. "I heard you scream in my sleep and felt your pain and fear."

"I had a nightmare," I said. I lowered my right arm. "And don't you think my own wardens would have responded if I had screamed?"

"With our luck lately?" He grinned up at me, that mischievous one that broke the walls I'd placed around my heart the day Gerd sold me to Balance in return for attaining Orrin's seat of Love.

"I warded the passage," I said, glaring at him.

"I've always been able to deactivate your wards."

"You don't even have a weapon with you," I pointed out.

He reached toward his waist and pulled his crutches through the opening. "These can give a Germanian war hammer a good run in a fight."

"You're incorrigible," I muttered.

"And you're naked." His leer was so ridiculous I couldn't help laughing at him.

"You said you wanted to talk," I said. "Or was that simply an excuse earlier tonight?"

"Not at the time, but I was also expecting you to be wearing clothes."

"Don't blame me for this," I snapped.

"Can we save the arguing until later?" He tried to give me a sad, pitiful expression. "I really missed you."

"So, you weren't really coming to my rescue?" I gave him the look that meant I wasn't falling for his act.

"I *was* coming to your rescue," he protested.

"So why the change of heart?" I cocked my head.

"Change of heart?"

"You have been quite adamant about blaming me for the edict," I pointed out.

"And I was wrong to do so," he said seriously.

"Who knocked some sense into your head? Because it definitely wasn't me."

"Would you believe it was Brother Garbhan?"

"Garbhan?" After the afternoon meeting at Thief, I had to wonder what else the young priest had told Luc.

"Yes, Garbhan," Luc said. "Now, may I please get up from the floor if we're going to continue this conversation? The marble is very uncomfortable."

"I don't know. Maybe I should leave you down there." But I switched the dagger to my left hand before I grabbed his right hand with mine and pulled him to his foot. I crouched to retrieve his crutches and handed them to him.

Luc headed straight for my bed.

"Pardon me?" I continued giving him the look. "What do you think you're doing?"

"I'm getting comfortable." He propped his crutches against the wall and flopped on my pallet. The wooden frame squeaked and groaned in protest. "And don't you want to hear an interesting story our newest brother of Light told me?"

"Let me guess." I let the sarcasm drip from my words. "He admitted he's spying on us for Father Farrell."

Luc placed his hands behind his head. "And that you already knew so he figured it was better to confess before you told me."

I blinked. Surprise didn't begin to cover the surge of emotion through my body. What had Talbert said to Garbhan after I left Thief this afternoon?

"Nothing to say about his confession, Chief Justice?" Luc said.

I sighed, strode to my bed, and stowed the dagger beneath the pallet before I climbed in next to Luc, pulled my knees to my chest and wrapped my arms around my shins as I sat facing him. "You didn't give me a chance to tell you before you picked another fight."

"I picked the fight?"

"You're the one who made the nasty comment about me truthspelling you," I pointed out.

Luc blew out a deep breath and stared at the ceiling. "Is that what we're going to do? Rehash every argument?"

"I don't want to rehash anything," I said softly. "I want you to stop accusing me of laying with Quan to assuage your own guilty conscious. And I want you to give me some time to deal with my own emotions about you and Claudia."

"That was the other thing he told me," Luc murmured.

"Who?"

"Garbhan." Luc turned his head to look at me.

"What?"

Luc chuckled. "My newest priest lectured me on how to deal with women, you in particular."

"Stop." I waved my right hand. "I need you to start over. When did Garbhan speak with you?"

"After I returned from the duke's manor."

At least, it wasn't while I and the rest of Balance were at Yellow Fin's funeral this evening. Maybe Garbhan was trying to impregnate Cedar Grove or another priestess at Thief after all.

"And?" I prompted.

Luc laid out exactly what had happened during my meeting with Talbert, Garbhan, and Cedar Grove. "Garbhan said there was no sense keeping the truth from me since Talbert made a point of letting you know. The Temples need to have a unified front if we're about to take down another seat. I should be there to witness your interrogation of the butcher you caught."

I smiled. "No offense, but I have someone else in mind."

"You can't use Shi Hua, and I've arranged for Jeremy to go see Mya in the morning—"

"I know you want to do this, but I think Dragonfly will be a better choice."

Luc rolled over and propped his head on his fist. "Why her?"

"To show the Temple of Love is serious about cleaning up Gerd's mess here in Orrin." I shifted and stretched out beside him. "Dragonfly has been working so hard to rectify everything. She deserves to be there."

One corner of Luc's mouth quirked. "Maybe I've been jealous of the wrong person."

I groaned. "Are we starting that again?"

"No." He leaned over and kissed me on the forehead. "No, I'm not. I'm sorry I didn't listen to you last year."

"Last year?"

"When you suggested we run away to Cant." He leaned over again, and this time, his kiss was full of his regrets and his love.

# CHAPTER 21

The next morning, I summoned Little Bear and Gina to my office.

"I need some suggestions for approaching families on the south side whose children were allegedly abducted," I said.

The wardens exchanged looks before Gina said, "So you believe Ela's story about missing children?"

"She was under a truthspell when she made the statement."

"She also said you were the culprit under the same truthspell," Gina said dryly.

"If there's a crime that's been committed and knowledge of such crime comes out during a trial, the Temple of Balance has a responsibility to investigate the accusation," Little Bear said.

"How fast do we need the information?" Gina asked. "Tomorrow's Rest Day. I'll be down there at First Morning."

I clasped my fingers together and rested my chin on them. "Maybe we take a hint from the south side landlords. Tomorrow, people will either be sleeping in or attending Temple services. I don't like waiting, but if children are truly missing, the parents should have come to us or the magistrate before now."

A little niggle of frustration ran through me. Katarina had been afraid of reporting Marco as missing to DiCook when the noble had been held prisoner by Samael DiRoy. That had been over a year ago, and here we were, still in the same damn position. I hated the fact Talbert was correct about how hard it was to regain the public's trust.

"What about the prisoner?" Little Bear asked.

I smiled. "I'll interrogate him as soon as High Sister Dragonfly arrives."

Little Bear's eyes narrowed. "Has Light been notified?"

"Yes." I tapped my temple. "Silent speech has its advantages. The high brother agreed with my plan to ask the high sister to witness. If you doubt me, feel free to cross the street to ask."

"I was not disparaging your honor—" Little Bear started.

"You have every right to, Chief Warden." I gave him a wry smile. "Our behavior last night upon leaving the duke's estate was abominable."

"I wasn't about to point that out either, Chief Justice." He pursed his lips before he added, "But it would be best not to repeat it. Perhaps counseling by someone from Child—"

I tossed a scroll at his head.

Little Bear ducked and left my office, laughing.

When Dragonfly arrived at my office a candlemark later, I rose and waved at my desk. "Leave the ledgers here. I have a special project for us."

She placed the set of scrolls and books on top of the scarred oak surface and flung her veil back. "The audit has taken us nearly three months, and we're almost done. What could you possibly want to do that takes precedence over these aggravating accounts?"

"I want you to witness an interrogation," I said. "I have reason to believe the person currently in my gaol is selling children for sexual use, but I think he is working for someone else."

Her lips formed a moue of disgust. "I hope the interrogation is the only reason you haven't executed him yet."

"Technically, I only caught him looting a murdered woman's belongings." I folded my arms over my chest. Despite Luc's efforts to put me in a better mood last night, I wasn't looking forward to this interrogation. "And I hate to say this, but I'm following a street rumor."

"You don't pursue a clue without a damn good reason." Dragonfly's attention flicked to my office safe hole and back to me. "Do you think he has something to do with the coded ledger I found?"

"I don't know." I gestured in the general direction of the south side. "It may be as simple as this Robin and whoever he may be working for are taking advantage of Gerd's absence to grab the children and the money."

"This is about more than street children, isn't it?" she asked.

"Allegedly, children on the south side are being abducted." I shrugged. "My wardens are working on putting out word that it's safe to come here to make a report. Hopefully, I have some parents visit since tomorrow is Rest Day."

"A good plan. Robin," Dragonfly murmured before her frown deepened. "The name isn't familiar to me as one of Gerd's regular visitors. Who is he?"

"A butcher on the south side of Orrin."

Dragonfly made a disgusted sound deep in her chest. "I doubt he worked for Gerd. He's not the type she'd use for her social climbing."

"The only way to find out is for me to truthspell him." I cocked my head. "So do you want to witness for me?"

"What's the real reason you don't have someone from Light here?"

"We're going into delve into some horrible topics. Frankly, I don't think the junior clergy can handle it. Garbhan's too young, and Jeremy and Shi Hua are expecting a baby themselves."

"And the high brother can't because . . ." Dragonfly's frown faded into a slight smile.

"Since he and Claudia are also expecting, I can't deal with beheading Luc for shoving one of his crutches through Robin's eye socket," I answered. "If it's any consolation, I've already told the high brother I planned to ask you."

Dragonfly laughed. "All right, but just so you know, Chief Justice—" She waggled her right forefinger at me. "—I'm quite aware you are playing a game with your prisoner, but I'm willing to go along if it means saving any more children from that murdered boy's fate. However, I want the full story when we're done."

I exhaled, not looking forward to the next couple of candlemarks one bit. "You may hear more of the story than you care to before we are done, High Sister."

"And I know damn well you wore out Luc last night," she added. "Which is the real reason you don't want him here."

"I have no idea of what you're blathering about," I said, but I could feel blood heating my cheeks.

"Mmm-hmm." Dragonfly shook her head and flipped her veil back into place. "Do you need me to truthspell this Robin?"

"No, I will."

Her sigh fluttered the edges of her veil. "You can't kill this one during an interrogation, Anthea. Even I know it sets a very bad precedent."

"I won't," I said. "I'll need him to testify against his employer."

# CHAPTER 22

Dragonfly's warning was the main reason I rarely ever truthspelled any-one. I usually compared Luc's technique to a butterfly net and mine to a sledge hammer. However, I had a feeling I would need that sledge hammer. Whether Robin realized it or not, he was facing capital crimes if he was involved in child selling.

And I honestly didn't regret allowing the fake Light priest Micah to die under my truthspell.

The high sister and I collected Donella to record the questions and an-swers of the interrogation. Little Bear selected Long Feather to accompa-ny us to the gaol. I understood why. Long Feather was a handspan taller than my chief warden and an excellent wrestler. There was a certain intim-idation in having my two largest wardens with us. And if something went wrong during the interrogation, we had a fighting chance of keeping Robin contained.

As long as he wasn't secretly a demon.

"Is our prisoner still alive?" I asked as we headed down to the winding stone staircase to the cells. Our gaol was carved into the granite bedrock beneath the city, deeper than even the tunnel system.

"According to Gina, he was when Jonata brought his morning meal to him," Little Bear said. "I only wish we had some way of making sure he isn't a demon wearing a human skin."

"I don't think demons would stoop to stealing coins and an old woman's wedding dress," I muttered.

"You hope." Little Bear said the words I was afraid to add to my statement. He grunted as he hit the bottom step. His way of letting the justice with him know they were in the gaol proper.

I'd given up on trying to correct that habit when it came to me. At least, he no longer attempted to aid me in mounting Nassa.

Jonata waited outside the first cell along with two stools on the floor beside her, one for me and one for Donella. The warden saluted as we approached her.

"This prisoner is alive, he's eaten all his meals, and he hasn't tried to kill himself," Jonata reported. A mischievous smile crossed her face. "He also hasn't threatened me through word or deed, nor has he shed his skin. However, I'm merely a junior warden at Balance."

Behind me, Dragonfly chuckled. "Your staff is picking up your perverse sense of humor, Chief Justice."

"So I've noticed." I gestured for Jonata to unlock the cell door. When she did so, I entered along with my entourage.

Robin laid on the wide bench, wearing the roughspun long tunic all prisoners donned when arrested. He scrambled to his feet at our presence. His chains cuffed to his wrists and ankles rattled with his movements. Long Feather inserted himself between me and the prisoner.

"I suggest you sit down, Robin," I said. "Neither of us would want my wardens to accidentally think you mean me harm.

He quickly sat, his face glowing beneath the green stubble along his chubby jowls. The stink of fear emanated from him.

Little Bear placed the two stools within the cell before he had Jonata close and lock the door once more. Donella and I took our seats. Dragonfly made a point of leaning against the wall on the opposite side of the cell from where I sat.

"Robin," I began. "You have been charged with entering a tenement apartment illegally with the intent to steal the contents within, for the actual theft of coins from a woman formerly known as Old Anne, for knowledge of the deaths of Old Anne and a boy named Yellow Fin and failing to report them to either Orrin's peacekeepers, the duke of Orrin, or any of the Temples, and for knowledge of children abducted from their families on the south side of Orrin which you again failed to report to the proper authorities."

He shivered more violently with each named offense.

"This interrogation will determine whether we will proceed to a public trial," I continued. "You will be truthspelled during this interrogation. Do you understand these charges?"

In response, he snatched up his chamber pot. Both of the male wardens drew their knives. However, Robin proceeded to lose his morning meal. I closed my eyes and rubbed my forehead.

It was going to be a long morning.

Dragonfly laughed. "I think that answers the question of whether or not our butcher is a demon."

"Demon?" Robin squeaked. He looked up at us and wiped his mouth on the back of his right arm. "I'm not a demon."

I opened my eyes and shrugged. "We've already had demons wearing human skins manage to enter the Temple of Balance. You'll have to excuse us for that being our first suspicion. Do I need to repeat the charges?"

"No, m'lady." His voice wasn't much more than a hoarse whisper as he set the chamber pot back on the floor. "I'll tell you everything."

"Yes, you will," I said. "That's why I'm placing a truthspell on you."

"Wait!" That squeaky voice of his was really beginning to annoy me. He looked around wildly. "Aren't the priests of Light supposed to do the truthspelling?"

"Under normal circumstances, yes." I smiled. "I would have someone from Light doing the truthspell. But given that I have reason to believe you know quite a bit about Yellow Fin, I'll be doing the truthspell myself."

"Who's Yellow Fin?"

"The boy who was left for dead in the alley off of Maiden Street."

"I didn't kill him!"

If anything, Robin's voice grew higher-pitched with each comment. Balance, help me. I don't know what made me angrier, his squeaky voice or his total lack of compassion for the child who was murdered.

"That's why I'll be doing the truthspell," I growled. "To learn whether that's the truth."

My words finally penetrated his thick skull. He turned a pale shade of green. Yellowish green beads of sweat rolled down his face.

"B-but you killed a man by truthspell," he whispered.

"He was a renegade who chose death rather than answer my questions." I leaned forward. "Somehow, I don't think you'll be able to endure the pain long enough to die."

Robin scrabbled across his bench as far from me as his chains allowed.

I whispered the words of the two spells. My magic settled over him. Penetrated him. "What is your name?"

"You know my name." Which was true.

Oh, Blessed Balance, this was going to be a very long morning. The slight ache between my eyes threatened to become a full-blown headache. I just hoped it wouldn't turn into a brain storm.

"Is your name Robin?"

"Yes."

"Where were you born?"

"In my parents' apartment."

Maybe that brain storm was closer than I suspected. Robin didn't seem the type to play word games. I didn't think he had the mental capacity. Which meant he definitely wasn't the mastermind behind the abductions from the south side. I took a deep breath and dragged my shredded patience back to me.

"In which city was your parents' apartment located at the time of your birth?"

"Orrin."

The rest of the questions and answers to establish Robin's identity, residence, and occupation proceeded smoothly now I understood how to ask in the way he could comprehend my inquiries.

"Did anyone give you permission to enter Old Anne's apartment?"

"No."

"Why did you go into her apartment?"

"To see if she was really dead."

A shiver of anticipation ran up my spine. "Why did you have reason to believe Anne was dead before you entered her apartment yesterday morning?"

Robin's tongue flicked across his lips. "Because two days ago, I told Drest Anne said she saw him leave the dead boy's body in the alley, and yesterday morning, he said he taken care of the problem."

I leaned my elbows on my knees. "What exactly did Old Anne say to you?"

"It wasn't to me."

"How did you hear what Old Anne said?" I asked.

"She came down to the fountain to get drinking water same as everyone else."

I dug my nails into my palms to keep from showing anything on my face. The lack of water in Gregorius's tenement gave me a reason to speak with him during the meeting of the city leaders. There was no reason for someone like Anne to walk down four flights of stairs to fetch drinking water. Was that the reason she wasn't paying her rent? Failure of this Gregorius to keep up the maintenance of the tenement's plumbing?

"Was this the fountain in Dancer's Square?"

"Yes."

"Was Anne speaking to someone in particular?"

"She was talking to Kushala the laundress, but she was talking loud enough for everyone to hear."

It was exactly what Talbert feared. His aunt tried to flush out the culprit, and she ended up paying the ultimate price for the information.

"What did you hear?" I asked.

Robin looked up and inhaled. "I heard her say she saw the face of the man who left the corpse in the alley."

"Did you know Yellow Fin's body was already in the alley before you heard Anne talk about it?"

"You mean the boy?"

"Yes. Did you know about the boy's body lying in the alley before you heard the news from Anne?"

"Yes."

"How did you know about the boy's body?"

"One of my neighbors told me on our way to the fountain. He'd seen it on his way home from the woman he's been keeping company with. We walked past the alley, and I looked, but I didn't enter the alley. There were a bunch of people looking."

"Why didn't you report the boy's body to the peacekeepers?" I could no longer keep the disbelief from my voice.

"I didn't want any trouble from the peacekeepers." Robin shuddered. "Or from you. Old Penelope was mean. Real mean. But the stories about you are worse."

"Do you have any idea what a demon can do with a dead body?" I hissed.

He shrugged. "They eat 'em."

"Or they can animate them and use them to fight other humans. Or they can wear the dead person's skin." I shook my head. "Why do you think we burn our dead?"

"I always thought it was just tradition."

His answer made me want to strike him, and we hadn't even gotten to the more difficult parts of this interrogation.

"Did you kill Old Anne?"

"No. Drest—"

I held up a hand to stop him from his hearsay and excuses. "Did you see Drest kill Anne?"

"No."

"Why didn't you report Old Anne's death to the peacekeepers?" I asked.

Robin gulped. "I'm afraid of Drest, and I didn't want the peacekeepers to think I was the one who slit her throat."

Did I continue with the subject of Drest? From the expression on Robin's face and the color of his skin, he wouldn't last much longer before passing out, and ironically, it wouldn't be from my truthspell.

Little Bear must have seen the same thing in Robin I did. He surreptitiously checked the bucket of clean water provided for the prisoner. It wouldn't be the first time we had to splash water in a prisoner's face to wake them up after they had fainted.

Maybe it would be better if I finished establishing the facts for the charges we already had on Robin.

"Did you take a bag of coins from Old Anne's chest without her permission after her throat was slit?" I continued.

"Yes." Robin hung his head. "I was about to take her wedding dress, too, but you caught me. She didn't have any family, so I didn't think anyone would miss them."

As much as I wanted to tell him Anne's nephew was a Temple seat here in Orrin just to see his reaction, it wasn't my secret to tell.

"Did you know about families living on the south side whose children were being abducted?"

Robin hung his head and whispered, "Yes."

"Did you personally take any of the children?"

"No."

"Do you know who did?"

"Yes."

"Who took the children?"

"Drest and his cronies."

Fury boiled up inside of me. Fury at both Robin and myself. I should have taken Nathan's stories about the street children more seriously. Yellow Fin would still be alive if I had.

"How did Drest know which children to take?" I bit out.

"I told him," Robin said with a sob. He bowed his head, unable to meet my gaze.

My shoulders tensed beneath my clothing. "Why did you assist Drest?"

"He said he'd take my children if I didn't help him!" Robin wailed.

# Chapter 23

My lungs ached, and I released the breath I didn't know I'd held. "When did Drest threaten to take your children?"

"'Bout five months ago." He wiped at his face while he wept, and he still couldn't look at any of us.

Little Bear and I exchanged glances. From his scowl, he was thinking the same thing I was. Five months ago was when Gerd was arrested, the homeless orphan Nathan became my squire, and Sivan started taking food to the street children who refused to go to the Temple of Mother for aid.

In other words, when the sources dried up for those with the predilection for fornication with children.

"Why haven't you tried to lie to me, Robin?" I asked softly.

"There isn't any use." He sobbed between words. "You'll execute me, and either Drest will take my children to be misused or you'll drink their blood. Either way, they're dead."

I was getting quite exhausted of that rumor about me. An idea flashed though on how to convince Robin to let us help his wife and children. Maybe this was the chance we needed to get ahead of the tensions on the south side. I straightened and said, "High Sister Dragonfly, would you be kind enough to truthspell me?"

Her veil fluttered as if to ask whether I'd gone mad. Little Bear, Donella and Long Feather had similar shocked expressions.

Robin raised his head and met my gaze. "Why would you do that?"

"To show you who and what I really am," I said.

"But how do I know you're really under a truthspell?" he asked.

"Because I'm going to lie to the first question you ask." I grinned.

Dragonfly made a sound in the back of her throat and shook her head, but she whispered the two spells. Like a gentle caress, Love magic settled over me. I nodded to Robin.

"What's your name?"

"Little Bear." The pain shot through my abdomen before the last syllable left my lips. Even though I prepared for it, I doubled over in agony. "Anthea." I gasped. "My name is Anthea." I blew out a deep breath and straightened as the pain ebbed.

Robin's expression was still suspicious. "How do I know you weren't acting?"

Dragonfly snorted in humor. "Robin, lie to me. What's your name?"

"Little B—aauugghh!" The butcher fell onto his side and his cries continued. His color changed so rapidly, I feared for his life.

"Answer her question, Robin. Answer truthfully to make it stop," I commanded.

"R-r-robin," he whimpered. His body sagged, and his ragged breathing gradually gentled. "Th-that would be very hard to resist."

"There's other factors to consider when truthspelling someone," I said. "But now you understand why it's effective."

He pushed himself upright on the bench. "I'm glad I didn't lie to you before, Chief Justice."

"High Sister—" I began.

"Wait," Robin said. "Please." He turned back to me. "Can I ask you a couple of questions before she removes the truthspell from you?"

I cocked my head and considered his request. Once again, my instinct said this was the right thing to do. "Go ahead, Robin."

"Do you drink blood?"

"No."

"Do you eat flesh?"

"Yes."

At his appalled look, I shook my head. "This is why the justices train for years in questioning techniques. I had roasted lamb last night for my evening meal. That's technically flesh."

"Oh!" He rocked on his bench a moment, a thoughtful expression on his face. "Have you ever eaten human flesh?"

"No."

"Have you ever summoned a demon?"

"No."

"Have you ever had intercourse with a demon?"

Balance, help me. These rumors were getting damn ridiculous. "No."

"Why are your eyes red?"

"Because I tried to give myself sight like you have." I laughed. "The spell didn't quite work correctly. Since I was born blind, I had no concept of what your sight is really like so the spell turned my eyes red."

"Did you get punished for trying to avoid Temple service?"

I sobered. Robin was brighter than I gave him credit for earlier. He understood why I'd performed the spell to give me sight. "Yes, I did."

"How-how were you punished?"

"Fifteen lashes."

Dragonfly was the only one in the cell who had actually seen the scars on my back. Though from Little Bear's expression, Sivan had never shared that bit of information with him.

"Will you lash me?" Robin asked softly.

"If I don't behead you, then yes. It depends on the rest of your answers. You did take the coins from Anne though she was dead, and yes, she does have family still living, which means your actions are theft. Then there's the matter of putting everyone in Orrin at risk by not reporting two deaths."

My answer prompted him to cover his face with his hands and start crying again. I nodded to Dragonfly. She murmured under her breath. The warmth of her magic faded from my body, and I shivered at the effect.

"You can survive the lashes, Robin," I said softly. "The question is whether you're going to try to change your behavior to avoid punishment in the future."

"If you have to take my head, will you find a place for my wife and children?" He looked up at me. Fat yellow tears rolled down his cheeks and into the beginnings of his beard. "They haven't done anything wrong, and I know the Temple of Mother won't help them."

I frowned. "Why do you believe Mother won't come to your family's aid if they lose you?"

"'Cause the High Mother won't help them." Robin's sniffed loudly.

"By High Mother, do you mean High Mother Bianca?" I asked.

"Yes."

"Why won't High Mother Bianca help your wife and children?"

Robin sniffed again. "'Cause she and Drest have been selling children since High Sister Gerd was arrested."

# CHAPTER 24

My mind roiled with Robin's statement. It was a step closer to the evidence I needed to stop Bianca. Beside me, Donella gasped. The wardens had expressions that said, "We're not surprised." I wished I could see Dragonfly's face, but no, she wore the traditional veil of Love.

And I realized she had kept very careful control of her emotions since we came down to the cell. I didn't get any mental impression from her at all, not the way I did from everyone else, including Robin.

I turned back to our prisoner. "How did you meet Drest?"

"We grew up on the same block." Robin shrugged. "His family moved to Orrin after their village on one of the Anacapa Islands was destroyed by pirates. I don't remember which one."

"When did you first learn Drest was abducting children?" I said.

Robin sagged on the cell bench. "When I learned he was back in Orrin. About midwinter."

"When did he leave Orrin?"

"Three years ago, a month after DiCook was elected as magistrate."

"Why did Drest leave Orrin?" I asked

"DiCook found out Drest was offering extra protection to certain folks on the south side for a price and was going to arrest Drest."

"Was Drest a peacekeeper?"

"Yes."

"Were you a peacekeeper?"

"Yes."

"Did you warn Drest the magistrate was about to arrest him?" I said.

Sometimes, it helped to already know some of the answers to the questions I asked.

"Yes."

"Did you leave the peacekeepers of your own volition after Drest's arrest warrant was issued?"

"No." Robin shook his head. "The magistrate asked Brother Mat to truthspell me and a bunch of other peacekeepers. Once the magistrate knew I was the one who'd warned Drest, he fired me."

I repressed a shudder at the mention of the renegade we'd known at Brother Mat. The man had nearly been my downfall. Maybe it was a good thing I had a traumatic childhood. I was suspicious of everyone.

However, the butcher was definitely holding nothing back. I guessed Robin cooperated with DiCook after he'd been caught since he had no knowledge of the pain a truthspell could produce. Or maybe the men's friendship went deeper than I realized until Drest crossed Robin's personal line when it came to his family. But it was time to dig into other subjects.

"What do you mean Drest offered certain folks on the south side extra protection?"

Robin seemed to fold in on himself. "His cronies would threaten some of the shopkeepers or the craftspeople who didn't belong to the guilds."

"Are you one of his cronies who threatened people?" I asked.

"No, I collected the money or goods for him." Robin sounded like he regretted his previous actions. Or else he was an excellent actor. A truthspell couldn't detect a person's real thoughts.

"Did Drest only demand money and goods from these folks?"

"No," Robin whispered. His face glowed crimson. "If the person was good looking and they didn't have any other way to pay, they could provide sexual favors."

I swallowed the bile that burned my throat. "Did you partake of any of these sexual favors?"

"Yes." Another sob caught in his throat and he bowed his head again.

"Were all of these people you had sexual relations with of the age of majority?"

"Yes."

My own morning meal churned in my stomach. As much as I didn't want to hear the answers, I had to continue.

"Have you ever knowingly had sexual relations with anyone who had not reached their majority at the time of the relations?"

"No."

Part of me breathed a sigh of relief. Sexual assault and extortion were lashing offences. Assaulting a child was a capital crime. I found I didn't want to execute this man for his wife and children's sakes.

Now, I could dig into the juicier matters. "Did Drest have sexual relations with anyone who had not reached their majority?"

"I-I don't know."

"How did you first learn Drest was back in Orrin?"

"It was a couple of weeks after High Sister Gerd was arrested. He came to my shop and asked for a place to stay."

I cocked my head. "Did you give him a place to stay?"

"Yes, m'lady." Robin looked up at me. "He was my best friend. I couldn't say no."

"Is Drest being your best friend the reason you warned him Magistrate DiCook was about to arrest him?"

"Yes."

"Is he still staying with you?" I asked.

"No, m'lady." Robin's skin glowed a brilliant red, and his voice became terse. "I kicked him out yesterday morning after he told me what he'd done to Old Anne and because he was wearing Temple robes. I've done some awful things in my life, but I won't stand for out-and-out sacrilege."

Out of everything Robin had said so far, this one took me by surprise.

"You saw him in Temple robes?"

"Yes, m'lady." Both of Robin's chins jutted forward. "He was wearing black robes just like yours when he came back to my place this morning."

"Do you know where he obtained the robes?"

"No, and I didn't ask because I didn't want to know. I just told him to get his belongings and get out of our home."

"How do you know Drest was abducting children on the south side?" I said.

"One of my regular customers Onawa has a babe on the way." Robin sighed. "She made the comment that she didn't know how she'd deal with another mouth to feed. I repeated the story over dinner that night. Drest was at the table as a guest should be. My wife pointed out Onawa's oldest girl could be put to work."

Robin swallowed hard before he continued. "Onawa's eldest daughter disappeared three days later."

"How do you know Drest took Onawa's daughter?" I asked.

"I didn't at first." Robin stared at the granite floor of the cell with a dejected expression. "It wasn't until Rest Day two weeks ago that I realized how stupid I was.

"My wife and children went to the duke's estate. He allows citizens to pick berries as long as they pick one box for the duke for every box they pick for themselves."

"I'm aware of the tradition." I waved my hand to try to speed Robin along. "What does your family picking berries have to do with Drest?"

"They weren't in our house when Drest came in that afternoon." Robin heaved another heavy sigh. "He didn't realize I was in the kitchen working on the shop's accounts instead of going with my family. I didn't think much of it until I heard a child cry out.

"I ran upstairs. There was a girl on his bed. She couldn't have been more than nine or ten winters. I didn't recognize her. He was forcing her to drink something."

Robin looked up at me again. "I asked him what he was doing. I'd seen him get angry before, but I never had that rage aimed at me. He said if I told anyone what I'd seen, my children would disappear and be sold to pedophiles like all the other children I led him to. That's when I realized he was taking my neighbors' children. The ones I mentioned over supper while he was there." Slow yellow tears rolled down his face again.

"Is there anyone else Drest would have gone to for help after you kicked him out of you home?" I said softly.

"Not that I know of personally."

"How do you know High Mother Bianca is involved?"

An odd half-sob, half-chuckle burbled from Robin's throat. "After Drest threatened me, I said there wasn't anything he could do to me now. That's when he said the high mother was his partner, and she had the power to destroy me while he did terrible things to my wife and children before he sold them for other peoples' use."

"So you haven't actually witnessed the high mother take any children herself?"

"No, m'lady."

"Have you seen any of the abducted children in High Mother Bianca's presence?"

"No."

"Have you seen any of the abducted children at the Temple of Mother since their families said they were missing?"

"No."

"Have you seen either Drest or High Mother Bianca sell a child to another person?"

"No."

I inhaled deeply. Robin's testimony was disappointing, but it was more of lead to Yellow Fin's murderer than I had yesterday. I exhaled.

"That is all the questions I have for you now, Robin," I said. "I may be back later today with more." I raised my hand to dissolve my spell.

"Wait," Dragonfly said. "Before you release him, Chief Justice, may I ask a few questions?"

It was unusual, but the Love priestess may have some insights I was missing. I nodded.

"Robin, how did you end up with a butcher shop after you were dismissed from the peacekeepers?"

"It was my father's. My brother Bruce inherited it since he was the elder brother." Real sadness descended on Robin. "He let me work at the shop after I was dismissed as a peacekeepers. Then a few months later, he and his son got caught in a riptide on North Beach and drowned. His wife signed the shop over to me because she wanted to go back to her people at Mountain Gate."

Bruce's wife was from a village on my old circuit? Had I ever met her?

Dragonfly's next question interrupted my musings. "Did you in any way talk, manipulate, or threaten your brother's wife to get her to turn over the shop to you?"

"No!" For the second time, anger rolled off of Robin's psyche. "I paid her a fair price for the shop."

"Where did you get the coin to pay Bruce's wife?" Dragonfly continued.

Robin's anger turned to embarrassment. "From my share of the extortion take."

"Did you go to the beach the day your brother Bruce and your nephew died?"

"No, I was minding the shop." Robin shook his head again. "I didn't know what happened until one of the squires from Child came to fetch me. His wife had gone mad with grief. That was part of the reason she wanted to leave Orrin once she was able to."

"That is all the questions I have for now, Chief Justice." Dragonfly shifted, and the bells on her robes and veils tinkled softly, as if they too grieved for Robin's family.

I gestured and murmured the words to dissolve the truthspell.

"If I may ask, what happens next, Lady Justice?" Robin peered curiously at me.

"Frankly, you'll need to stay here." I stood, and my back and leg muscles complained from being in one position for so long. "Drest will know about your arrest by now. I don't want to put your life in danger by releasing you."

"But my family—"

I held up my right palm. "I'll make arrangements to keep them safe."

He bowed his head. "Thank you, Lady Justice."

I just prayed to Balance Robin's family was still alive.

# CHAPTER 25

After leaving Robin's cell, I ordered Long Feather to change into civilian clothing and to go to the south side and check on Robin's family. Little Bear added that he should take Dezba with him to avoid rousing suspicions. Then my chief warden decided he should brief Dezba himself.

Thankfully, Long Feather merely smiled and shook his head before he headed for the male wardens' barracks.

Dragonfly and I returned to my office while Donella rushed back to hers to make both inked and stamped copies of Robin's statement. My clerks would be busy the rest of the afternoon once court was completed.

Outside, Temple bells pealed the hour. Only Second Morning? It felt like we'd be in the gaol far longer than that.

"You need to be careful how you go after her, Anthea," Dragonfly murmured. She flipped back her veil with a sharp motion that set her small decorative bells ringing. "Arresting Gerd was one thing, but imprisoning Jerrod last winter—"

"I know. I know." I sat in my chair and wiped my hands down my face before I looked at Dragonfly again. "It was a stupid thing to do on my part, but I couldn't think of how else to protect him while I tried to outsmart the renegades."

"Bianca could say you're obsessed with taking revenge on her because Gerd used her to call the convocation and lay charges of wrong doing on you. And it's not just the other clergy you need to worry about."

"What do you mean?" I regarded Dragonfly. Once again, I couldn't get a sense of what she was thinking. Her psyche was pulled tight around her.

"Four seat changes in a city in less than half a year unsettles the populace as well as the Temple personnel," she pointed out. "Bianca would be the fifth. She's probably already telling worshippers you're the reason she can't move freely through the city to minister to them. With the tensions on the south side—"

"What do you know about that?" I asked.

"The same rumors and resentment you and everyone else has been dealing with, Anthea." She smiled. "My Temple is doing what it can for worshippers, but our efforts aren't enough. Sooner or later, violence will explode if we don't find a way to ease the tension. I'm afraid Bianca's arrest may be the spark that sets the south side aflame."

"Are you saying we ignore what Bianca has done?"

"Love, no!" Dragonfly lowered herself gracefully into one of the visitor's chairs. "You and I both know she's involved in these sick practices, but she's been very careful to make sure she's kept clean by letting others do the dirty work. We need to find this Drest first. A disgraced peacekeeper would be a decent sacrifice for the peace."

I chuckled. "Magistrate DiCook would dispute that idea."

"If Drest was working with Bianca and Gerd—" Dragonfly jabbed a forefinger in the direction of my safe hole. "—he might have an idea of the key to that ledger since Robin didn't."

I smiled. "I thought you said Gerd wouldn't stoop to dealing with someone from the south side."

Dragonfly smiled back. "Gerd wasn't the one snatching children from the streets. It would mean getting her hands dirty. That doesn't mean Drest's partner wasn't taking them when they walked right through her doors. She cleaned them up, and Gerd found buyers for her."

"You're speculating, High Sister." I leaned my elbows on the table. "Weren't you just telling me to be careful with any accusations against Bianca?"

"Which is why we need to find this Drest," Dragonfly said.

"*We* need to find Drest?" Luc looked at me askance from across the table in his private dining room during our midday meal. This joint Balance and Light clergy meeting cum meal had one extra person besides our chief wardens. Luc turned to Dragonfly. "How exactly are you contributing, High Sister?"

"Are you saying I haven't contributed to solutions to our recent issues?" she replied haughtily.

"No, that's not what I'm saying." Luc waved his spoon in the air. At least, he hadn't dipped it into his soup yet. "But even under a truthspell, Robin had no idea where Drest might be hiding."

"What I don't get is why he's wearing the Temple robes?" Garbhan reached for a slice of bread. "His grievance is with the magistrate, not the Temples."

Luc and I looked at each other.

"Oh, we are such idiots," I muttered.

"We still need more than our suspicions to go charging into the Temple of Mother," Luc pointed out.

"Are you two using silent speech again and forgetting that the rest of us can't hear you?" Yanaba said.

"No, Lady Justice," Little Bear said with a bit of a smirk. "These are people who've worked so long by themselves they can communicate through body language."

"So basically, yes, they are using silent speech," Elizabeth said. "Just a different type."

"They've realized Mother has the material and patterns to create our robes," Shi Hua said. "If the Orrin Temple of Mother is corrupted, it could be where the renegades who abducted High Brother Luc got the robes they were wearing."

"Oh," Yanaba said. "I'm sorry. I'm usually quicker. Master Bly wasn't jesting about pregnancy affecting a woman's mind."

"Sister Shi Hua is pregnant, too," I teased. "I don't think that excuse will hold up to logic anymore."

Yanaba stuck her tongue out. I wasn't sure if the gesture was aimed at me or Shi Hua.

"So does that mean the plan for me to infiltrate the renegades is out?" Garbhan asked. "High Mother Bianca will be extremely suspicious if I try now."

I leaned my head back and groaned. "I hate to say it, but you're probably right."

"Not necessarily." Elizabeth waved her hand. "We now have a huge clue as to how the renegades are financing their operations. Once Bianca is out of the way, either Garbhan or I could offer to assist them in restarting their child selling."

"Let's stick to solving one problem at a time," Luc said. "Solving Yellow Fin's murder and stopping the sale of children should be our first priority."

"Has Gina had a chance to talk to Maebh?" Jeremy asked. It was the first time he'd spoken since lunch began. He looked miserable, but neither he nor Shi Hua showed the tension that marred our last meal here.

I shook my head. "Not with two murders in the last two days. She plans to approach her tomorrow. There's an inn on the waterfront Maebh goes to when she isn't on duty on a Rest Day."

Luc shook his head. "There's not much more we can do openly. Let us hope the inquiries we've made about Drest's whereabouts produce some fruit."

Long Feather and Dezba waited for me when Little Bear and I returned from the midday meal and meeting at Light. I entered my office and gestured for the three wardens to follow me inside.

Once we were seated, I asked, "Where's Robin's family?"

Long Feather and Dezba looked at each other before turning their attention back to me.

"She refuses to leave their shop and home," Long Feather said.

"I told her Robin was in protective custody because his life was in danger." Dezba shook her head. "She replied that if Drest killed her husband, then he deserved it for bringing Drest into their home."

I leaned back in my chair and crossed my arms. "Does she realize her own life is in danger? That Drest may kill her and their children to spite Robin?"

"Yes, she does," Long Feather said. "Dezba even added that our mistress could protect her. She laughed and replied, and I quote, 'Can your mistress stop a Temple seat from doing whatever she damn well pleases?' When I said yes, she snorted in derision and ordered us out of her shop."

"We considered taking her into protective custody," Dezba added. "But after the last two days, the neighborhoods on the south side are claiming we're failing to protect them from a murderer."

Balance, this was worse than I suspected.

"All right. Thank you for doing your best, Wardens." I inclined my head in the direction of our kitchen. "Go get yourselves something to eat."

Once Long Feather and Dezba left my office, Little Bear fixed me with a stare. "I understand High Sister Dragonfly's concern for you and your position, m'lady. But we may have to raid Mother and arrest everyone before any more trouble is stirred up."

I shook my head. "When we raided Love last winter, Magistrate Di-Cook had already given us enough to hang Gerd by her pretty little fingernails. All we have right now is a disgraced butcher's say-so that Bianca is selling the children for ill use."

Little Bear grimaced. "I know what you're going to say, but maybe it's time to put Nathan and Ming Wei to use."

# CHAPTER 26

Govind arrived at Balance shortly before the bells tolled Third Afternoon. I appreciated his promptness. However, my word as to Govind's character meant less than nothing to my wardens. In the foyer of the Temple, Gina searched him thoroughly for weapons, a measure he tolerated with a bemused smile.

"This way." I beckoned with a finger.

His unease grated against my psyche as he realized which section of the Temple we passed through.

"Uh, Lady Justice?" he stammered.

"No questions just yet." I smiled over my shoulder. "And Gina will be accompanying us to protect both our honors."

My slight jest did nothing to alleviate Govind's concern. We entered my bedchambers, and Gina locked the door from the inside.

I crossed to the stone guarding the passage into the tunnel system before I looked at the former silversmith again. "I must ask that you do not repeat anything you see or hear during this meeting, even to your family."

Suspicion crossed his face. "What exactly are you getting me into, Chief Justice?"

"Both I and another Temple seat need someone we can rely on in these difficult times." I shook my head. "I can't say anything beyond that."

Govind crossed his arms over his chest, and his eyes narrowed. "After hearing your proposals, what happens to me if I say no? I have a wife and four children to care for."

"Your memory of this meeting can be erased." I held up my hands. "After all the work I put into saving the populace of Tandor, I won't do anything more to you than that."

Govind blew out a deep breath and his arms dropped to his sides. "Very well then."

While we spoke, Gina lit and shielded a lamp. "To let you know, Govind, I won't open the lamp until the chief justice closes the passage. While we have guards on the main entrances to the tunnels, we still try to be as cautious as possible."

The silversmith shuddered, and a bit of grief leaked from him. "After shielding clergy from skinwalkers and demons for months, I'm willing to go on a bit of faith for now, Warden."

I crouched and murmured the words to dissolve my wards and open the passage. The marble folded back on it self.

A little gasp of surprise burst from Govind. "I've heard of such magic, but I've never seen it in action before."

I slipped through the opening. Govind and Gina quickly followed, and I sealed and warded the opening. Piercing white light enveloped my warden, and I tried not to wince at it.

"This way." I beckoned with my forefinger once again and set off at a brisk pace toward Thief.

"They've done nice work cleaning up the floor down here," Gina murmured.

"Cleaning up the floor?" Govind asked.

"Between High Brother Luc losing his foot, and the Temples of Tandor using the tunnels as an escape route to get help, we thought it would be best to clear any debris," I said. "The Orrin tunnels weren't used for several decades except by Love. Father has been shoring up the tunnels with the help of the Mining Guild, and every one else helped take care of the debris."

Gina chuckled. "You should have seen what the chief justice and Sister Shi Hua of Light did to the exit by Death's Gate."

"We had some help," I grinned at the memory. "Jing flashbangs come in rather handy at times when attempting to kill a demon."

"So that's where High Sister Reby gets her recklessness from," Govind said.

"Do not blame Reby on me," I retorted. "She was like that when I first met her, and she is damn lucky she's not sitting in gaol instead of holding a seat."

Govind and Gina laughed rather than respond to my argument.

I held up my hand and stopped as we approached the entrance to Thief. My companions halted. *Talbert?* I called silently.

*One moment, Anthea.*

The warding faded, and marble groaned as it folded back. Gina strode in front of me and ducked through the opening.

"All clear," she called out.

When I entered, both Talbert and his warden wore bemused smiles. "Do you now fear for your safety during our visits, Chief Justice?"

"I fear I'm the reason for her warden's caution," Govind said as he straightened. "As I'm sure I'm the reason for your own warden being here."

"High Brother Talbert, may I present Govind the silversmith?" I said. "He was one of the Tandoran citizens instrumental in the city's defense. Govind, this is High Brother Talbert of Thief."

After both men acknowledged each other politely, Talbert looked at me. "Chief Warden Sabine will be present during our discussion unless you have any objection, Chief Justice?" From the slight curve of Talbert's mouth, I had an excellent idea of why his second wouldn't be joining us this afternoon.

"I have no objection, High Brother," I said.

Talbert gestured for us to sit at the same table in his bedchambers, and once again to my delight, he had a steaming pot of Jing tea for me. He turned to Govind. "I wasn't sure who the chief justice might be bringing with her. Since she probably won't share her tea, I have a bottle of azul wine you may be interested in."

A pleased expression crossed Govind's face. "How did you know that is my favorite? Did you read my mind?"

"It's has nothing to do with magic or talent," Talbert said as he poured the Mecan spirits. "It's a matter of logic." He shot me a look I couldn't decipher. "The Temple of Balance doesn't own the market on deductive reasoning."

"Why, High Brother, that almost sounds like a challenge," I said as I poured my tea.

"Why would I be foolish enough to challenge the Demon Slayer of Orrin?" he replied.

I tried to hide my surprise at the epithet, but Talbert didn't miss much. "Fool is never a word I would associate with you, High Brother."

Both wardens politely declined Talbert's offer of azul wine. I didn't blame them. The Mecan beverage was far more intoxicating than the strongest Pana Valley wine.

"Let us dispense with the pleasantries if you don't mind," Talbert said.

"Not at all," I replied.

He turned his attention to Govind. "Did Anthea tell you that anything said, seen, or heard here must remain here?"

"Yes, High—" Govind stopped himself as if saying the words would erase them from his memory. "Yes, sir."

Talbert chuckled. "A simple yes or no will suffice." He took a sip from his goblet of azul wine. "Anthea tells me you live on the south side of Orrin."

"Yes," Govind said. The suspicion returned to his features.

"And I'm assuming you're having a bit of a problem with the Smiths Guild here in Orrin," Talbert continued.

"Surely, the chief justice told you that as well," Govind said.

"Not in so many words." Talbert smiled. "You're not the only guild member with issues. In fact, Chief Healer Aaron is the only guild leader with enough sense to welcome his fellow members from Tandor."

"What exactly do you wish from me?" Govind said.

"Old Anne was one of my watchers," Talbert said. "She was also my maternal aunt."

"I share your grief." Govind responded as if he meant it. "No one should have to pass into Death's arms in such a manner."

"Would you be willing to take Anne's place until I can recruit an additional two watchers?" Talbert asked.

"What would it entail and how would I protect my family?" Govind replied.

Talbert raised his goblet to me. "He's a smart one. Thank you, Anthea."

I nodded and sipped my tea.

Talbert returned his attention back to Govind. "We would train you on what to watch for. It will be in the evenings since you care for your children during the day. You will also receive a stipend. If Anthea doesn't mind, our story will be you were hired by Balance for maintenance work. It will explain the money and your presence at Balance. On the evenings she's unavailable, go to Child. High Sister Mya will bring you to me."

"How long will it take for you to find Anne's replacements?" Govind asked.

"I won't lie. It may take a year," Talbert said. "But I have a feeling Anthea has something more in mind for you."

Both he and Govind faced me, and I set my empty cup down on the table. "My request is twofold. The blacksmith my stablemaster has been using is planning to leave the business, and he has no apprentice."

Govind frowned. "My skills aren't the same as a blacksmith's—"

"I know, but please let me finish." I smiled to take the sting from my words.

Govind nodded and gestured for me to go on.

"Surely, you know a Tandoran blacksmith in the same position as you?" I said.

Again, Govind nodded.

"I suggest you two become business partners," I continued. "You'll already have the contract with the Temple of Balance. In addition, the Healers Guild has been needing someone to do fine quality work for their medical tools. Master Aaron would like to see some samples of your work before he signs the contract—"

"But I have no tools!" Govind protested.

"Does your wife have any jewelry that you made still with her?" Talbert asked.

"She has her earrings . . . are you suggesting I sell my dowry gift?" Govind was truly appalled now.

"No, he wants to see the quality of your work." I smiled as I poured myself some more tea.

"And if you can do the fine work the Healers Guild requires," Talbert said. "I want to hire you for some work for Thief as well. After examining your work, I would pay you an additional advance so you can purchase the necessary tools."

After a brief look of joy, Govind's expression faded. "But I will still need to register with the Orrin Smiths Guild. Another smith I know has family in the city. Her father-in-law fronted the money for her tools and the guild refused to sell them to her."

Talbert turned to me. "The meeting the duke called is for Second Evening tonight, isn't it?"

"Yes, I believe it is." I didn't like how Thief worked at times, but it seemed to be warranted in this situation.

Talbert faced Govind again. "The situation with the Orrin Smiths Guild and the Tandoran guild members will be rectified by tonight."

"But—" Govind started. I laid a hand on his arm.

"When it comes to Thief, it's best not to ask too many questions," I murmured.

Talbert released an exaggerated sigh. "I was beginning to wonder if you would *ever* learn that lesson, Anthea."

# Chapter 27

Half a candlemark before Second Evening, I still didn't like Little Bear's plan to use our squires, but I couldn't come up with an alternative. We needed more information, and Orrin's street children were the only direct path to that knowledge. Nathan was the first to point out his old friends would only talk to another child.

While my chief warden supervised the plan to gain additional intelligence on Bianca and Drest through our squires, I dealt with the duke's city meeting.

All twelve Temple seats rode up the main thoroughfare toward Government House because all twelve chief wardens insisted on a place from which to adequately guard us by giving them room to maneuver. Good to know some people within the Temples took their duties seriously.

In Balance's case, Little Bear ceded his duties to Gina, saying she needed the practice for when she was promoted. Frankly, I believed Gina and our squires were simply an excuse to get out of this particular duty by Little Bear.

I didn't blame him. I didn't like this parade of power either. Whether we walked or rode, this was a move designed to intimidate the nobility and civilians by displaying the unity of the Twelve Temples. If the rest of Orrin were as tense as the south side, I could guarantee the feared riot would happen tonight.

When Bianca and her wardens joined the procession, she studiously ignored everyone but High Father Jerrod, who pointedly shot me a nasty look.

I'd tried to apologize to him more than once for imprisoning him last winter. It's not like I tossed him in a gaol cell. I had my wardens take him to one of the second floor guest rooms. Apparently, no apology was sufficient. How would he react when I arrest Bianca? Because it was a matter of when and not if. Maybe I should speak with High Sister Mya about how to deal with some of the Temple seats. Luc repeatedly pointed out the social graces were not my strong suit.

The slow pace of the procession up the Duke's Road irritated me to no end. I clenched my jaw. The ride to Government House would not be the worst thing of the evening, but I wanted to get the posturing and preening over with and settled down to the real business. How many of the former Tandoran residents on the south side besides Govind had helped defend their city from the demons only to lose their homes, their businesses, and their family members? The cost of that siege and battle still squatted like a poisonous toad in my gut.

*Settle down*, Luc whispered in my mind. *We'll get nowhere by browbeating the civil leaders in this meeting.*

*If the civil leaders did their damn duty, I wouldn't feel the need to browbeat them*, I shot back.

*Did you notice Chief Warden Maebh?* he said.

At first, I believed Luc was merely trying to distract me from my petty thoughts. But I watched her posture as I rode behind her. Her shoulders were hunched, and the way she sat in her saddle was terribly stiff. No wonder her horse walked in such an awkward manner. Temple mounts were highly trained fighting animals. The poor mare was getting mixed signals from Maebh on what she should be doing.

*What has Maebh riled up?* I asked.

*Guilty conscience?* Luc asked in return.

*Maybe Gina can use it to her advantage*, I said.

As we approached Government Square, I could see the Temples weren't the only ones who rode to this meeting. Carriages and horses parked around the edges. The nobles and business people wore their finery. The guilds didn't look quite so ostentatious, settling for their guild patches in metallic thread on the shoulder of their nicest clothing. Peacekeepers ringed the area and scattered through the crowd, attempting to keep an eye on everyone. A rumble of voices filled the area until someone spotted the Temple leaders. The conversations around the square abruptly died.

*If there are renegades still in Orrin, this would be a perfect time for them to strike*, Luc murmured in my head.

I glared at him. *You'd better hope Thief didn't hear you.*

He merely smirked and shrugged.

And he was totally correct. Balance help us, what were we thinking by suggesting this plan of action to Duke Marco? I prayed any renegades didn't have time to plot against us with the short notice of this gathering.

A horn blew four short blasts announcing the arrival of the duke of Orrin. The crowd parted on the north side of the square. His four horses pulling the ducal carriage trotted forward. The driver reined them to a halt in front of Government House.

If it had grown quiet when we arrived, it was even more silent with the arrival of Duke Marco and Lady Alessa. His sister had been standing in for his wife at formal functions since the last third of Lady Katarina's pregnancy. At least Alessa wasn't a power-hungry shrew like her mother had been.

Temple personnel dismounted as one a moment before the duke and his sister alighted from their carriage. Two of their personal guards followed them up the steps. The Temples seats lined up in the same order we rode, with our chosen warden at our sides, and followed the nobles inside.

The primary place for meetings of this type was the rotunda in the middle of the two-story building. A raised dais sat at the west end of the rotunda for the duke and his companion. To the duke's right sat the current magistrate and the elected city leaders. Then came the chiefs of the guilds, and between them and the nobles on Lady Alessa's left, the Temple seats took our places. Citizens who wished to view the proceedings sat in the gallery on the second floor.

Magic tingled against my skin as city bureaucrats with passive talent activated the Light spells on the alabaster globes situated around the rotunda. It took a few moments for everyone to file in and take their places.

*Anthea?*

I recognized the delicate touch of High Sister Mya of Child, but I didn't dare look behind me. *Yes?*

*Talbert asked me to point out Gregorius to you. He is the third man on the second row behind Magistrate DiCook.*

*Thank you to both you and Talbert, Mya.*

Her presence literally disappeared in my mind, meaning Talbert was protecting her. If it weren't for Talbert's quicksilver ability shielding her mind, Mya wouldn't be able to attend any public function at all. The same demon attack that left Yanaba unable to leave the city had shredded Mya's psychic shields. As an empath, she was already ultra-sensitive to the moods of people around her. Without a way to shut them out, too much emotion could literally drive her mad.

I examined the person she mentioned. He looked to be average height. His features indicated Toscan descent, but the receding hairline confirmed it. Plenty of jewels decorated his silk-clad body. It should be an interesting talk with him after the public meeting.

DiCook stood and stamped the official staff he held against the floor. "This emergency meeting of the leaders of the city of Orrin now begins. Since this assembly has been called by His Grace, Duke Marco of Orrin, the floor is his."

Marco stood, and his gaze swept around the rotunda. "Thank you for coming on such short notice. We have a predicament brewing in our duchy, and frankly, it's one of our own making. We haven't been as welcoming to the displaced citizens of Tandor—"

Gregorius practically leapt off his bench. "Lazy bums if you ask me, living off the queen's dole—"

"Of which you've been pocketing quite a bit from your tenements." Marco's light tone caused a good number of the assembly to titter, or in a couple of cases, laugh outright.

Gregorius sat down, but from the dark look he shot at the duke, he wasn't finished.

"We need to give these people a purpose and a reason to believe Orrin can be their new home," Marco continued. "Representative Gregorius is correct in that the queen cannot continue paying the way for the former residents of Tandor. Nor do they want her to. Most of them came with literally nothing but the clothes on their backs. I ask you to put yourselves in their position. What would you want?"

The guilt he shoveled into the assembly seemed to have the effect he intended. However, here and there, I felt pockets of anger.

"What about the murders down on the south side?" The chief of the Textiles Guild rose to her feet. "Many of my people are afraid to go down there. Have been for years!"

DiCook's chest puffed, and his body tensed. He looked about ready to jump up and tear into the guild chief.

I reached out with my talent. *Malven, don't.*

With an effort, he calmed himself. His motions actually looked natural when I stood and his head turned toward me.

"If I may speak, Your Grace?"

Marco nodded. The guild chief sank onto her bench, partly irritated with me properly asking for the floor and partly annoyed with herself for not doing so.

"With all due respect to this august body, one person cannot fix our problems alone." I pitched my voice lower and amplified it with a touch of magic. "Our own problems are threefold. The first is the . . . unorthodox way both my predecessor and Magistrate DiCook's performed their jobs. While we've both worked hard to regain the public's trust in fair and just outcomes in disputes, we realize we have a long way to go.

"Second, it has come to our attention a great many crimes are going un-reported. These crimes are not committed by outsiders, but by our own citizens. Blaming the Tandorans who sought refuge here only exacerbates our problems.

"Last is the matter of false accusations." I let a bit of anger seep into my voice. "Just yesterday in court, I had an Orrin woman accuse a Tandoran man of theft simply because he refused her advances."

I took a deep breath to calm myself. It was time to use Marco's emotional flagellation. "As for the murders, it has only been two days since the corpse of Yellow Fin was found. None of you cared about the orphaned street boy when he was alive, so I would think twice before accusing either me or Magistrate DiCook of shirking our duties. As this is an ongoing investigation, I can say nothing further on the matter."

A noble I didn't recognize rose to her feet. "Your Grace, may I ask the chief justice a question?"

"You may, Lady Flavia." Marco inclined his head.

Flavia turned to me. "Chief Justice, how do we know none of these Tandorans are demons in disguise? The horde infiltrated Orrin once already dressed in human skins."

"I understand your concern, Lady Flavia, since I have the same one." I waved in Marco's direction. "As I told the duke, I offer my assistance to verify any Tandoran hired is human. Therefore, you do not have the responsibility or the risk if you choose to hire them."

Clothing rustled behind me. "The Wildlings will assist the chief justice in her interviews," High Brother Jax said. "Does that soothe your worries, Lady Flavia?"

"Yes," She nodded firmly. "Yes, it does."

The rest of the meeting devolved into borderline arguments about tax incentives for the nobles and business people to hire more Tandorans. It wasn't hard to notice all the guild chiefs except Master Aaron kept quiet and, according to Luke, they all looked slightly guilty.

The assembly broke up at Third Evening with no one totally happy with the results. In other words, it was a sign of a productive meeting.

"I'll be right back," I whispered to Luc.

I spotted the person I needed to address. I didn't have to dodge the milling groups talking on the main floor. They seemed quite eager to step out of my way. Representative Gregorius was speaking with three other merchants who had been watching the proceedings from the gallery when I approached.

"Representative Gregorius, may I have a private word with you?"

He quickly swept his initial surprise away with a genial smile. However his expression didn't match the pointed edges of his psyche. "Of course, Chief Justice." He inclined his head to his companions. "If you'll excuse us, my friends."

We retreated to one of the pillars supporting the rotunda.

"How may I help you, m'lady?" he murmured.

"I'm sure by now you are aware one of your tenants at your tenement building on Maiden Street was murdered yesterday morning," I said.

"Yes, I was informed of the matter." Gregorius shook his head. "A terrible thing to do to an old woman who harmed no one."

"I understand from the other residents Anne had not paid her rent over the last three months."

"You think I would kill someone over rent for one of my cheapest rooms?" He stared at me, disbelief written all over his features.

"I merely wanted to give you the opportunity to file a claim of recompense," I said. "Minus the lack of running water in the entire building, of course."

Gregorius stiffened. "Surely, the person who informed you about Anne's lack of payment also told you the water tanks had to be emptied due to a leak in the pipes."

"Which was more than three months ago," I said.

"Maybe because my money had to go to supplying the queen's army on its way to Tandor shortly before the Spring Equinox," he bit out. "To save your hide, I might add."

"No offense was meant, and the Temple of Balance thanks you for your service, Representative." I sighed. "Alas, it is my misfortunate responsibility to inform citizens of all their legal positions."

Gregorius huffed and looked away a moment before he turned back to me. "I recognize a bargaining ploy, Chief Justice. What is it you really want to know?"

"What have you heard about child abductions on the south side?" I said.

He shook his head, and his skin remained a constant golden yellow. "Most of the folks down there scrape by." He shrugged. "They don't like the fact their children leave in search of something better. Doesn't happen often, but when more than a handful run away in a short stretch, those people are sure someone's out to get them. Our lives are just a roll of Thief's dice at times."

I gritted my teeth to keep from decking Gregorius. His callous disregard was appalling, but nothing I could say would shake him out of seeing beyond his own nose.

"Thank you for your information, Representative." I forced a smile. "Is there anything I can do to assist the repairs to your tenement on Maiden Street?"

He smiled in return, no doubt thinking he had the better of me. "I assure you the repairs will be completed within the week."

"I can ask no more."

We both inclined our heads, fake smiles plastered on our faces. I pivoted as gracefully as I could manage under the circumstances and headed across the tiled floor back to Luc.

*To lighten your mood, Talbert says he accomplished his mission,* Luc whispered in my mind. *Govind's friend will have permission to take over Odysseus's forge on First Day.*

*That's one thing that went right on this Twelve-forsaken night.*

*Thing's not go well with Gregorius?* Luc asked.

*I learned he wasn't involved in Anne's murder.* My anger seethed inside of me as we walked toward the entrance, Nicholas trailing behind us like Luc's second shadow. *She was too far beneath him to warrant his notice of her existence.*

*And the missing children?*

*The same.* I slowed to match Luc's pace as he navigated the front steps.

*Is there anything I can do to make you feel better?* Though his visage showed no sign, his lascivious thoughts gave him away.

Gina left Chief Warden Sabine standing on the top step and jogged over to Luc and I. "My apologies, m'lady. I didn't see you exit."

"Was your conversation more productive than mine?" I said.

"Definitely." She grinned.

Daniel led Nassa and the other Balance Horses to us. I turned to Luc.

"I must decline your offer of a second supper, High Brother. I have matters to deal with at my Temple."

"Of course." Luc inclined his head. "Until tomorrow, Lady Justice."

Daniel, Gina, and I mounted and headed back down Duke's Road.

"You two really need to be taking advantage of the edict while you can," Gina murmured.

"What are you saying, Warden?" I glared at her as she rode beside me.

"Since you and the high brother have feelings for each other, no sense ignoring them," she said. "Especially since he's done his duty."

"You are treading on dangerously inappropriate ground," I snapped.

"Then make sure you ward your damn bedchambers from now on," she said dryly.

Behind us, Daniel snickered.

I was thankful I had left my hood up the entire evening. From the warmth of my cheeks, even those with normal sight would see my skin glow. And knowing my wardens and staff, they all were now aware of mine and Luc's relationship. Yet, until now, they'd mentioned nothing.

"How about you tell me about your conversation with Sabine before I decide to lash you for impertinence?" I said.

"Maebh definitely noticed us speaking," Gina said. "Sabine made a point of waving in Maebh's direction and calling her over to us, saying she wanted Maebh's opinion. However, Bianca nipped our attempt in the bud."

"So tomorrow?" I glanced at Gina.

"Maebh's been primed so definitely tomorrow."

I exhaled, adding a little prayer to the Twelve that Gina could get Maebh to cooperate willingly.

As usual, they didn't bother to reply.

# CHAPTER 28

At a candlemark after First Afternoon the following day, I was in the practice yard with Elizabeth working on combat forms when Gina passed through the postern door. I was about to make a flippant comment when another hooded figure followed her onto the Temple Grounds. Someone far too covered for such a warm, sunny day.

"We need to speak inside, Chief Justice," Gina said as she and her companion hurried past us. I didn't have to guess who would want to hide themselves should someone in one of Mother's towers be observing our practice yard.

Elizabeth lowered her staff. "I guess that means we're done for the day."

"This should be more interesting than smacking around a blind woman," I said.

My fellow justice made an amused sound as I wrapped her left hand around my right elbow and led her to our back porch. We left our staffs on the equipment rack. I hoped we could return to our practice, but I knew from experience it might be wishful thinking on my part.

I squinted against the yellowish-white light of the oven and main fireplace as I guided Elizabeth into the kitchen. The oven wasn't as hot as Deborah normally kept it. Luckily, I remembered Lailani was on meal duty for the evening before I panicked. Rest Day was the one day Deborah and Hogarth would actually rest as long as we had a schedule for who was covering for their duties.

From the pounding sound, my junior clerk was beating a taro root to death.

"Lailani—"

She paused in her plant assault. "Gina grabbed a bottle of Hogarth's whiskey and said she'd be waiting for you in our reception room. And once again, may I please build a proper imu in the back? It would be a good way to improve cultural relations with the Sea People—"

"No," I said.

"I'll keep feeding all of you poi!" she shouted as we exited the kitchen and strode down the corridor.

"I know!" I shouted over my shoulder.

"What's poi?" Elizabeth whispered.

"It's a traditional Sea People dish," I explained. "Apparently, it looks quite disgusting to people with normal sight. Don't tell anyone, but I love it."

Elizabeth laughed. "All right then, what is an imu?"

"It's an outdoor underground oven. Lailani says our stone oven doesn't cook her kalua properly."

"I'm afraid to ask—" Elizabeth began.

"It's meat wrapped in taro leaves," I said. "On the good side, it means fresh meat tonight for our evening meal rather than dried or salted."

"Oh, that explains why I haven't eaten it yet," Elizabeth said. After a moment, she added, "Are you sure you want me in there during your talk with Maebh?"

"Yes," I said firmly. "Unless you're planning to kill her before she spills her secrets?"

"Not this time," Elizabeth murmured. I chuckled.

We entered the reception room, and I closed the door behind us. Once Elizabeth was settled in one of the chairs, I looked at the other two women and folded my arms across my chest. "Would someone like to tell me what is going on?"

Gina turned to the cloaked figure. "You need to tell her exactly what you told me."

The person pushed back their hood, revealing Maebh's pale yellow visage. "You need to truthspell me, Chief Justice."

I sighed and took another seat, my sweaty bare thighs sticky against the varnish. No sense wishing for a bath first. I'd have to deal with my perspiration soaking my short practice tunic. "First, I need to know why you're here so I know the proper questions to ask."

"High Mother Bianca is selling children. She has been for several years." The anguish in Maebh's voice was telling. Her spirit could no longer deal with such evil.

"I understand not wanting to approach Chief Justice Penelope," I said softly. "But you could have told High Brother Kam or any of the other seats—"

"Like High Sister Gerd?" Maebh laughed bitterly. "Who do you think the high mother was selling the children to?"

"I know," I said. "Gerd should have been—"

"Executed," Maebh hissed. "But instead she's escaped. Your own Reverend Mother let her escape!"

"Are you willing to offer testimony against High Mother Bianca?" I asked.

Maebh sank inside of her robes. "I might as well. If she doesn't kill me, my career is over anyway. And there is a girl inside Mother who Bianca plans to sell this week."

I leaned back in my chair. I was tired. So, so tired. All the lies, all the fears, they seemed to pile around me, threatening to crush me at any moment. And now, another child's life sat on my shoulders.

"Do you know to who?"

"Theodosius's eldest son Maximus," Maebh spat. "A sadistic little piece of work. You already saw what he did to that boy." A sob wrenched its way from her throat.

"Theodosius?" I looked at Gina.

"He was one of the merchants with Gregorius last night when you approached him," she said. "The one with the braid coiled at the base of his neck."

I nodded at the memory before I turned back to Maebh. "Do you know why Yellow Fin was wrapped in a blanket with the emblem of the Temple of Mother on it?"

Maebh muttered a curse. "It was mine. I couldn't leave the boy naked on the floor. Not like that. He told me he'd burned my blanket and taken the boy to a healer."

"Who did?"

"A man named Drest. Bianca hired him to help her acquire children when they stopped coming to the Temple for succor." Maebh shook her head. "He used to be a peacekeeper."

"Wait," Elizabeth interjected. "The boy was alive?"

Maebh nodded. "Maximus tortured the boy, then sent a messenger to the high mother when he couldn't rouse the child. She sent me and Drest."

I leaned my elbows on the table. "Chief Warden, do you know where I can locate Drest?"

She shook her head. "He comes and goes from Mother, but he never sleeps there. I don't know where else he might be staying."

Damn. Even if I truthspelled Maebh, I knew it my gut she didn't have the last piece of the puzzle I needed to convict Bianca.

So, how did I find that final clue?

While Gina settled Maebh in one of the second floor guest rooms and Sivan assisted Elizabeth with her bath, I sipped some iced white wine and mulled over my options as I faced the four children before me as we sat on Balance's back porch.

As far as last night's city assembly went, I now had the excuse of hiring some assistants for Sivan, Deborah, and Hogarth. However, I needed Drest to pin down Bianca and slice my sword through her pretty little neck for her atrocities. That was my first priority.

I still didn't like Little Bear's plan to send Nathan and Ming Wei down to the south side together either. I especially didn't like the fact he left them down there on their own overnight. But their mission had proven quite successful. Shortly before Second Afternoon, they returned with some witnesses.

Two older children stood before me on Balance's back porch, a boy and a girl. They were probably in their mid-teens though their malnourished frames seemed to indicate otherwise.

Nathan and Ming Wen looked rather proud of themselves as Nathan made the introductions.

"Chief Justice, this here's Dog and Cat." Nathan waved to indicate our guests. The boy glared at me while the girl executed a proper curtsy. "They're the ones all of us kids listen to on the south side."

"Sure, ya listen," the boy said sarcastically. "I tole ya to stay away from adults and not to filch from the same place more than once a month."

"Don't mind Dog, Lady Justice," the girl who must be Cat said. "His manners leave something to be desired."

Cat addressed me properly. Along with the curtsy, something didn't quite add up.

"How did you two end up on the streets?" I asked.

Dog snorted. "Because no one gives two rats' asses what happens to us. Ya may have fooled Nathan here, but I'm a wondering what yar game is. Ya as perverted as your granddad?"

The other three children gasped.

On the other hand, I found myself liking Dog for his bluntness.

"As far as Nathan's status, I don't believe a hungry child's hand should lopped off because he had no other method than theft for obtaining a meal." I glanced at my squire. "Nathan worked off his debt some time ago. However, I'm glad he decided to stay at the Temple. He's a smart, capable young man. As for High Brother Kam, I do object to you calling him a pervert. His and Chief Justice Thalia's relationship was illegal and unwise, but he never stooped to drugging and raping children."

"Ya still haven't tole me what yar game is," Dog declared defiantly and folded his arms over his chest.

"Your logic is inescapable, Master Dog." I smiled. "I want information, and I'm willing to pay you for it."

Now, even Cat looked suspiciously at me. "What type of information, and how much?"

"Five coppers each to start," I replied. "For looking at a drawing and telling me whether you recognize the man in the picture, and if so, where I can find him?"

"Ten coppers each," Cat replied. "Just for looking even if we can't tell you who the man is or where to find him."

"That isn't a fair bargain," Nathan blurted.

"Our time coming all the way up here on just yar say-so is worth something," Dog argued.

I bit my lip to keep from laughing. Nathan appeared totally serious, but Ming Wei stood behind the larger kids and grinned at the negotiating.

"That's too steep for the lack of information," Nathan said. "Five coppers each for your time. If you can give the chief justice the answers she needs, then an additional two coppers each."

Dog and Cat looked at each other before they turned to me and nodded. "Deal," Cat said.

I unrolled the parchment beside me on the bench and held it up to show the children. "Do either of you know this man?"

The sudden greenish pallor of their skin said I'd found gold.

"The Dog Catcher," Cat whispered. She nudged Dog. "I told you I saw him."

Dog trembled violently. "Why ya asking 'bout him?" His voice shook more than his scrawny limbs.

"He's the person who dumped Yellow Fin's body in the alley." I rolled the scroll back up. "He's also the person who killed Old Anne. From the matching knife marks on Yellow Fin and Anne's throats, he may have killed Yellow Fin, too."

Dog bowed his head. Both he and Cat made warding signs against evil.

"Yellow Fin was a good kid," Cat murmured. "Just a bit of bad luck like the rest of us."

"So why do you call him the Dog Catcher?" I asked.

Despite the waves of grief rolling off Dog, he smirked. "Because he's been trying to catch me for a long time."

"Do you know where he lays low when he's not chasing you?"

Cat grinned. "For a couple of extra coppers each, we can even show you."

I smiled back. "If you can lead me to him, I'll do better for you than two extra coppers."

# CHAPTER 29

Between Gina's information from Maebh and the tidbits gleaned from Nathan's friends, Dog and Cat, we narrowed the warehouses where Drest could be hiding down to two. One was a DiMara building, empty thanks to the lull in trade due to the Battle of Tandor. The other had been owned by Amarantha DiRoma, a prominent Tandoran merchant until her murder over a year ago. Elizabeth never had the opportunity to inventory DiRoma's estate before the renegades had poisoned her staff and taken her prisoner.

We waited until First Night before I led a team of wardens, Conflict priests, and Wildlings to the DiRoma warehouse. Meanwhile, DiCook took peacekeepers he trusted along with High Brother Jax and a few more Wildlings to the DiMara warehouse.

As I crept toward the DiRoma warehouse, Brother Sisquoc scouted ahead. The man was sheer beauty in both his human and panther forms. I could understand why High Brother Aduba found him attractive.

When Sisquoc came back, he butted his head against my thigh five times. Damn. I didn't realized how much I counted on Drest being alone when we found him. With hand signals, I passed the word back through the ranks.

High Brother Han of Conflict led a group to the rear doors of the warehouse. Sisquoc and a few others headed for the windows along the roof. Little Bear and the rest followed me to the front doors.

My chief warden quietly tested the door. Locked, as we suspected.

He pulled two flashbangs from his equipment bag and tossed me one. Since we deliberately didn't bring anyone from Light with us to protect them, we had to ignite the fuses the normal way, using the flames from covered lanterns.

We placed the flashbangs, and our team took cover.

The twin explosions rattled everything along this side of the harbor. The falling double doors added another crash to the cacophony. Before the dust even settled, Little Bear tossed me another flashbang. This kind consisted more of powdered Cantan peppers than Jing flash powder.

Once again, we used the lanterns to light the fuses. This time, we rolled the devices into the warehouse. They exploded, and that's when the screaming began.

Three men rushed out of the warehouse, running blindly and hacking as if they had whooping cough. Their eyes watered, and snot ran from their noses. It didn't take much to tackle and bind them. However, as I checked each face, none of them were Drest.

"What the demon do you think you're doing, woman?" one of them shouted.

Little Bear thumped him on the head. "You will address the chief justice of Orrin properly, or else suffer the lash."

A few moments later, Han came around the corner of the warehouse. Behind him, his people dragged two more prisoners. I couldn't help my smile when I saw Drest was one of them.

Han pulled off the Inuit goggles he wore to protect his own eyes from the Cantan pepper. "No one else, including children, were inside the warehouse, Lady Justice."

We'd brought a wagon for prisoner transport. As the wardens loaded the five into it, DiCook and Jax jogged up to us.

"The other warehouse was empty," DiCook reported between puffs of air.

"No one had been in there for months," Jax added.

"Han found no children here either," I said.

I turned and leaned my forearms on the side of the wagon. While his cronies stank with fear, Drest glared at me defiantly.

"You shouldn't have killed High Brother Talbert's aunt in her home," I said.

I shouldn't have been delighted at the look of horror on Drest's face as he realized his fatal mistake, but I was.

# CHAPTER 30

I had known it would be a long night when we planned the raids on the warehouses. My wardens moved Robin to the Light gaol prior to us setting out for the warehouse district. DiCook took Drest's four compatriots to the Government House gaol while Drest himself stewed in one of Balance's cells. I headed for the kitchen in search of my Jing black tea. I would need its strength to question the ass.

Deborah was still in the kitchen. A pungent scent came from the ceramic pot she was preparing. An odor I hadn't smelled since Bertrice's death.

"Why in Balance's name are you making Meca bean tea?" I asked.

"Did you know that in the Cradle it is called kaffa?" Deborah smiled, piling more orange wrinkles across her yellow wizened features. "High Brother Aduba told me the story from his youth about a goatherd discovering the plant after his flock became very excited."

I cocked my head. "You're avoiding my question."

"I've been drinking our store since the high sister no longer visits," she said softly. "Would you like some?"

I wasn't prepared for the anguish that seized me. Bertrice had given her life to stop the demon army once we had lured it inside the wall of Tandor. Deborah kept the bitter beans for those times when the high sister of Death had visited me. It had been her favorite drink. And now, there was no sense of keeping them.

"Kaffa, hmmm? I think I like that name better." I laid a hand on Deborah's shoulder. "Yes, please."

She patted my hand before she shuffled to the shelves to retrieve a second ceramic mug.

"The kaffa doesn't explain why you are up this late," I said. "It's less than two hours before First Morning.

Deborah shuffled back. Her hand gripping the mug shook. I grabbed the handle of the pot with one of the thick padded mittens she used to prevent burns and the first empty mug before I retreated to the prep table the kitchen girls used during the day. Deborah followed and dropped heavily into one of the chairs. I carefully poured the kaffa into the mug she held.

"You shouldn't be serving me, Chief Justice," she protested.

"Allow me this little kindness." I smiled at her before I poured the dark pink liquid into the mug I claimed. "You have taken care of all of us with no thought of your own needs. If you like this drink, please continue ordering some for yourself."

"Thank you, m'lady." She raised the cup to her mouth and blew on the hot liquid before taking a sip. "Neither Hogarth or I could sleep. Not until we knew all of you were back, safe and sound."

"The raid was successful, and there were no injuries on our part." I clasped my hands around the warm ceramic.

She reached over, grabbed my wrist, and fiercely whispered. "Don't you dare feel guilty about taking these unholy men's lives." Her fury sparked and jabbed my mental shields. "They don't deserve the Twelve's mercy."

"Deborah." I released my mug and took her left hand in both of my own. "It's all right. We'll stop them."

She shook her head and wiped away a tear that escaped. "Hogarth and I wanted children for so long, but the only one that survived birth died seven days later. To see these people's disregard for the Twelve's most precious gift . . ." She placed her right hand over mine. "You did right by taking in Nathan and Ming Wei. They've given all of us hope." She patted my hands. "Good eventide, m'lady."

"Good eventide, Deborah." I watched her rise and shuffle from the kitchen.

She left behind her nearly full mug of kaffa.

So, I wasn't the only one feeling sick over the things going on right under our noses. I should have listened to Nathan. Should have acted sooner. Yellow Fin would still be alive if I'd paid more attention to what was happening in Orrin.

I swallowed the rest of my mug before I started drinking Deborah's. No sense wasting the expensive beans.

However, I stalled by doing so, and I knew it. I feared losing control of myself and plunging my own dagger into Drest's misbegotten heart.

"Chief Justice?"

I raised my head at Noko's voice. "Yes?"

"High Sister Dragonfly has arrived."

I could stall no longer.

Once again, the high sister of Love acted as my witness in my interrogation of a suspect.

Maybe Aduba's story about the goats finding the kaffa beans was true. I had gulped down the contents of Deborah's mug before Dragonfly and I headed down to the Balance goal. Now, I felt like an entire colony of ants crawled underneath my skin.

Drest's expression was sullen as we worked through my initial questions. However, when I asked about his relationship with Bianca, he crumpled over in agony.

"I don't know what you're blathering about," he managed to spit out.

"Of course you don't," I said. Something wasn't quite right. He was resisting my truthspell somehow. Well, partially resisting the pain. Almost like how the demons had resisted Yanaba's truthspell by sharing the load.

I reached out with my senses. Yes, there was a link there. The same delicate, subtle magic as the trap spell on Yellow Fin's body.

*Dragonfly, can you detect a link to Drest?* I asked silently.

She closed her eyes. I could feel her gently probe the bit of magic I'd noticed. *Yes. It doesn't go very far. Shall we break it in order to question him more thoroughly?*

*No.* My intention was petty and totally beneath my rank. *I want to continue the interrogation.*

*Bianca isn't foolish enough to link to him,* Dragonfly said. *Not after she's been so careful. Nor can I see her suffering for anyone else.*

*But what are the odds she would keep the person linked with Drest close to her?* I asked. *So she would know if he tried to betray her?*

*One of the other Mother priestesses?*

*Or a non-Temple talent she controls through threats or greed,* I suggested.

Dragonfly made a face. *That sounds more like Bianca.*

"I know you are lying," I said to Drest. "Else you'd be feeling no pain at all."

"I'm not a sick, perverted creature with a taste for demons and blood." He glared up at me, clutching his abdomen, but the truthspell couldn't exert its full force.

I smiled. "If that awful rumor were true, you'd fear to be in such a small, enclosed space with me, wouldn't you?"

Drest blinked in the moment before his gut started burning. He groaned at the load of two questions he hadn't answered.

Outside of Drest's cell, Little Bear passed word to get a warden up on the north side of our roof. Feet scurried down the gaol's corridor. Stone vibrated beneath my boot soles as the heavy steel door opened and shut. The reconstructed gaol door, designed by Orrin's chief blacksmith with input by Shi Hua and Han, would test how small a demon could make itself in attempting to escape the Balance gaol.

Though I prayed events would never come to that test.

However, Drest wasn't acting like Yanaba and Shi Hua's descriptions of the demons who had been wearing human skins. That small measure relieved me.

"Are you afraid of me?" I asked.

"Yes!" he spat.

"Why are you afraid of me?"

He writhed so wildly he fell off the wooden bench. None of us moved to help him.

Dragonfly caught my eye. "Chief Justice?"

I nodded.

She knelt next to Drest. "You are going to die one way or another, my child. Balance doesn't care how as long as Her scales are even in the end. You cared enough to wrap Yellow Fin in a blanket and placed him where he would be found. Do you want more children to die?"

"Yes," he snarled. "Why should they have happy childhoods when I didn't?"

"What happened when you were little?" Dragonfly asked gently.

"What would you call pirates raping and slaughtering your sister in front of you?" He groaned, but not from the physical pain. "The high and mighty Temples didn't do a damn thing. You're all just like the pirates. Using people as you please with no thought. No remorse."

"Yet you abduct children for one of the very Temples you resent," I said. "Why?"

Drest stared at me, the mental and emotional dissonance of his suffering then and his actions now caused him more distress than the physical pain of my truthspell. "At least you pay me."

"Do you mean High Mother Bianca pays you?"

"Yes." It wasn't the pain of the truthspell breaking him. The link to a third party eased his physical pain, but not the emotional agony he'd carried for so many winters.

"Do you know the code Gerd used to record the child sales?" I asked.

Drest stared at me for a long time before he choked out, "She'll . . . kill . . . me."

Do you mean Bianca will kill you?"

"Yes.

I shrugged. "So will my truthspell if you don't start answering my questions. It's not a pretty way to die for you or whoever is shielding you. However, I can offer you a quick and merciful death by sword if you cooperate."

"There's nothing you can do to make me talk," he sneered.

Dragonfly snorted and crossed her arms. "He's not worth the effort of your sword, Anthea. I say release him. Let Gerd deal with him."

Drest's skin turned a sickish green-yellow. "Gerd was executed for de-mon dealing."

I ignored him and stood. "That's not a bad idea. Bianca will tell us the code in an attempt to save her pretty little neck. We just spread the word it was Drest who confessed."

"No!" Drest roared. "Don't release me! I'll talk!"

A candlemark later, poor Donella shook the cramps from her writing hand as we climbed the steps out of the Balance gaol. However, I was too tired to be pleased we now had enough evidence to arrest Bianca.

It worried me even more that a man like Drest was terrified of my birth mother. So what exactly was her end game?

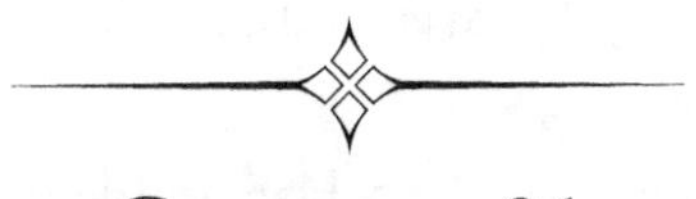

# Chapter 31

I didn't plan another raid. I simply assigned wardens to watch and make note of who entered and left the Temple of Mother while I got some sleep after interrogating Drest. Luc, Donella, and Dragonfly worked on deciphering the coded ledger Gerd had left behind now that we had the key from the murderer. There was nothing I could do to help them since everything was in ink and paper.

Dragonfly was right. Bianca had been the one to recruit Drest, but he knew everything about the deals between the two priestesses.

Honestly, I could have stayed awake and helped the three in deciphering the ledger by translating it to Balance code. Maybe I couldn't deal with anymore pain and blood on my hands.

At Second Morning, High Brother Han and Brother Jeremy insisted on accompanying me as I strode toward the main doors of the Temple of Mother accompanied by a contingent of wardens. When I protested over needing that many people, Han said, "Bianca is far more dangerous than you give her credit for, Anthea. By now, she knows her chief warden is missing and Drest had been questioned under truthspell. You've made it clear you have a death wish from the first time I met you. Today is not the day. As you've pointed out, too many lives are at stake."

"And I owe you for my behavior last week," Jeremy added.

I didn't have time for their arguments, so I threw my hands in the air and shut my mouth.

There was no warden on duty at the main doors. When we entered the Temple of Mother, one attendant waited in the vestibule. She bowed. "High Mother Bianca is expecting you, Chief Justice."

Several priestesses and, from my quick head count, the remaining Mother wardens sat in front of the holy hearth. While Little Bear and his group took the surrendering people into custody, Han's clergy and wardens spread out to search the Temple.

I followed the Mother attendant, Han and Jeremy trailing behind me, to a different receiving room. It was designed to look like a common farmwife's living space with a spinning wheel, a loom, and a basket of thread in one corner. In another corner were large lumps covered by a blanket. A butter churn, a cheese press and other food preparation utensils decorated the area around the fireplace. For all the cozy impression it was supposed to make, it felt like a trap.

Despite the heat of summer, a large fire burned on the hearth. I angled my body to block some of the blaze's white light, but I kept it in the corner of my vision. The ability to manipulate fire was on of the primary talents of the adherents of Mother.

High Mother Bianca sat at a roughhewn table in the middle of the room. The odor of spirits filled the air. She sipped from a ceramic cup.

"You can leave, Red Leaf." Bianca waved at the servant, who quickly departed. She poured a healthy dose of liquor into her cup. Her attention remained on the fire. "I was wondering how long it would take you to put everything together, Anthea."

I kept a grip on the handle of my dagger. "You successfully managed to hide your activities since the Reverend Mother of Balance assigned me here. I would say the congratulations goes to you."

Bianca took another drink before she said, "I should have known Drest would spill everything."

"Have you ever met anyone who could resist a truthspell?" I asked.

She rubbed her temple and finally faced me. "If you want to truthspell me, you'd better do it soon."

I released my dagger and pulled my sword before I even consciously registered her words. The whispers of Han and Jeremy doing the same sounded incredibly loud. We all shifted to face the covered lumps in the corner.

Bianca giggled. "They're already dead."

Han eased closer and poked the piles. A corner of the blanket fell, displaying a woman's face. Her skin had already turned green. He reached down and yanked the covering away.

Two women in Mother's robes huddled in the corner, hugging each other. Or their bodies did. Han stepped away though his eyes remained locked on the corpses. I'd need Devin and Bly to confirm what I couldn't see, but I'd wager the tips of the dead priestesses' extremities were cherry red.

If they were, I knew what was in the liquor Bianca drank.

She smiled at me. "You can question the rest of priestesses, but they were the only two involved in child selling."

"Brother Jeremy, truthspell her," I ordered.

"Yes, Brother Jeremy, why don't you truthspell me?" Bianca mocked.

"I can't, Justice," he whispered. "The mere effort could kill her immediately, and if she survived and I'm still bound to her when she passes—"

"Enough." I understood. Any first-year student at a temple school knew the danger. There was quite simply not a demon-damned thing I could do. It almost made me wish I still had that blasted demon grimoire so I could tie the bitch's soul to her rotting body.

Almost.

"Do you know where Gerd is?"

Bianca shrugged. "No. Probably out trying to find a way to summon some demons."

"Like Samael DiRoy and Cora DiMara?"

"No." She giggled. "Her feud is with you for arresting her. And Dragonfly for betraying her."

"And with you for screwing up the convocation," I said.

"Me?" Bianca couldn't quite focus on me, but I wasn't sure if the cause was the liquor or the poison. "She wanted to hurt Kam by destroying you. And she was so sure she had DiCook under her spell. But now?" She waved her forefinger at me. "Now, all that rage she's carrying will be focused solely on you."

Bianca started laughing. She laughed until she choked, and blood poured from her mouth and nose. The odd gurgling sounds finally stopped, but somehow, she still sat in her chair.

"What do we do now?" Jeremy murmured.

"Find the girl." I couldn't take my eyes off Bianca. Three more dead on the tally of my mistakes in handling this damn city.

The two priests left the room, and Little Bear entered.

"Your orders, Chief Justice?"

"The standard." I sighed. "Fetch someone from Death and Masters Devin or Bly."

He nodded and left as well.

I glared at Bianca's corpse. I could play the same game. I counted silently until I was sure no one would come in and see me, and I warded the room. The priestesses of Mother would feel my magic, and I had the excuse of securing an area where questionable deaths occurred.

My dagger made quick work of strands that had loosened from Bianca's intricately braided hair. I pulled a clean cotton bag I carried for such purposes and placed the locks inside. Shoving my dagger back in its sheath and the bag into my robe pocket, I crossed the overly warm room and stared at the corpses.

What I contemplated was sheer insanity. According to the lore of my order, I would be condemned to non-existence for breaking the very laws of nature, much less my own oaths.

But we had at least one traitor within Balance, and I was fairly certain Bianca knew who it was. Someone had helped Gerd escape, and Bianca wasn't worried a bit about her own safety until I got too close to her child selling business.

I squeezed my eyelids shut to squelch the threatening tears. That could have been Nathan with his throat slit.

As Samael and his demons learned to their detriment, I wouldn't go down without a fight. But was winning the battle worth my soul?

# Chapter 32

By Third Morning, all of Orrin knew about Bianca's suicide. The rumors flew faster than migrating birds fleeing winter. And as Dragonfly had predicted, Bianca was the catalyst that flamed the tensions on the south side.

First, Govind brought his family to Balance. Then Robin's wife and children sought shelter with us. My staff and wardens' family and friends trickled in. And I found out how little I knew about them. Daniel had been born and grew up on the south side, and his parents were so very proud of him.

By First Afternoon, roiling yellow smoke filled the dark blue sky from my perch in Balance's bell tower. The volunteer firefighters fled when they were assaulted by roving bands and their pumps destroyed.

A half-candlemark later, noise deafened as the crowd marched up the Duke's Road. Temple gates and doors closed. Wardens lined the walls, arrows and crossbows pointed at the crowd. DiCook rallied his peacekeepers. They formed a prickly line between Death and Vintner.

And I knew they wouldn't last long.

I climbed down from the bell tower and headed for the main doors. Little Bear grabbed my arm.

"What do you think you're doing?" he hissed. I looked pointedly at his hand, and he released me.

"They blame me," I said.

He shook his head. "You're just a convenient target."

"Maybe High Brother Han was right." I smiled. "Maybe I do have a death wish, but hiding in here isn't going to stop that mob." I jabbed my forefinger in the direction of the street.

"Do you actually have a plan?" He stared at me as if I were truly mad. Maybe I was.

"Of course, I do."

"Liar," he muttered. "At least take one of us with you."

"Not this time, my friend." I clapped him on the shoulder. "Keep Elizabeth and Yanaba safe."

He nodded.

I glared at Gina and Long Feather next. She pursed her lips, but he wore a wild grin. They unbarred the doors and opened them. I walked outside. With a series of clangs and bangs, they secured the doors again.

I jogged down the steps of Balance and strode toward the line of peacekeepers. The voices of clergy tickled the back of my mind, but I shut them out.

"Peacekeepers! Retreat!"

The folks looked behind them. DiCook whirled and stomped toward me.

"What in Father's mighty penis do you think you are doing?" he roared.

Even the mob coming toward us quieted at his bullhorn voice.

"They want a sacrifice." I projected my own voice with a bit of magic. "Fine. I will be that for them if it means saving Orrin. I will *not* lose two cities to our foes in the space of a season!"

Maybe DiCook understood what I was doing. Or maybe he was simply tired of arguing with me for the last year.

"Retreat one Temple!" he roared.

I had to give the peacekeepers credit. They didn't argue the way my wardens did. The peacekeepers stepped back, keeping their eyes on the crowd. They managed to part around me and continue their retreat.

"Kill the red-eyed witch!" someone screamed from somewhere in the middle of the crowd. A rumble of agreements ran through the people. Most of the ones I could see carried tools or bricks or stones. Brooms or hammers or spades.

In response, I unbuckled my harness and laid it on the cobblestones. I did the same with my knives and daggers. I unlaced my robes, and they followed my weapons to the pavers.

"Now, whoever called me a red-eyed witch gets the first chance to kill me," I called out.

Whatever the mob expected, my lack of fear and lack of defiance unbalanced them. There were a few murmurs, but none of them moved.

"I have killed demons. The Assassins Guild has a contract on my head for interfering with their plans to take over Orrin. I can never, ever leave this city." I held my arms out wide. "But please, go ahead. Blame me because one of you summoned demons! Blame me because Tandor fell! Blame me because none of you reported your children were missing!"

The mob quieted. Maybe I was getting through to them. But I couldn't keep my emotions leashed any more.

"Four children with parents, families, are gone because none of you would talk to me! I don't know if they're alive or dead. I don't even know where to look! And the one person who knew drank poison rather than tell me where those children are!"

Magic crackled along my body. Not someone else's. Mine.

"And in your anger, you're burning your own homes to the ground! So take that anger out on me! Kill me!" I roared. "Kill me!"

No one moved. DiCook stepped to my side.

"That's enough, Anthea," he murmured to me before he bellowed, "Go home, people! Enough deaths have happened!"

Another rumble went through the crowd, but this one wasn't filled with violence. When the people started shuffling back to their homes and businesses, they felt . . . afraid.

The tension didn't flow from my shoulders. I bent to pick up my cloak and weapons. When I turned toward the Temples, I realized everyone stared at me with shocked looks.

"My speech wasn't that good," I whispered to DiCook.

"No, it wasn't," he said. "In fact, I'd say you need to make an appointment to talk to High Sister Mya just like you forced Brother Jeremy to do."

"Because I was screaming like a mad woman in public?" Even I knew my joke was poor.

"I think it had more to do with the lightning."

"Lightning?"

DiCook gestured at the trees on either side of the street. "I know your vision is different, but take a good look at the bark."

I did, and my gut clenched in horror. The two closest trees displayed scorch marks similar to lightning strikes. And the burning smell wasn't the buildings on the south side, but the leaves smoldering in a thirty-foot radius around me.

"What . . ."

"You could have killed them all," DiCook said before he looked at me. "But you didn't."

No, I hadn't killed the mob. But fear wasn't a successful tool either.

Some day, my unconscious actions would come back to bite me.

# Chapter 33

Luc and I lay in his bed, spent and out of breath. He swiped at a trickle of sweat between my breasts. I wasn't sure if it were the summer heat penetrating his bedchambers or if we were simply that overenthusiastic in our bedplay.

"I don't understand you," he said softly.

"What do you mean?"

"Between the riot two days ago and the executions yesterday, I thought I wouldn't see you for at least a fortnight."

"Are you saying I need to find someone else for bedplay?"

"Of course not." He took the palm of my hand and kissed it. "I missed you."

"I noticed." I chuckled.

"I also know how executions affect you," he murmured.

I considered his words. He knew me better than anyone else, and he was right.

"I think I took my feelings about Bianca, Drest, and their cronies out on the mob from the south side." I wasn't sure where the power I released came from during the confrontation with the crowd. I was simply glad I hadn't aimed that power at the people, and I prayed Child would forgive me for burning so much of her vegetation.

"Does that mean we are done being angry with each other, too?" he asked.

I rolled over to look at him. "It was never you I was angry with. Gerd took so much from me." I hesitated a moment before I told him the other things I'd been struggling with. "After Bertrice saved my life, Thalia contacted my birth father. They made arrangements for me to go live in Diné when I was born. But—" I waved my hand and blinked to keep the burning tears from falling. "Not being able to have your child was just another choice Gerd took from me. I think about what could have been, and I get so furious . . ."

Luc pulled me on top of his body and stroked my back. "If you'd gone to live in Diné, we might not have ever met."

"I know." I rested my chin on my hands on top of his chest. "I still haven't received any word from the Reverend Mother regarding Gerd's escape. I don't like finding out things from another Temple."

"Has Dragonfly heard anything more?" he asked.

"Only that her Reverend Mother offered to send additional wardens to Orrin." I pursed my lips before I added, "After what happened last winter, I don't think there are enough wardens in the world to deal with Gerd."

Luc looked at me askance. "I know a couple of chief wardens in particular who may not be happy with that assessment."

"Before or after Gerd and her allies poison their ale?"

"Fair point."

"And I owe you an apology," I said.

"Wait. I need pen and paper for this." He reached for his night stand.

"Stop it." I lightly tapped him on the tip of his nose with my forefinger. "I'm being serious. I shouldn't have handled the issue of Jeremy the way I did. I'm sorry."

"No, you were right to bring it up. I was ignoring obvious problems within my own Temple. I'm sorry for not listening to you."

"How are things going with him?" I said.

"Brother Turtle has helped a lot." Luc exhaled and stared at his ceiling a moment. "I didn't realize how badly the battle affected him. But things are getting better, and he's treating Shi Hua with a little bit of affection."

"So his crush is gone?"

"They're treating each other more as colleagues. She wants him to be involved since she knows their child will never be Jing." Luc's hands paused, and he was quiet for a long moment before he said, "Can I ask a favor without it starting a fight between us?"

"Probably not." I smirked. "But go ahead."

"Claudia doesn't want me there for the birth," he said softly. I could feel the hurt as his psyche brushed against mine. I reached up and ran my hand through his thick curls.

"Did she give you a reason?" I asked.

"Only that after everything Gerd did to her and the other sisters, she often has the urge to kick men in the balls. Luckily, her personal assistant Ichik doesn't have any. She's had to go to Child everyday while we . . ." Luc waved his right hand before placing it under his head. "I hated putting her through that."

"You shouldn't feel guilty over someone else's wrongdoing," I said.

"I wanted you to understand why I would ask this of you." He sucked in a deep breath. "Would you please attend the baby's birth for all of our sakes?"

"Does it mean that much to you?"

"Yes." He cupped my cheek with his left hand. "I totally understand if you say no. It's a lot to ask after all the pain Gerd has put you through, too."

"All right," I said softly. "I'll do it, but for the baby's sake, not anyone else's."

"Thank you, m'love." And he kissed me like I meant everything in the universe to him.

If you are enjoying the adventures of Anthea
and the people of the Justice universe, drop me
a line through my website, Twitter or Facebook.
Recommending the Justice series to your friends
or writing a review would be even better.

Turn the page for a sneak preview of the next
Justice story, *A Twist of Love*

# A Twist of Love

I sat at my scarred oak desk in my office and stared at the pile of morning dispatches from the home Temple of Balance in Standora, the capital of the Queendom of Issura. Summer's heat was upon us even this early in the morning. Despite my office being located within the cool marble depths of my own Temple, I hadn't bothered with my formal robes. It was too warm.

So I perched on my chair in leggings and tunic, considering if taking my boots off was a move too close to breaking etiquette for my station, and I stared at the pile. There shouldn't be this many dispatches from Standora. Not during the height of the growing season.

My city of Orrin was the third largest city in Issura and its second largest port. Normally, we would only have our share of petty crime, property damage from brawling sailors, and the occasional stabbing when a brawl got out of hand before the city peacekeepers arrived to break it up.

But ever since I was assigned, or rather sentenced, as the city's chief justice a little over a year ago, it seemed like the Twelve decided to up the ante. Especially over the last six months. And I was hoping for, or dreading, some more information in today's dispatches about one problem in particular.

I ran my fingertips over the seals of the various pieces of parchments until I found the one with the personal sigil of the Reverend Mother herself. I cracked the wax and brushed my fingers over the raised symbols of the Temple of Balance to read them. Even though I was no longer totally blind like the rest of my sisterhood, I couldn't discern the difference between ink and parchment as sighted people did. There wasn't a large enough difference in the level of heat for me to read ink writing.

As I suspected she would but I desperately wished otherwise, the Reverend Mother failed to give me any more details about Gerd's escape from custody in Standora. I wanted to throw the tiny scroll across the room. Gerd, the former high sister of Orrin's Temple of Love, may be my birth mother, but she was insane and dangerous and on the loose.

Not necessarily in that order, and I was at the top of her list of people she wanted dead.

The Reverend Mother should have tried and executed Gerd months ago after she was discovered demon dealing among her multiple other crimes. Once again, the Reverend Mother failed to explain in her letter why Gerd was still alive, much less how the Mad Whore removed shackles designed to inhibit her magical talents, killed a warden and escaped from the capital. I crumpled the parchment and threw it anyway, knowing my senior clerk Donella would merely give me disapproving looks when she carefully smoothed it out and added it to the official records.

The wadded ball barely missed Sivan's head as she entered my office with my breakfast. I received the disapproving look earlier than expected. My personal assistant and head of household shoved aside some other documents with her elbow, set the tray on my desk, and turned to close the door.

"I'm sorry Sivan," I said.

She bent to pick up the wadded parchment and examined the broken seal as she straightened. "I'm assuming you weren't happy with whatever the Reverend Mother said."

"More like her lack of saying anything," I grumbled. "Dragonfly has gotten more information from the Reverend Mother of Love than I have from Balance. If I didn't know better, I'd think my own Reverend Mother hopes Gerd will succeed in killing me this time around."

"I doubt it," Sivan said dryly. "She went to too much trouble to force you to be Orrin's chief justice." She carefully straightened the parchment I'd thrown and laid it on the pile of dispatches I hadn't read yet. "Not to mention, it's been over a month since Gerd escaped. She's a lot of things, but stupid isn't one of them. She probably hightailed it for the Gray Mountains.

Get through those before the snows start, especially with a death sentence here."

"The Reverend Mother of Love seemed rather certain Gerd would head south to seek revenge," I said.

"As I just said, Gerd's—" Sivan started.

"Not stupid," I finished while I poured a cup of tea from the steaming ceramic pot on the tray. "But she makes less sense than a Wixáritari Wildling priestess using peyōtl."

Sivan shrugged. "Let's try a different subject. How long are you planning to mope about the Temple?"

"I am not moping," I said. "And definitely not about Gerd."

"You've been moping ever since you found out Sister Claudia is carrying High Brother Luc's child." Sivan folded her arms across her chest. "And it's gotten worse now that she's showing. You say you've accepted the edict—"

I leaned my elbows on my desk and propped my chin on my fists. "She asked me to attend the birth."

"Oh. Oh, dear." Sivan dropped into one of the visitor's chairs without my permission, but I didn't have the heart to chide her over the etiquette misstep.

Maybe I wanted someone to talk to about this situation. I couldn't talk to Yanaba. She was also pregnant thanks to the stupid edict.

I couldn't talk to Elizabeth either. She had been raped and tortured for nearly a year when the renegades secretly took over our sister city Tandor, so she had a special dispensation from Child excluding her from the order to procreate. Feeling pity for myself because I was barren seemed like a terrible thing to complain about to a friend and fellow justice who'd suffered so much.

And I'd been born barren and blind thanks to my birth mother's attempt to illegally abort me.

"What did you tell Claudia?" Sivan said softly.

"I tried to jest about it, saying we should see how I handle Yanaba's delivery first." I sighed. "I don't know what to do. Part of me hates her for giving Luc what I can't—"

"Stop right there." Sivan held up her right palm. "This isn't about what you want. Or even what Luc and Claudia want. They would never have lain together if it weren't for that damn edict."

"And the other, logical, part of me knows that. This is about breeding as many children with Light and Balance talent as we can." I groaned and laid my forehead on my desk. "What is wrong with me, Sivan?"

"Felicitations, Chief Justice. You've finally joined the human race."

I rolled my head to the side so I could look at her. "What's that supposed to mean?"

"You hold yourself, and everyone else around you, to impossible standards." Sivan shook her head. "As a result, you make yourself and everyone around you miserable."

I sat upright and glared at her. "Excuse me for trying to adhere—"

Someone banged on my office door. "Chief Justice Anthea!" my head warden Little Bear called out. Another round of banging as Sivan rose and opened the door.

"What the demon are you carrying on about?" she snapped.

He shot her a sheepish grin and whispered, "Sorry, m'love," before he turned to me and inclined his head. "I apologize for intruding before you've finished your first pot of tea, Chief Justice, but there's a messenger from Love who says it's quite urgent he speak to you."

"Send them in."

Little Bear gestured. It wasn't one of the stablehands or one of the priestesses' children as I expected. Ichik, Sister Claudia's personal assistant, appeared in the doorway. They wore the standard uniform of the staff of the Temple of Love, but their long hair was loose. Whatever had happened, they hadn't had a chance to do one of the intricate hairstyles the staff of Love were known for before rushing to Balance. They were also slightly out of breath.

Ichik bowed. "Please forgive the intrusion, Chief Justice, and my disarray. The high sister begs most urgently for your presence in her chambers."

The alarm rolling off the eunuch spiked a rush of my own nerves. Why hadn't Dragonfly sent her own personal assistant if it were that urgent to meet with me?

"What happened?" I rose and reached for my formal robes, sword and harness hanging from their pegs. "Is Dragonfly all right?"

"No, Lady Justice." Ichik's voice shook. "She is not all right. No one in the Temple of Love is. She asks that you come immediately." Between their fear and their loyalty to Dragonfly and Claudia, I wasn't going to get anything more out of them.

I glanced with longing at the steaming cup on my desk as I donned my gear. So much for having my first pot of Jing tea before disaster struck.

Sivan caught my yearning look. "I'll brew a fresh round for you when you return, m'lady."

Little Bear exited my office, and his bellow for Gina and Dezba echoed through the Temple corridors. The two female wardens were a better choice to accompany me. After the awful things Gerd and her cohorts had done to the sisters of Love, the priestesses had a tendency to draw weapons first and ask questions later when it came to armed men. The eunuchs that served them were barely tolerated right now as it was, despite the Temple of Child doing their best to heal the priestesses' spirits.

Gina and Dezba ran up to me as I entered the courtroom with Ichik trailing behind me. Balance didn't have a true sanctuary as the other eleven Temples did. The citizens didn't worship her. Balance meted out what a person deserved, and no amount of pleading or prayer swayed her. That was why her priestesses, like Yanaba, Elizabeth, and me, meted out judgement for wrongdoers and restitution for victims.

"Horses, m'lady?" Gina asked as I strode toward the main doors.

"No, it's not worth the time to saddle them, but let's give Dezba a moment to fix her attire." I raised an eyebrow as the young warden attempted to secure her padded leather jerkin. From her damp hair that was merely braided instead of pinned up like Gina's, Dezba had been rousted from her bath.

"My apologies, Lady Justice," she murmured as her skin went from orange to red while she struggled with the laces.

I shook my head. "If Ichik here had been half a candlemark earlier, I would be in the same position. However, we do have an image to maintain in public."

With Gina's assistance, Dezba was presentable within three breaths.

I exited through the main door with a nod to Warden Ahiga who stood guard, jogged down the marbles steps, and strode at a brisk clip toward the Temple of Love. My wardens and Ichik trailed behind me.

It was early enough in the morning that traffic was light on Orrin's main thoroughfare. A few people gave us curious looks, but for the most part everyone ignored us. It probably had something to do with my lecture to the citizens of Orrin last month about knowing when to mind their own business and knowing to speak up when they learned of an injustice.

It also meant there were fewer spies watching me these days.

When we reached the Temple of Love, Sister Shada met us in the foyer. She wasn't wearing her formal robes or veil. For a brief instant, I feared something may have happened to Claudia and her unborn child. But surely, Dragonfly would have sent for a master healer, not me.

Shada bowed. "This way, Chief Justice."

From the whispers of the other priestesses and servants, not everyone knew what was going on. Like Shada, none of the priestesses were dressed in their formal wear. It wasn't like Dragonfly or Claudia to keep secrets from the sisters either. My gut clenched as I matched Shada's pace back to the priestesses' private quarters.

Shada knocked softly on the door. Love's Chief Warden Citana opened the door to Dragonfly's bedchambers just enough to see who it was. Citana relaxed a bit when she saw me. Shada inclined her head to me.

"Call if you need additional assistance, Chief Justice." The silence as she walked away was unnerving. I was too used to the tinkling of the silver bells that adorned the robes of the Love priestesses.

Citana opened the door wide enough to admit me and my companions. The weeping and jingle of bells drew me past the sitting room into the main bedroom.

Claudia sat on the huge wooden platform bed and held a crying

Dragonfly. Claudia wore a plain linen nightshift, her braids cascading down her back. Dragonfly was the first person in Love I saw in formal robes though her public veil had been removed. Her bright yellow tears soaked the shoulder of Claudia's shift.

Dragonfly's second nodded toward the door to the bathing room.

I didn't want to see what had disturbed Dragonfly so, but I forced my boots in that direction. I stopped at the doorway. Gina peered into the room beside me.

A body floated in the pool of jasmine-scented, orange-hot bath water. Equally orange writing marred one of the deep blue marble walls.

"Please tell me the message was written with bath water," I whispered.

Gina swallowed hard. "It's not m'lady."

In large orange letters, the message read, "You're next, bitch."

# GLOSSARY
## WORDS AND PHRASES SPECIFIC TO THE JUSTICE SERIES

APPRENTICE – lowest rank of a trade or craft guild

BRITANNIA – Toscan name for a series of islands off the western coast of the Old Continent. The two largest are Eire and Albion. Four hundred years before Anthea's time, the queens of Eire and Albion were losing their battle against the demons. They ordered the islands evacuated and the Temples of Death to launch their last resort spells. The islands are now barren, and no one who steps on them lives for long.

BRITON DIASPORA – refers to the survivors and their descendants of the evacuation of Britannia who are now scattered around the world

BROTHER – title for any fully ordained priest of any Temple that accepts men, except for the Temple of Father

CANT – Issura's neighboring nation-state to the south

CHENGZHOU – the capital of Jing, a nation-state in the western shore of the Old Continent

CHIEF JUSTICE – title of the highest ranked priestess at a Temple of Balance

CHIEF [NAME OF TRADE] – the highest ranking master guild member of a trade in a city or region

THE CRADLE – according to legend, the continent where Child created the first members of the human race

DUKE/DUCHESS – highest ranking noble of a region

DISTANCE-VIEW GLASSES – a telescope

FATHER – title for any fully ordained priest of the Temple of Father

GRAY MOUNTAINS – a mountain range that runs the entire length of the western side of the Long Continents

THE GRAND CANAL – a human-built canal that passes through the isthmus connecting the Long Continents

THE GREEN LADY INN – an inn near the Embassy District of Orrin, it has the only entrance/exit to the tunnel system with the city wall that is not a Temple

GUILD – a civil organization for a trade or craft

GUILD MASTER – an expert tradesman's rank based on analysis of his/her peers

HEALER – a person with the magical ability to heal illness and repair wounds

HIGH BROTHER – title of the chief priest of a city Temple, except the Temple of Father

HIGH FATHER – title of the chief priest of a city's Temple of Father

216

HIGH MOTHER – title of the chief priestess of a city's Temple of Mother

HIGH SISTER – title of the chief priestess of a city Temple, except the Temples of Balance or Mother

IBERIA – nation-state on the southwestern corner of the Old Continent

ISSURA – queendom on the western coast of Northern Long Continent; the Peaceful Sea forms its western border with the nation of Pagonia to the north, the nation of Cant to the south, the nations of the Cliffdwellers and Diné to the southeast and the Gray Mountains to the east

JING – nation-state on the eastern side of the Old Continent

JOURNEYMAN/JOURNEYWOMAN – middle rank of a trade or craft guild

JUSTICE – title for any fully ordained priestess of the Temple of Balance; alternate term of address is Lady Justice

KEMET – nation-state on the northeast corner of the Cradle

THE LONG CONTINENTS – the two continents separating the Peaceful Sea from the Panthalassa Sea, they are connected by a narrow isthmus

THE LOST CONTINENT – southern continent between the Peaceful Sea and the Storm Sea. By Anthea's time, the original inhabitants were believed to be slaughtered by demons 500 years before. Sailors from the Sea Peoples and Maurya who landed there after the inhabitants' disappearance reported screams but found no one. Those with magic talents went mad. Not even the priests and priestesses from Child could save them. Those who tried went mad themselves.

MAGISTRATE – elected official of a city or town in Issura who is responsible for civil and criminal law enforcement and the city or town's defense/care in an emergency

MASTER – senior member of a trade or craft guild; the clergyperson who is primarily responsible for the training of a novice class

MAURYA – the southern-most nation of the Old Continent

MIDDLE SEA – shallow sea that separate The Cradle from the Old Continent

MOTHER – title for any fully ordained priestess of the Temple of Father

NATIONAL ROAD – main, paved road through the nation of Issura. It roughly parallels the western coastline.

NEW THENOS – an island city/state on the eastern coast of the Northern Long Continent

NOVICE – a person in training to become a priest/priestess of the Twelve

ORRIN – third largest city in the queendom of Issura with the second largest port

PAGONIA – Issura's neighboring nation to the north

PANTHALASSA SEA – ocean that separates the Long Continents from the western part of the Old Continent and the Cradle

PEACEFUL SEA – ocean that separates the Long Continents from the eastern part of the Old Continent, the islands and archipelagos of the Sea Peoples, and the Lost Continent

PEACEKEEPERS – men and women who act as a city's police force. They report to the city's magistrate. They also act as an auxiliary defense force if their city or nation is attacked.

RAMBLA – a city in northern Cant, its people were used to hatch demon eggs off-screen during the events of *A Modicum of Truth*

REVEREND FATHER – senior-most priest of a Temple order, the leader of that sect in the nation in which he resides

REVEREND MOTHER – senior-most priestess of a Temple order, the leader of that sect in the nation in which she resides

SEAT – person holding the highest ranking position of a Temple

SHAKYA – nation-state in the western portion of the Old Continent, southwest of Jing and northeast of Maurya

SISTER – title for any fully ordained priestess of any Temple that accepts women, except for the Temples of Mother and Balance

STANDORA – capital and largest city of Issura

STORM SEA – ocean bordered by the eastern part of the Cradle, the southern part of the Old Continent, and the western part of the Lost Continent

TANDOR – Issuran city that guards the border with Cant and Diné

TEMPLE – a collection of people dedicated to the service of one of the twelve gods; a building that houses such people; the primary place of worship for one of the twelve gods

TIWAN – the capital of Cant

TOSCANA – nation-state on the southwest section of the Old Continent; location of the first battle against the demons

THE TWELVE – the collective name for the twelve deities of the Justice universe

VALENCIA – duchy in the nation-state of Iberia; know for their innovative shipbuilding designs

WARDEN – security guard of a Temple, they act as supplementary military personnel in the event of a demon invasion

**MOTHER**

CLOAK COLOR – Light blue

MOTTO – "To give without thought; to forgive with love."

**THE TEMPLE OF MOTHER** is responsible for the teaching of household arts, such as spinning, weaving, food storage and preparation. The order is also responsible for caring for those who have lost their families.

**FATHER**

CLOAK COLOR – Dark blue

MOTTO – "All tools are weapons, and weapons tools."

**THE TEMPLE OF FATHER** is responsible for the constructive arts, such as carpentry and smithing.

**BALANCE**

CLOAK COLOR – Black

MOTTO – "Balance in all things."

**THE TEMPLE OF BALANCE** runs the judicial system. A justice is the judge in criminal and civil cases.

**LIGHT**

CLOAK COLOR – Medium brown

MOTTO – "Light brings truth, for without truth, there can be no justice."

**THE TEMPLE OF LIGHT** is responsible for codifying contracts and mediating contract disputes. A Light priest also acts as the bailiff for a justice, and is often the one to truthspell a witness or the accused. The Temple of Light also provides military support to a nation's civilian army.

**KNOWLEDGE**

CLOAK COLOR – Gold

MOTTO – "With patience, knowledge comes."

**THE TEMPLE OF KNOWLEDGE** is responsible for education and for recording historical events. They essentially act as the library system for the Justice universe.

**THIEF**

CLOAK COLOR – Grey

MOTTO – "Hiding in plain sight."

**THE TEMPLE OF THIEF** acts as the intelligence-gathering arm of both the Temples and the civilian leaders. They finance their efforts through gambling dens.

**CONFLICT**

CLOAK COLOR – Dark Red

MOTTO – "Destruction is the necessary evil, for it clears the way for new growth."

**THE TEMPLE OF CONFLICT** focuses on strategy and all martial arts. They are the primary support and teachers of a nation's army.

**LOVE**

CLOAK COLOR – Medium Red

MOTTO – "Pleasure is life."

**THE TEMPLE OF LOVE** are the holy prostitutes. They also deal with sex education and lead the Spring Rituals, the annual fertility rites which were first used to breed as many humans with magical talent as possible. Don't underestimate them. They fight just as hard and as nasty as their fellow clergy in Conflict.

**CHILD**

CLOAK COLOR – Light green

MOTTO – "All things are new once."

**THE TEMPLE OF CHILD** is responsible for the emotional health of citizens. They also develop and teach agriculture and animal husbandry techniques.

**WILDING**

CLOAK COLOR – Dark green

MOTTO – "All creatures return to us."

**THE TEMPLE OF THE WILDLING GOD** deals with management of wild animal populations, forestry, and the protection of ecosystems.

**VINTNER**

CLOAK COLOR – Purple

MOTTO – "The line between wisdom and madness is one sip."

**THE TEMPLE OF VINTNER** not only deals with the cultivation of grapes and the production of wine, but they also promote the gathering, cultivation and processing of all medicinal herbs.

**DEATH**

CLOAK COLOR – Black

MOTTO – "For every life, there is a death."

**THE TEMPLE OF DEATH** takes care of the gathering of the dead, the last rites, and disposal of the corpses. They also act as a repository for the last wills and testaments of all citizens.

# QUEENDOM OF ISURRA
## ORRIN
### TEMPLE OF BALANCE

CHIEF JUSTICE ANTHEA – a circuit justice for ten winters until her appointment as Chief Justice of Orrin at the age of thirty winters ("Justice")

CHIEF JUSTICE PENELOPE – deceased, predecessor to Anthea as Chief Justice of Orrin

CHIEF JUSTICE THALIA - deceased, predecessor to Penelope as Chief Justice of Orrin, maternal grandmother to Anthea

JUSTICE YANABA – junior justice assigned to the city of Orrin after the events of *A Question of Balance*

JUSTICE ERATO – junior justice assigned to the circuit of the eastern section of the duchy of Orrin and the southern tip of the duchy of Pana Valley after Anthea is sentenced to the seat of Orrin in "Justice"

SIVAN – personal assistant to Chief Justice Anthea and head of the household staff

DONELLA – senior clerk

LAILANI – junior clerk

CHIEF WARDEN LITTLE BEAR – head of the Balance wardens

WARDEN TYRA – junior warden, killed in the Battle of Tandor (*A Matter of Death*)

WARDEN GINA – junior warden

WARDEN AGLAIA – junior warden, died in the battle to retake the Temple of Love (*A Question of Balance*)

WARDEN DANIEL – junior warden

WARDEN NOKO – junior warden

WARDEN JONATA – junior warden, Aglaia's replacement from the Standora Wardens' Academy

WARDEN DEZBA – junior warden

WARDEN TAHOMA – junior warden

WARDEN AHIGA – junior warden

WARDEN LONG FEATHER – junior warden

HOGARTH – former chief warden under Justices Thalia and Penelope, now stablemaster, husband of Deborah

DEBORAH – Head cook, wife of Hogarth

NATHAN – squire to Chief Justice Anthea after he was sentenced to pay
reparations for stealing bread, an orphan, age ten winters at the time of his
sentencing in *A Question of Balance*

MING WEI – squire to Justice Yanaba, nine winters old at the end of *A Question
of Balance*. Originally from Jing, she was sold by her parents to a Jing noble as
a sex slave and brought to Issura. When the noble's crimes were discovered,
he immolated himself and his slaves. Ming Wei was the only survivor and has
severe scar tissue on her face, back and arms.

### TEMPLE OF LIGHT

HIGH BROTHER LUC – a circuit priest for twelve winters until his appointment
as chief priest at the age of thirty-two winters between the events of "Justice"
and "Diplomacy in the Dark"

HIGH BROTHER KAM – semi-retired, predecessor to Luc as chief priest,
poisoned and died during the events of *A Question of Balance*

BROTHER MAT – Second to Luc. His birth name is Micah. He murdered the
real Mat on his way to Orrin from Standora. Died under Anthea's truthspell
interrogation in *A Question of Balance*.

BROTHER JEREMY – youngest junior priest until he is promoted to Luc's second
after the events of *A Question of Balance*.

BROTHER GARBHAN – junior priest who is assigned permanently to Orrin after
the events of *A Matter of Death*

ISTAQA – personal assistant to High Brother Luc and head of the household
staff

EDBERTH – former personal assistant to High Brother Kam, he now acts as
evening assistant to High Brother Luc

HENRY – stablemaster

CHIEF WARDEN NICHOLAS – head of the Light wardens

WARDEN GIBB – junior warden, died shortly after the renegades' kidnapping of
High Brother Luc in *A Question of Balance*

WARDEN MATEQAI – junior warden, becomes Sister Shi Hua's personal
bodyguard during the events of *A Modicum of Truth*

WARDEN YAR – junior warden

WARDEN TADHG – junior warden

WARDEN GAD – junior warden

222

## Temple of Love

HIGH SISTER GERD – chief priestess, biological daughter of Thalia and Kam, biological mother of Anthea. She was removed from office on charges of fraud, bribery of a public official, unlawful magic, and conspiracy to commit murder. Later, the charges of dealing in demon artifacts and treason were added.

SISTER DRAGONFLY – Gerd's second, BERDA (genderfluid), is acting High Sister after the events in *A Question of Balance*, becomes High Sister after the events in *A Modicum of Truth*

SISTER GRETCHEN – junior priestess, deceased. The discovery of her body in one of Duke Marco's wine barrels precipitates the events in *A Question of Balance*

SISTER CLAUDIA – junior priestess, Dragonfly's second

SISTER SHADA – junior priestess

SISTER ZIHNA – junior priestess

WARDEN JOCASTA – junior warden, one of the replacement wardens after the events of *A Question of Balance*

ICHIK – a eunuch who is Sister Claudia's personal assistant

## Temple of Conflict

HIGH BROTHER HAN – chief priest

## Temple of Death

HIGH SISTER BERTRICE – chief priestess

HIGH BROTHER KAI – deceased, predecessor of Bertrice, retired in Bertrice's favor as the temple seat and became a teaching brother in Standora until his death

BROTHER XANDER – Bertrice's second until her demise during the Battle of Tandor, succeeds her as Orrin's High Brother of Death

SISTER RAVEN CLAW – Xander's second when he becomes high brother

CHIEF WARDEN AXTON – head of the Death wardens

WARDEN HITARI – junior warden

## Temple of Vintner

HIGH BROTHER BEN – chief priest

## Temple of Mother

HIGH MOTHER BIANCA – chief priestess, she commits suicide when Anthea discovers Bianca has been selling children

CHIEF WARDEN MAEBH – head of the Mother wardens

## Temple of Father

HIGH FATHER JERROD – chief priest

## Temple of Child

HIGH SISTER MYA – chief priestess

BROTHER TURTLE – junior priest, helps to save Justice Yanaba by pulling her soul back into her body during the events of *A Modicum of Truth*

## Temple of Wildling

HIGH BROTHER JAX – chief priest, second form is a wolf

SISTER FARRAH – Jax's second, second form is a fox

## Temple of Thief

HIGH BROTHER TALBERT – chief priest

SISTER CEDAR GROVE – Talbert's second

CHIEF WARDEN SABINE – head of the Thief wardens

## Temple of Knowledge

HIGH SISTER MARIANA – chief priestess

## Nobility

DUKE BENEDETTO DIMARA – father of Marco, Alessa, and Isabella, husband of Cora, convicted of conspiracy and conspiracy for illegal magic to mind wipe his son Marco during the events of "Justice"; imprisoned at Standora for life.

LADY CORA DIMARA – mother of Marco, Alessa, and Isabella, convicted of treason and demon dealing, executed by the Reverend Mother Alara of Balance during the events of "Justice".

DUKE MARCO DIMARA – duke of Orrin, inherited his post at the age of eighteen winters after his parents were found guilty of numerous offenses and stripped of their titles and property

LADY KATARINA DIMARA (NEE' DILOVE) – common-born wife of Marco, animal healer. Her mother Sister Ilina was a priestess of the Temple of Love and died of the wasting sickness shortly before Katarina's eighteenth winter.

LORD KAM DIMARA – eldest child of Marco and Katarina and heir to the Duchy of Orrin, named for High Brother Kam of Light, godson of Chief Justice Anthea and High Brother Luc

LADY ALESSA DIMARA – sister of Marco, a latent talent, lover of Sister Gretchen of Love

LADY ISABELLA DIMARA – sister of Marco, attends the University of Standora

BARTHOLOMEW – retainer of Duke Marco's until it was learned he'd assaulted

224

Lady Alessa and Sister Gretchen, Lady Alessa subsequently asked Chief
Justice Anthea for clemency and hired him to manage the estates Sister
Gretchen had bequeathed to Alessa

WILLIAM – retainer of Duke Marco's

JULIAN – retainer of Duke Marco's

ARTURO – former captain of Duke Marco's flagship, his murder is the
precipitating event of "Diplomacy in the Dark"

TITUS – captain of Duke Marco's flagship, the *Mars Tranquilus*

## CITIZENS

MALVEN DICOOK – duly elected magistrate of Orrin

DANTE – one of Orrin's peacekeepers, dies at the beginning of *A Modicum of
Truth*

BARBORA – wife of Dante, dies at the beginning of *A Modicum of Truth*

JAIME – one of Orrin's peacekeepers

LEYTI – one of Orrin's peacekeepers

DREST – a peacekeeper, dismissed by DiCook for extortion

ROBIN – a peacekeeper, dismissed by DiCook for warning Drest that DiCook
was coming to arrest him

## GUILDS

CHIEF HEALER AARON – head of the Healers' Guild

MASTER HEALER DEVIN – second to Aaron in the Orrin Healer's Guild,
originally from New Thenos

JOURNEYWOMAN BLY – a junior healer, often assists Master Devin at autopsies

## TANDOR

HIGH BROTHER DAV – chief priest of the Temple of Light

CHIEF JUSTICE ELIZABETH – chief justice of the Temple of Balance

MINERVA – the new clerk with the Temple of Balance, a renegade, killed during
the fight within the Temple of Balance (*A Modicum of Truth*)

HIGH BROTHER ADUBA – chief priest of the Temple of Conflict

BROTHER TIGHAN – second of the Temple of Conflict, a renegade, killed by
Aduba during the fall of Tandor

HIGH BROTHER NANTAN – chief priest of the Temple of Death

SISTER REBY – second of the Temple of the Wildling God, first introduced as a
shapeshifting thief in "The Perfect Partner", second form is a polecat

BROTHER SISQUOC – surviving priest of the Temple of the Wildling God,
second form is a panther

BROTHER TRAJAN – priest of the Temple of the Wilding God, second form is a wolf

SISTER JUMPING MOUSE – priestess of the Temple of the Wildling God, second form is a kangaroo rat

DUKE ENZO DITOSCANA – Duke of Tandor, murdered by a skinwalker possessing his wife

DUCHESS NADINE DITOSCANA – the widow of Duke Enzo of Tandor

URAL DISAND – merchant from Tandor, implicated in the Assassin Guild plots in Orrin, killed while possessed by a skinwalker (*A Modicum of Truth*)

AMARANTHA DIROMA – Tandorian merchant, rival of Ural DiSand, murdered by renegades shortly before they poisoned most of the personnel of the Tandorian Temples

GOVIND – a silversmith who assisted with the defense of Tandor against the demon army, settled in Orrin after the evacuation and fall of Tandor

*THE WAVE DANCER* – Duchess Nadine of Tandor's flagship, one of two remaining ships in Tandor prior to the Battle of Tandor

## STANDORA – CAPITAL CITY OF ISSURA

REVEREND MOTHER ALARA – head of Issura's Temple of Balance

JUSTICE ROSE – novice training priestess of the main Temple of Balance in Standora when Anthea was a novice

REVEREND FATHER FARRELL – head of Issura's Temple of Light

BROTHER ELROY – a Light priest, aide to Reverend Father Farrell, and a distance speaker who accompanies the Isurran and Sea Peoples' fleets to Tandor in *A Matter of Death*

BROTHER LONG WIND – a Light priest and aide to Reverend Father Farrell; he accompanies the queen's army to Tandor in *A Matter of Death*

BROTHER GARBHAN – a Light priest and aide to Reverend Father Farrell; he remains in Orrin during and after the events of *A Matter of Death*

BROTHER JON – novice training priest at the main Temple of Light in Standora, murdered by the skinwalker at Samael DiRoy's abandoned manse prior to *A Question of Balance*

HIGH SISTER IMALA – a Love priestess, considered to be the lead contender for position of Reverend Mother of Love; she accompanies the queen's army in *A Matter of Death*

CHIEF WARDEN CATHERINE – Imala's chief warden; she was a classmate of Mateqai's at the Warden Academy and the two had a physical relationship

WARDEN HOTOTO – a junior Love warden

BROTHER WHITE WOLF – a senior priest of Thief; he's a personal friend of High Sister Imala

QUEEN TEODORA – reigning monarch of Issura

CROWN PRINCESS CHIARA – eldest child and heir of Queen Teodora of Issura; lady general of the queen's army

DUKE WHITE EAGLE – former Conflict brother, left the order to marry Crown Princess Chiara; honorary title duke of Standora as the future queen's consort; lord general of the queen's army

## PANA VALLEY

LORD ALEISTER DEGROVE – noble noted for his vineyards

## JING EMPIRE

### CHENGZHOU

EMPRESS BAO DE – ruler of Jing a century before Bao Yu, she sacrificed herself to stop a demon army

EMPRESS BAO YU – ruler of Jing until her death from natural causes during "Courting Trouble"

EMPEROR BAO CHENGWU – current ruler of Jing, succeeded his mother Bao Yu during "Courting Trouble"

AMBASSADOR QUAN PO – half-brother of the current Jing emperor Bao Chengwu; was heir to the throne until his nephew was born

REVEREND FATHER JIN – head of Jing's Temple of Light

SISTER SHI HUA – a priestess of Light, who was tapped as Po's bodyguard. She received additional training from Conflict, Thief, and Love. Originally from the town of Yintze in the southern province of Chu.

BROTHER LIN – novice master of Light

BROTHER JIAN – a priest of Light, classmate of Shi Hua during their novice years

BROTHER FA – a Wildling priest, his second form is a tiger, a friend of Shi Hua and Jian during their novice years

JUSTICE MEI WEN – a priestess of Balance, Shi Hua's closest friend other than Jian during their novice years

SISTER YIN LI – a priestess of Love, Shi Hua's maternal aunt

REVEREND FATHER CHEN – head of Jing's Temple of Conflict

BROTHER SHANG – a priest of Conflict, Shi Hua's instructor when she was a novice

REVEREND FATHER BIMING – head of Jing's Temple of Thief

*THE UNBRIDLED* – a spy ship used by the Temple of Thief, a four-masted carrack built in the Iberian duchy of Valencia, captained by Reverend Father Biming during *A Modicum of Truth*

BROTHER HADAR – a priest of Thief from the Kingdom of Hejaz, serving on board *The Unbridled*

## ISLANDS OF THE SEA PEOPLES

### KINGDOM OF O'AHU

PRINCE ALIKA – youngest son of the king of the Sea Peoples, one of Sister Gretchen's worshippers, the father of her unborn child

CAPTAIN IAKEPA – senior captain of the O'ahu trading fleet

## DINÉ NATION

REVEREND FATHER NIZHÉ'É' – head of the Diné Temple of Conflict

JUSTICE SPOTTED FAWN – the western circuit justice for the Diné Nation, killed in the Battle of Tandor

BIDZII – Spotted Fawn's clerk, he's fluent in Issuran so the justice speaks through him; killed in the Battle of Tandor

BROTHER BUMBLEBEE – junior priest of Light with the Diné army

SISTER LIZARD – junior priestess of Knowledge with the Diné army

## CLIFFDWELLERS

HEALER KOTORI – a physician with the Diné army during the siege of Tandor

## PLAINS NATIONS – COMANCHE

HIGH BROTHER PECOS – a senior Conflict priest with the Diné army during the siege of Tandor

# Acknowledgments

The Justice world started as a whim of a short story seven years ago. It's hard to believe I've already started writing the fifth novel as well as writing six more short stories in this universe. For those of you buying and reading my books, thank you from the bottom of my heart.

I can't say enough about my gratitude to Jaye Manus and Elaina Lee for making my books look so damn professional and awesome. Thank you so much, ladies!

This book was never meant to come out on Valentine's Day. So a super thank you to my Darling Husband for staying out of my way as I finished this book. There isn't enough treasure in the world for my personal hero and his dedication to the needs of my fluff mop of a dog and her multiple trips to the yard for poo duty in the dead of winter.

And to Angie, Becky, Jo, Roshonda, Shelley, and Valerie, thank you for all the support and encouragement. Now, we just need to plan a trip to Vegas for everyone at the same time!

**Suzan Harden** transitioned from writing information technology manuals for companies and legal articles for a law enforcement magazine to her first love, fantasy and science fiction in all their forms. She's the author of the Bloodlines, the 888-555-HERO, and the Justice series.